HOPEFUL

LOUISE BAY

Published by Louise Bay 2017

ISBN – 978-1-910747-01-8

BOOKS BY LOUISE BAY

Hollywood Scandal

Duke of Manhattan

Park Avenue Prince

King of Wall Street

Love Unexpected

Indigo Nights

Promised Nights

Parisian Nights

The Empire State Series

Hopeful

Faithful

Sign up to the Louise Bay mailing list

www.louisebay.com/newsletter

Read more at www.louisebay.com

You pierce my soul. I am half agony, half hope.
Tell me not that I am too late, that such precious feelings are
gone for ever.

ONE

Saturday nights in the country were much like Saturday nights in London—friends gathered around the TV, figuring out whether or not we'd move our drinking from the sofa to a bar or restaurant or a combination. Tonight I'd voted for staying in the warm. I'd lost.

"I thought we were going to the pub, you boring bastards," Adam said, diving into one of his increasingly regular rants. Adam's temper flared more and more often the closer he got to the Big Three-O. He was partying as hard as possible, rejecting any evidence that he wasn't a kid anymore. I was pretty sure we'd all handle it badly. Adam was just first of our group to be hitting the milestone.

"We're going when this is over, so shut the hell up," I replied, lifting my chin at the television. The six of us—even Matt and Daniel—were engrossed in sequin-covered, ballroom-dancing celebrities, but Adam was restlessly pacing. He'd been in a bad mood all day.

"Ava, I'm surprised at you, liking this glitter and sequins and dancing shit. You're such a girl," he spat.

"IQ points are wasted on you, aren't they?" I replied. "Get lost so we can watch this in peace." I hated humoring Adam when he acted like this, but reacting was pointless.

"Thank God I'm getting my wingman back for good. I'm going to nail a different girl every day this summer," Adam chuntered under his breath.

"Yeah, I'm sure." Daniel chuckled as he headed to the bar. "I guess there will be plenty of leftovers."

"No one says 'nail' anymore, Adam," Leah said, flipping her hair, which dismissed Adam and showed off her beautiful hair in one efficient gesture. "This isn't 1996."

Jules raised her glass, asking Daniel for a top-up. Perfect man that he was, he brought the half-empty wine bottle over from the bar. "Has someone not snapped that delicious man up yet?" she said as she watched the alcohol slip into her glass.

Who? What delicious man? My stomach did an inexplicable flip. I felt as if I was missing something and although my eyes stayed fixed on the television screen, I tuned out the music and tried to listen more carefully to what Daniel, Adam and Jules were talking about.

"Nope. And I don't need his leftovers, so fuck off, Daniel. We're going to tag team it all across London when he gets back," Adam said, tipping back his beer.

"Not if I snap him up first!" Jules bounced on the sofa.

Who were they talking about?

"And you can fuck off, Jules. Don't go near him when he gets back. The boy is back in town. And we're going to have a summer of fun."

My breath caught and I had to close my eyes to stop the

world from spinning as I realized the subject of their discussion.

Joel.

He's coming home.

Fuck.

ADAM HAD PERSUADED us to brave the cold weather and move our Saturday night drinking to the pub in the village. It had three-hundred-year-old slate floors and ceilings so low Daniel and Matt both had to crouch to make it to our table without banging their heads on the beams.

It was so hot I couldn't breathe. The jumper I had on wasn't helping. Nor was the open fire . . . or the mention of Joel. The conversation had moved on to other things, but I was desperate to know more. When was he coming back? *Why* was he coming back?

I hadn't seen him for so long—years. Seven years, nine months and fifteen days if I wanted to be exact.

"You okay, Ava?" Jules asked.

"Just a little hot," I said. My lips, already dry from the Scottish wind, cracked under my too-wide grin. I was going to have to work on my poker face. And my hearing. The pub was in the middle of nowhere, but it looked like the whole of Scotland had descended on it tonight. I was having a hard time figuring out what my friends were saying over the clatter of cutlery, the chatter of the other customers, and the boom in my ears that thudded *Joel, Joel, Joel*. My friends' voices just came out as incomprehensible vowel sounds. I wanted to get back to the house and crawl into bed, but I'd volunteered to be the designated driver. Thank God tomorrow was the end of our annual weekend away in the country, and we'd all be heading home to London. I needed to organize my thoughts, figure out if breathing was possible at the same time as being face-to-face with *him*.

I took a deep breath and tried to focus on what Adam was saying across the solid pine table. What had originally started as just an Easter lunch over the years had morphed into a weekend in the country. Daniel always found us the most glamorous places to stay, which he insisted on paying for as he was the richest man in England. Or technically, the third richest man under forty in England, but whatever he was, he was far wealthier than the rest of us. At first we'd resisted, but it had been futile and we had all long since given in. This year we were in a beautiful old castle in Scotland that had turrets, sweeping driveways, and staff. It felt like a hotel, but with only us as guests. I wasn't sure why we'd had to come to the pub—we had a cook and a bucketful of booze back at the castle.

Still, it was a comforting ritual. Various girlfriends and boyfriends came and went, but the six of us—friends since university—went away every year. This year Daniel had brought Leah. They hadn't been together long but they were the perfect couple. Would they be married by this time next year? Everyone's lives were moving forward.

Neither Jules nor Adam had brought significant others this year. Jules had disposed of her latest victim last month, and Adam, for all his talk, was still licking his wounds over his girlfriend of five years rejecting his proposal this time last year. I wasn't sure if he really was out "nailing" half of London, but I doubted it. He had never been good at casual sex. He was far too needy—one of several reasons there would never be anything romantic between us. Needy wasn't sexy. Strong. Confident. Knowing. That was sexy to me. The ying to my yang.

Matt and Hanna teased us about it from time to time. They were convinced Adam and I would end up a couple. Or Adam and Jules. They'd kissed the first term at university and married just after graduation. They were the constant in our group—like the patient parents of four unruly children. They were settled and happy and wished that for everyone in their orbit.

I'd never brought anyone along to our annual weekend in the country.

There'd been nobody since Joel.

God, I had to get out of here. My head was full as if someone had slipped open the catch on all my thoughts about him and I was drowning. Over the past eight years, I'd pushed him to the very corners of my memory. Within weeks of his leaving, I'd started at law school and then training on the job for one of the best law firms in the country. I'd loved the long hours, the lack of sleep, the mostly unspoken competition between the junior lawyers, the whole brutality of the culture.

It had been my punishment for my previous weakness.

I'd reinvented myself during those first few years, determined not to repeat past mistakes. And I'd stepped back from our little group. I'd joined in on the odd night out, and of course we did our annual Easter thing, but generally it was all too painful so I'd deliberately kept my distance. The group reminded me too much of our shared history and of what was missing, who was missing. Of who I'd been. Work had been the perfect excuse, and nobody questioned my absence, really. After a couple of years, I bought my first flat in Clapham, near Hanna and Matt, and slowly began seeing more of them, and eventually, more of Adam, then everyone.

It took years, but I resurrected my life outside work and

the new, confident Ava who was a successful lawyer started to have friends again.

But, I didn't date. Not even a little. I knew no one would ever be what Joel had been and so there was no point in trying only to be disappointed and have him back in my thoughts again. There were times that my lack of sex life was questioned. Jules regularly asked me if I was shagging my boss and Adam occasionally enquired if I was a closeted lesbian. But eventually my singledom stopped being a topic of conversation. Hanna and Matt were married. Daniel divorced. Jules was a serial monogamist and incorrigible flirt. Adam was a pretend uber-shagger either side of a long-term girlfriend. And I was single. That's just how we were.

But Joel's return had the power to change everything.

TWO

The library was always busy at the beginning of the term. Given it was my final year, I should have figured that out by now and come earlier, rather than waiting until mid-morning. The place was packed, and after twenty minutes searching I still couldn't find a free desk. I had two or three secret spots on the first floor that were so tucked away I could always guarantee one of them would be empty, but today I'd been forced off the first floor that held the law library to the third floor.

As I turned the corner, I spotted Joel. There was a space open opposite him. I wanted to grab it before anyone else did, but I felt awkward, shy almost. We didn't really know each other. Joel was Adam's friend. They were classmates—both economists—while the rest of us were thrown together in the same block of bedrooms in the dorm. Joel lived on his own off campus, so I only saw fleeting glimpses of him when he came to visit Adam. On nights out, he would sometimes be around, but he always seemed slightly at arm's length from our group. He and Adam were kind of a package deal. Whereas the rest of us were all firsthand friends, Joel was a secondhand friend—we knew him only through Adam.

Looking—no staring—at Joel from this distance, I took him in. I usually avoided watching him, desperate to ensure I didn't become one of the quivering women who seemed to be constantly buzzing around him.

I stood, partly concealed by a bookshelf, and watched him, his head bowed and his forehead creased, flicking between two books as if they were saying completely opposing things and he was trying to make sense of it. He had developed a bit of a half beard, which made him look even more masculine than usual. He still had his summer tan, and his shirt clung to his broad chest. His sleeves were pushed up, emphasizing his strong arms and his very capable-looking hands. Had he always been this handsome?

And so totally out of my league?

As if he could feel someone watching him, he raised his head and glanced around. I knew I should look away and busy myself with the bookshelf in front of me, but I couldn't. His eyes found mine and he broke into a grin. I forced a goofy smile, did a stupid half wave, and walked toward him.

Jesus, I was pathetic.

"Hey, Ava. You studying or picking up books?"

"I'm trying to find a spare desk to start my thesis, but the world's conspiring against me. This library's packed!" I said, my voice at least an octave higher than any sane person's should be.

Calm the hell down, Ava.

"What bad luck, and I suppose the free desk in front of you right now is completely useless? Anyone who sits there will be infected by a curse that will cause them to fail their finals?"

Funny *and* handsome. Not to mention cool and charming.

"You heard that, too? Well, coming from an economist, I guess I have to believe it—I thought it was just a rumor. See you around." I pulled my eyes away from his and turned to leave.

"Sit, Ava."

Saying nothing and avoiding his eyes, I set out my books and papers and opened my laptop.

It was an indisputable fact, acknowledged by men and women alike, that Joel was *hot*. Even I couldn't deny it. Well over six feet tall, he had a swimmer's body and that slightly longer, messy hair that just begged to be tousled. Guys teased him about being pretty and girls flirted with him as a matter of course. But it was his confidence that sealed the deal for me, though I wasn't sure if he was confident because he was so gorgeous, or gorgeous because he was so confident. He wasn't cocky or arrogant, and he didn't enjoy other people's misery or disaster. He was just so comfortable with who he was, or so it seemed from a distance. I'd always wondered how people like that operated, what you found when you looked a bit deeper. Did their insides look just like mine?

The world Joel inhabited wasn't like most people's—he led a privileged existence. He was served at the bar before others, strangers smiled at him on the street, and shop assistants were at his beck and call. From the outside, the sun seemed to shine just a bit brighter for him. I'd never resented people like him and their smoother path in life, never thought it was unfair. I just knew it to be different from the world I lived in, and I understood that our worlds wouldn't collide. Ever.

But sitting opposite him did bring our worlds into convergence, just a little. I watched from behind my hair as people stopped by his desk to do that weird boy handshake stuff, or bat their eyelashes—women mainly, but not exclusively. Even library staff acknowledged him with an air of deference. None of his visitors gave me a second look. To my embarrassment, every now and again Joel spotted me distractedly watching his interactions with his numerous admirers. He never said a word when he caught me, just offered the occasional smirk.

Despite the floorshow right in front of me, I managed to achieve more than I expected. Joel always had good grades, and I assumed they, like the rest of his life, came easily to him. But when his admirers weren't distracting him, Joel worked hard—really hard. It seemed that like the rest of us, he had to study to do well in class. Now, I wasn't competitive, but I wasn't letting a pretty boy like Joel out-study me. I took fewer breaks than usual, which may have had something to do with my view, but more than that, I wanted him to know I worked hard too.

When one of his *almost* equally attractive friends came over to ask him to grab a snack, Joel asked me to join them, and I hastily refused. I needed a break from studying, but I also needed a break from being so close to him.

At just after seven I was ready to throw in the towel. Joel looked totally consumed by what he was doing—it looked complicated with graphs and numbers and stuff. Without saying anything, I started packing up my things. As I closed my laptop, he looked up.

"Hey, are you going? I'll come with you." He looked

exhausted—his eyes sleepy in a completely sexy way and his hair wild from his fingers' manipulations.

"Stay," I said, "you look engrossed."

"No, I'm done. I'll walk you back." He collapsed back in his chair and ran his hands through his hair.

"Adam will be around, I imagine." No doubt Joel wanted to catch up with him. Joel just looked at me and frowned.

Silently we gathered our stuff and headed out.

Following the pedestrian path back to the dorms, neither of us uttered a word. Joel seemed completely comfortable with the silence. I couldn't say the same. "So, you work hard," I blurted.

Joel tipped his head back and laughed. "You sound shocked. Did you think I had someone else do it for me?"

"No. Sorry. I just thought it would have come easily to you or something."

He stepped closer as a couple passed us coming the opposite way and bent to my ear. "Nothing worth having comes easy, Ava."

Warmth heated my cheeks. Was he flirting with me? I kept my eyes fixed on the path in front of me.

He laughed again.

He was making fun of me. Perfect.

"Maybe that's true for most of us," I said.

"Who's that not true of?"

"All I'm saying is that life is easier for some people. The planets align for some but not others."

"Oh wow, you're one of those." He chuckled again.

"One of what?" I stopped in the middle of the path.

"Come on," he said, stopping alongside me, pulling my backpack off my arm and tossing it over his shoulder. "It's just, girls have this fascination with astrology that I've never quite understood."

My temperature rose and my face contorted into a scowl.

"I'm not 'one of those,' as you put it." He was labeling women as people who didn't care about facts or science. I was smart. His frozen face told me he'd heard me. "I wasn't talking about bloody astrology—as if you'd get a better job because you are a Leo rather than a Virgo." I rolled my eyes. "I was talking about some people's lot in life being easier than others," I said. "It's a *fact* that attractive people are more likely to be promoted, less likely to get depression. You'll even be paid more if you're better looking. There have been scientific studies about it." Joel was in that elite group of people who would always have it easier than the rest of us.

Joel had stopped laughing but his smile was still there. He had a strange look on his face, as if he was saying something to me in his head but the words weren't coming out.

"What?" I started walking.

In two very long strides, he caught up with me "Well, I . . . You're right. I'm sorry. I misunderstood you."

"Okay." I'd probably overreacted but I hated for people, Joel, to think I was one of *those* girls.

"Okay?" he asked.

"Okay." I nodded and smiled at our to-and-fro.

"Oh, and you're cute when you swear," he said.

I swatted him on the arm. Joel Wentworth flirting with me was not something I wanted to encourage. It was far too dangerous.

"And you think I'm attractive. Nice." He looked ahead, grinning.

I hit him again. He was just too charming.

Back at the halls of residence, we bumped into Adam coming out of the block door.

"Hey, I just called you," Adam said to Joel as Joel and I went into our block. "Wanna grab a beer?" His eyes flickered from Joel to me and then back at Joel. "Where have you two been? Never mind." A bedroom door banged shut upstairs. "Come on, let's go."

I walked straight past them both and toward my room on the ground floor.

"Let me drop off Ava's bag and I'll follow you up," Joel said as I unlocked my door, kicked off my shoes, and collapsed on my bed.

Joel knocked on the still-open door. "Are you decent? I can come back later if you are."

"Err, come in." Did he mean to be suggestive? "Thanks for carrying my books back."

"It was my pleasure. You're a great study partner, and very easy to wind up. It's a winning combination. Let's do it again sometime."

Anytime, I thought, although I knew he was just being polite. I could be top of the class if I studied as intently as I did when Joel was around. "I'm going to have to live in the library this term if I'm going to get my thesis done."

"Okay," he said, sweeping his hand through his hair, his eyebrows narrowing, just slightly. "I'll pick you up tomorrow."

Was he serious? "Okay." I let the word linger over my lips, waiting for him to say *just kidding*. But he didn't and the corners of my mouth twitched as he held my gaze.

"Okay." He grinned.

"Get out of here, loser." I rolled my eyes in faux exasperation. He was pretty *and* funny and my heart did a little pitter-patter when he smiled like that. It just wasn't fair.

Why did all the great qualities end up concentrated in just one guy?

At least when he didn't pick me up tomorrow, he'd be *that* sort of guy. And then he wouldn't be so perfect.

———

TRUE TO HIS WORD, Joel picked me up and walked me to the library the next morning, and then walked me home that evening. The next day was the same. And just like that we were study buddies, firsthand friends, library geeks. I enjoyed his company and attention. And for some reason, he kept turning up and walking me to the library.

At first, our conversations were restricted to the walks to and from the library, but then we started to take lunch together and then the odd break. Pretty quickly, Joel became the person I spent the most time with out of all the friends I had at university, including my roommates. More than that, he was the one I *wanted* to spend every waking moment with. As well as being great eye candy and making me laugh all the time, he was kind and thoughtful. Not just to me, but also to everyone he came across.

I paused briefly as the automatic doors on the third floor opened. As I stepped through, I saw Joel immediately. I'd had an extra tutorial all morning so today was the first day Joel and I hadn't walked to the library together. I wandered up to our desk and found a jacket on the chair opposite and a couple of books on the desk. My heart sank. He had a new study mate.

"Hey, Ava," Joel whispered loudly.

"Hey." I faked a smile.

"How were lectures?"

"Good. Hard but good." I shrugged, glancing around to see if there was a desk nearby.

"You'd better sit down and study then." His gaze returned to his books.

"Yes, thanks, Dad. I'm going to find a free desk."

God, I was interrupting his studies by coming over to speak to him. How embarrassing. I went to step away but Joel grabbed my wrist and I froze.

Joel Wentworth was touching me. My heart thundered in my chest. "But I saved your spot. Hand me my jacket, will you?" he asked, dropping my hand and reaching in the direction of the coat on the chair opposite him.

He'd saved me a seat. *He'd saved me a seat!* I hadn't got it wrong. He wanted me here. Opposite him.

I concentrated on keeping my expression neutral. "Okay, thanks."

"Okay, you're welcome." He grinned his gorgeous grin at me.

"Okay, you loser." I couldn't help but grin back.

I pulled out my papers and laptop and got to work. About an hour into things, my concentration was beginning to waver and my imagination started to wander across the desk. What was Joel like in lectures? Did he sit at the front with his hand up all the time, or was he at the back, ignoring the lecturer and flirting with whatever girl was next to him? A scrunched-up ball of paper hit my keyboard and pulled me back into reality. I looked up and Joel was grinning at me. He nodded in the direction of the bookshelves next to him.

What? I mouthed.

Joel just nodded more vigorously. I strained my neck but I couldn't see anything. *What?* I mouthed again.

Come here, he mouthed back.

I pushed my chair back and walked around our table, my back to where he was looking. Why was he being so cagey? I leaned against his desk, my fingers gripping the wood either side of me. "What?" I asked softly. He made a *come here* motion with his finger so I bent forward. Wow, he smelled of the ocean and lemons.

"Some people have more of a physical approach to studying than we do," Joel whispered. "Look to your right."

As subtly as I could, I turned my head and through the books saw a couple who clearly thought they were better hidden than they were. They were kissing fervently, their hands desperately running across each other's bodies, feeling each other's contours through their clothes, as if any moment they expected to be pulled apart and separated forever. I couldn't take my eyes away.

"You like to watch," Joel whispered. It wasn't a question. And I should have corrected him, told him he'd got me wrong, but I didn't. Because he'd got it right. There was something compelling about the couple. Something I couldn't look away from.

Joel was so close to me that my skin prickled at his breath on my neck. In that moment, all I wanted was for Joel to kiss me like the guy I was watching was kissing his girl. My heart pounded and my pulse began to race.

"I guess it's a good way to blow off steam for them," I finally managed, straightening up. "Like stress relief or something." I was scrambling for words.

"Wanna give it a try?"

I flicked my head back to Joel, whose eyes were twinkling at me.

"Don't you twinkle at me, Joel Wentworth." I faked a dose of haughtiness and went back to my seat.

"What? I'm just thinking about your stress levels."

No wonder he was never short of female attention. He managed to combine flirting with funny so he never came across as arrogant.

"Okay, well, thanks for the offer."

"Okay, well, anytime." He raised his eyebrows and gave me that ridiculously handsome grin.

I put my head down and did a great impression of someone studying extraordinarily hard. There was no ambiguity. Joel was flirting with me. Worse, I was enjoying it. I had to remind myself that Joel couldn't help but flirt. He was genetically programmed to spread his charm and good looks around. I had to become impervious. It wasn't personal. It was just Joel.

THREE

I had spent the last eight years working hard to put my career front and center in my life, dodging any personal complications. I could control my career—the harder I worked, the more success I had. It balanced out the fact that I didn't have anyone special in my life. Of course, I'd tried. I'd dated in the first few months after he'd left—all part of my reinvention. But my heart wasn't in it. I wanted Joel. I was in love with *Joel*. No one else quite measured up. Adam came along to black tie events and dinners when I needed a plus one. And I had good friends.

Piece by piece, I'd managed to pull together a reality that worked for me.

Now Joel was coming back, and no doubt he hadn't lost any of his charm or good looks.

Eight years ago, Joel had left for New York and I'd never seen him again. Never even spoken to him. A part of me had assumed there would be some sort of resolution between us. That he'd come back, forgive me, declare that he couldn't be without me. I'd always believed that either we'd live happily ever after, or I'd fall out of love with him.

But neither happened.

Joel was gone, and yet, not. The thought of coming face-to-face with him brought the realization that my reality was twisted. I thought of Joel as still being with me because he *was* with me in my heart. I still had conversations with him in my head. Still smiled when I saw couples kissing when they thought no one was watching, if only because I knew it would make Joel smile. I followed his career, either through snippets from Adam or Matt, or through the occasional Google search.

I never stopped missing him.

It wasn't that I wasn't in love—I was. It was just that my love wasn't in my life. Love hadn't been enough.

Of course, he occasionally came back to London to visit or for work, but I'd always managed to be busy or away. A clean break was what he'd said he wanted, and it was the least I could do. Because our friends had no idea that there'd ever been anything between us, no one said anything.

But now he'd be home for good and I wouldn't be able to dodge him. My brain, which I'd managed to trick into thinking I was happy, into thinking I could live with a one-sided, long-distance relationship, had to face reality. I'd been in love with a man I hadn't seen or spoken to for eight years. *Shit.*

The waves of panic that had started on the drive back to London and got more violent when I was on my own were threatening to drown me. When I was panicked, there was only one thing to do. Take positive action. I was good in a crisis, and this was a chance to shine. I glanced at the empty ice cream carton on my coffee table and took a deep breath.

I pulled out my mobile from under my knee and muted the television I hadn't been listening to.

"Jules, hi. So, I need your help."

"Anything. Name it. Although, I'm going to take some convincing about participating in an orgy. I'd visit a sex club though. Is that what this is about? I've heard about one in Hammersmith—"

"What? No." I shook my head. "Listen, I know you're on those Internet dating sites . . ."

"Oh. My. God!" Jules squealed. "I've finally broken you, haven't I?" She was always begging me to start Internet dating and up until now I'd resolutely refused. "You know it's the only way to meet someone in London. This is going to be great."

I was pretty sure *great* was going to be far from what it would be. But hopefully if I was dating someone else, it would stop Joel thinking I'd been waiting for him this whole time. Wouldn't it? "I haven't even said anything yet."

"I can hear the resignation in your voice."

"Okay, so you'll help me put myself online?" I asked.

"Tomorrow night. You bring the wine. I'll bring my laptop. This is going to be so much fun."

"Fine, whatever. Just don't tell anyone." I'd managed to stop my lack of love life being the center of attention. I didn't want to disturb the waters. But I needed a focus to prevent me from falling apart when he came back to London. And as much as I knew no one could be Joel, maybe someone could dilute the part of me that was still hoping for him. "Especially don't tell Adam."

"Because you two are having a secret affair?" she asked.

"Because he will tease the shit out of me." If Jules told Adam, Adam would be sure to tell everyone, including Joel.

"Please, Jules," I whined, which I knew she absolutely hated.

"Fine. Whatever. No need to get your knickers in a twist."

I put down the phone and immediately felt sick.

Christ.

I was going to have to get over him before he got over here.

FOUR

Joel and I moved around the cafeteria in a now-familiar pattern. The yelling from the tables, the clatter of trays on metal, it all faded into the background. Not because Joel and I were talking. We were just focused *until* we could talk. We'd fallen into this dance over the last few weeks. We split our duties—him at the hot counter. Me at the cold. There were no words between us, just a pointed finger from him as I held up a Coke and a Lucozade or a smile from me as he got extra fries for me without me having to ask.

We met at utensils. "Did you get ketchup?" he asked. I tilted my head as if to say, *of course I got ketchup. I always get the ketchup.* And he grinned his shit-eating grin. He led the way out of the food section to the tables and found us a spot by the window.

"How was the mock exam?" Joel asked, shaking the sachet of ketchup and examining his burger as if he were considering different ways of tackling it.

"It was blah," I said, sighing dramatically.

He looked up at me as if he hadn't heard me right. "Blah?"

I nodded.

"You're a freak."

"I'm a freak? Because my mock was blah?" I took the cherry tomatoes out of my salad and put them on Joel's tray.

"Yup." He transferred the paper cup of fries onto my tray and I slid his Lucozade across the table to him. And we were set.

"Okay," I said and I shrugged.

"That's it?" He picked up his burger with both hands.

"What do you want me to say?"

"I want you to tell me how your mock went, you freak." He stuffed a huge bite of burger into his mouth as he rolled his eyes.

I laughed at his exasperation. "It was neither good nor bad." I swirled around my salad, trying to cover it with the dressing.

"Oh, well, that explains everything." His mouth was full and it should have been gross but like most things Joel did, he made it adorable.

I shook my head. Because I shouldn't be finding anything he did cute. "What? It was a European Law exam. How much detail do you want?"

He swallowed. "Well, did you get the question on the difference between direct effect and direct applicability in relation to the antitrust stuff?"

I didn't quite know what to say. Joel looked at me expectantly.

I raised my eyebrows. "And you think *I'm* the freak?"

He pulled back. "Hey, why am I a freak?"

"You're a freak because A, you are a geek about

economics and B, because you know way too much about *my* exams. *Le-gal* exams. And yes, I did get the question."

"I knew it." He punched the air and I shook my head again.

"A geeky freak."

"I'll take that." He grinned.

I glanced to my left to avoid the buzz I felt whenever we made eye contact when he was smiling like that. I knew he couldn't help it. Dave Johnson was coming toward us. We were on a table for four. I hoped he wasn't going to sit down.

"Hey, you at hockey practice today?" he asked and I faded into the background noise and concentrated on my salad.

I wasn't sure whether it was because I was so out of his league or whether it was because everyone was so wrapped up in their own worlds that no one noticed Joel and I were spending time together. Adam just put it down to our shared geek-like tendencies. He loved that maybe he could be cooler than Joel, although I suspected he really knew that could never be the case. He lacked the fundamental confidence Joel had. My friends saw him picking me up and dropping me off every now and then—okay, Joel dropped me off most evenings, but because he caught up with Adam afterward, it looked like my presence was coincidental.

I glanced up as Joel and Dave talked about practice and Lee Rigby's busted knee and whether he'd play again this term. Joel's chest expanded as he leaned back in his chair and the muscles in his arms bunched as if he were about to start press-ups.

Dave didn't look at me. Not once. And I didn't mind at all. Within the bustle of university life, Joel and I had carved out a secret world only occupied by him and me. Joel had stepped out of our world for a second, but he'd be back.

I wasn't delusional. I understood what we were—study buddies. Friends. But I still basked in the intimacy of it. He might be a ridiculously handsome study buddy, but no one, including myself, thought for a moment it could be more than that. He was way out of my league. I barely ever used makeup. I didn't give a shit what I wore, as long as it was warm. I couldn't remember the last time I got my hair cut—it just hung down my back. I didn't bother blow-drying it as it took too long. The girls that Joel and Adam surrounded themselves with were well groomed, pretty, vivacious, always ready to laugh at their jokes. Those women were almost a different species. I didn't resent them and they didn't notice me—that's just how it was.

Joel flirted with me, there was no doubt about that. But he was just wired that way. I continued to pretend to be impervious to his charms. The *actual* imperviousness wasn't going too well. I thought he was devastatingly attractive, of course, but more than that, I liked him. I liked spending time with him. I wanted to share my news with him and I wanted to hear all about his life outside the library. Him growing up. His hopes for the future.

I wanted to know every private thought he had.

IT WAS ONLY eight but I'd already been up two hours. I had three deadlines next week and needed to study as though it was my job if I had any chance of making it through. "Hey, come in," I whispered, in response to Joel's soft knock. Courteous, as always, he knew my roommates would be asleep for a long time yet. It was a sweet, thoughtful habit, and it always made me smile. "Sorry I'm not packed up," I said, reaching across my desk to gather my papers.

When he didn't reply, I glanced over my shoulder and he was leaning against the wall. Instead of his normal grin, he wore a slight frown as if he were almost in pain.

I looked at him, trying to figure out what he was thinking.

"God, you look beautiful in this light, Ava," he said, his voice soft and serious.

I turned my whole body to face him, wondering if I'd heard him right. I opened my mouth, trying to find a reply. His gaze dipped to my lips and then back to my eyes. My heart began to thud against my chest. What was happening?

I turned away. I must have imagined what he said, misunderstood the way he was looking at me. "No, I don't," I mumbled, in case I'd misheard. I reached for my bag to add my books.

His warmth heated my back; he was almost touching me. "Yes. Yes, you do," he whispered, his words curling over my body. I stood frozen as he ran his hand down my arm.

"Joel." My small voice cracked. What was he doing?

"Turn around, Ava." His voice was thick, deeper than usual and I shivered.

Was this really happening? Joel didn't pick girls like me.

Reluctantly, I turned. But I didn't dare make eye contact.

"Ava," he said again as he brought his hand to my throat, sliding it behind my hair as he cupped the back of my neck. Our foreheads met and our breath mingled. We stayed like that for a long moment, on the brink of something. Tentatively, I slid my hands up to rest on his chest. *Oh lord, that chest.* I'd sat across from his magnificent chest for the last few weeks, imagining how it would feel to touch, stroke, kiss. Broad and hard, it most definitely lived up to every expectation. I daren't move, worried I'd lose control and not be able to stop what he'd started and I'd fall and fall and fall.

He slowly pulled his forehead from mine and replaced it with his lips, kissing me lightly. My eyes closed as I stood still. He dipped his head to my neck and placed feather-light kisses from my ear to my collarbone. I gasped, and, as if he had been holding back until that moment, he found my mouth urgently and pressed me to him.

I didn't know which way was up, as if I were floating in space where there was no left or right, or sounds, and no light. I just sank into him. Just for a second. Just for a minute. Or two.

He ran his tongue along my bottom lip, placing gentle kisses at each corner of my mouth. I moaned as I let my tongue be surrounded by his. His arms moved around my back, pulling me into him so there were no gaps between where he ended and I began. His kiss deepened and I felt him thicken against my stomach. Slowly, I smoothed my hands across his shirt and up to his shoulders. I wanted to feel every part of him. I reached into his hair and he groaned. *Was I really making him groan?*

Suddenly he broke our kiss. *Had he realized his mistake?*

"You taste even better than I imagined." He sighed and then dropped another kiss on my lips, and another at the corner of my mouth, and then another. "You're so soft."

I recommenced my exploration of his shoulders and neck. "You imagined this?" The chemistry I'd felt between us all these weeks hadn't been all in my head? It wasn't just the normal Joel Wentworth charm . . . it had been meant for me?

"Oh, I've been having very inappropriate thoughts

about you, Ava Elliot," he said, then kissed me right out of my shoes.

My stomach flipped and I let my head tip back. His mouth fell on my neck, his tongue trailing across my skin between kisses. The sensation was so excruciating, I thought I'd burst.

"Stress relief, huh?" I mumbled, recalling an earlier conversation.

"Something like that," he said, just before I caught his bottom lip between my teeth.

The kiss seemed to go on for days, and I was happy to stay there until graduation. A bang of a bedroom door upstairs invaded our private world, and we both looked at my closed door toward the sound.

"What was that?" he asked, pulling his hands from my hair then intertwining my fingers with his.

I shivered. "Probably Adam. He's so noisy." Adam would not believe what was happening below him, here in this room. No one would.

"Please don't tell anyone," I blurted as I drew back a little and spoke into his lips that hovered over mine. "Promise." No one could know about this.

He nodded and pulled me toward him again, silencing me, just holding me.

They say a promise easily made is easily broken. But there was no doubt in my mind that Joel would keep his promise. Why would he want anyone to know about this either? He could have any girl on campus. No one would understand why he'd kissed me.

"So," I said, trying to fill the silence.

"So . . ." he whispered against my ear.

God, his breath on my neck felt *so* good. I leaned into

him, wanting to be closer. "Hmmm," was all I could manage as thoughts tumbled about in my head.

Joel jerked away. "So, stop distracting me. Come on. Library." He swatted my bottom and I jumped at his sudden change in direction. "Study break is over. If I stay in this room alone with you another moment, I may never leave." He grinned at me, and I captured my lips between my teeth to prevent myself from returning his smile.

My heart grew twice as big in my chest as we collected my stuff and he put my rucksack over his shoulder and guided me, with his hand on my lower back, out of my room.

No one could know about what just happened. I didn't want to be labeled the ridiculous geeky girl who thought she had a shot with Joel Wentworth. I'd be his study buddy, his friend, but I was nobody's fool.

FIVE

Tonight, Jules was coming over to help me with my dating profile, so I'd left work early. Mondays were never great but a weekend away and two nights where memories of my ex-boyfriend ensured I didn't sleep meant the day had been a complete write-off. I was a total liability. I just couldn't think about anything except Joel. When was he coming back? How would I feel when I saw him? I kept going over and over it in my head. I'd sat through a meeting for two hours and came out without a clue of what had happened and no notes to rely on. I sent an email with at least ninety typos in it to a partner and he'd gone completely apeshit. I needed a boyfriend, fast.

Jules arrived about three minutes after I'd changed into leggings and my favorite, very worn sweater. My style had evolved since university. After forcing myself to buy a whole new wardrobe after Joel left, I found I quite liked fashion. At work, I preferred shift dresses with higher-than-high heels and bold jewelry. My hair finally had a style:

long layers that made the most of my natural wave, with lowlights done by an actual hairdresser. At university, I had been known to cut off my own split ends. But we'd all grown up. We couldn't live in jeans and T-shirts our whole lives.

When I'd seen pictures of Joel on the Internet at the beginning of his meteoric rise as a successful entrepreneur, it'd seemed odd to see him in a suit. Though he had that innate style gene some people just seemed to be born with, I'd never known him in anything but casual clothes. He'd always looked so great, but in a suit, he looked like something else—a movie star or a model or something. But a little less like my Joel.

God, I hoped he didn't wear a suit when he came home to London. Partly because I was going to feel overwhelmed as it was seeing him again. But also because I still wanted him to be my Joel.

"Oh, this guy seems perfect for you. Complete workaholic," Jules said, taking a sip of her sauvignon blanc. She could open a bottle of wine quicker than anyone I knew, and before I could say "But is he marriage material?" we'd polished off our first glasses and she'd created my profile on a well-known Internet dating site. Jules was excited, but for me it was a means to an end. I needed to get over Joel. I'd had eight years, but now I had to do it almost overnight.

"Jules, I'm not a workaholic. I just do *work*. We can't all get paid to party." Jules was in PR and was out most nights.

"Whatever. You're going to need a guy who understands how important your career is to you. That's why you've been single for so long—most guys don't want to marry a career-focused overachiever. You'll intimidate them."

"Really, Jules, that's just too many compliments at one

time. I'm blushing." It was a good thing Jules and I had been friends for as long as we had. She could get away with talking to me like that. But she wasn't so wrong. I wasn't the girl that ended up with the guy.

"You know what I mean. You've always had a little too much Hermione in you."

"And who said I wanted to marry the guy?" I found it hard enough to imagine anyone *touching* me other than Joel. Marriage was not in my future. "Let's just find someone hot."

"Making up for lost time, I see. That's my girl." Jules was right again—I had eight years of lost time. "What about this one? He sounds nice. Accountant, good-looking, sporty. What's not to like? Wink at him! He's online now."

Oh Jesus. Was I really going to do this?

"There." Jules said, clicking the mouse. "I've done it for you."

Jules winked at three more guys before the gossip took over. "So my new boss' boss is totally hot," she said.

"The married guy?"

"Just because he's married, Ava, doesn't mean he's not hot."

"Yes, but it does mean that you shouldn't be *thinking* he's hot." Jules' glass was almost drained, and I reached for the bottle.

"I'm not saying I'm going to start dry humping him at team meetings. I just think he's hot. No big deal." But it was a big deal. Jules had had an affair with a married man before and, big surprise, it hadn't ended well. She shrugged it off now, but at the time she'd been broken. It had been heart-breaking to watch. She'd really thought she was going to marry the guy—when he left his wife.

"And, anyway, with Joel back in town, I'll have plenty to

distract me this summer." Jules grinned from ear to ear. Nausea washed over me. Jules and Joel together would be my worst nightmare. Watching him with anyone would be bad, but with my best friend, where I'd have to hear every detail, would be too much.

"So he's not bringing a wife or girlfriend?" Was that subtle enough? Everything about Joel became magnified in my head so, although objectively there was nothing wrong with asking about a mutual friend's relationship status, I couldn't help but worry that my need for him coated every word I spoke.

"Not from what Adam was saying. I think Joel's pretty wrapped up in his business, and now that it's gone global he wants to be based in London. I don't think he'd move if he had commitments in New York. Right?" she asked, taking another sip of wine.

"I guess." I'd been careful not to drink too much tonight. I needed to keep in control, so I just took baby sips to every other one of Jules' gulps.

"You guys were close at uni, weren't you? Haven't you spoken to him at all?" My cheeks reddened at Jules' question. I had to tread carefully, not give anything away.

"Not seen him for ages," I mumbled.

"But you were good friends, though? You had such a crush on him!"

"What are you talking about? We were study buddies." I got up to go to the fridge to get some more wine, hoping to change the course of the conversation.

"You so did. Oh my God, I remember now," Jules said, bouncing in her seat. "Didn't you kiss him in that nightclub at Adam's twenty-first birthday?"

"Like you'd remember anything from that night. We were all completely hammered. You slept on your doorstep." I stared into the fridge, enjoying the cool taking the edge off my embarrassment.

"It seemed like a good idea at the time." Jules was frowning as though trying to recall the reason behind that decision.

"Oh my God, yes." I pulled a bottle of wine from the door and headed back to the sofa. "You were trying to get away from Adam because you'd shagged him and left him lovesick."

"I don't know what you're talking about." Jules jutted her chin in the air a little indignantly. "I had part of my brain removed, so I don't have to remember that particular disaster."

I giggled at the memory. Adam had followed her around like a puppy for a couple of weeks.

"Saved by the bell," Jules declared. "Will, the accountant from Holland Park, just winked back at you."

Three glasses of wine ended up being all it took to convince me it was a good idea to meet Will the next day for a drink. And when Bruce, a salesman from Hoxton, suggested drinks on Thursday, I thought, *in for a penny, in for a pound*, and said yes straight away, much to Jules' shock.

Two dates in one week. Operation Get Over Joel was in full flow.

BEFORE I KNEW IT, I was headed for a bar in Soho to meet Will. It felt like business. And business I'd gotten good at over these past few years. I'd set myself a task and see it through. Will was my task for tonight. Last night I'd created a spreadsheet and listed all the things I should be looking for. I knew it was going to be difficult not to compare every man to Joel, so having a spreadsheet as my comparator seemed like a better idea.

I saw him as soon as I entered the bar. He wasn't twenty years older than his photo suggested, so that was promising. Tick. He looked up and his eyes found mine. He smiled and stood up. He was tall—not over six foot but not under five ten. *Tick.*

"Ava?"

"Yes. Will?" *Ava and Will, Ava and Will?* Did it sound right in my head? It didn't sound wrong, at least. *Tick.*

He leaned toward me and kissed both cheeks. "Can I get you a drink?" he asked.

"Sure, what are you having?" I tried to be breezy.

"A beer, but I'm happy to share a bottle of wine if you'd like. Have a look at the list."

Likes wine. *Tick.* I was going to need a couple of glasses to get through this evening.

"That sounds good." Did I want to commit to a whole bottle? *Don't overthink it*, I told myself. "You choose."

"Red or white?"

"Don't mind. I'll leave it to you."

"Oh, is this my first test?" he asked. I looked up and found him grinning at me, and I couldn't help but return his smile.

"Not your first," I deadpanned.

"Oh, I see, and how am I doing so far?" he asked, still grinning.

"All test results are confidential until the end of the evening." My smile was genuine. He was confident and at ease with himself.

"Okay, playing it cool. I can work with that."

"You like tests?" I asked.

"I'm an accountant. The only people who sit more tests than we do are lawyers. We have to like tests. Right? And I've never failed one yet."

Doesn't take himself too seriously. Flirty. *Tick* and *tick*.

The waitress joined us at our table. "We'll have a bottle of the New Zealand pinot noir," Will said, looking at me while he ordered. He was confident that if this was a test he would pass, and he was right. Not a cheap bottle, but not the most expensive. It wasn't an obvious choice if he were trying to impress. *Tick.*

I felt more relaxed than I had since I'd heard about Joel. I was doing something positive and I wasn't trying to impress Will. I was here to see if he was someone I could go on a second date with, not fall in love with, because I knew that would never happen.

"Have you been single long?" As soon as I asked the question, I knew I'd get it in return and I wished I hadn't raised it. What would I say? Eight years? I knew how ridiculous that sounded. How had I stayed stuck for so long?

"About nine months. You?"

"Longer." I took a sip of my wine.

"Longer?" His smile was warm without being smarmy. Generous without being forced.

"Yup. What happened with your breakup?" I didn't want a cheater. I'd learned enough from Jules to know some people were wired to cheat. Some weren't. I wasn't. Joel hadn't been.

He chuckled. "Are we ready for the previous relationship talk?"

I probably shouldn't be working my way through my checklist quite so quickly and obviously. I needed to row back. "Do we not do that on a first date? It's been a while. You'll have to refresh my memory of the rules." I tilted my head and held his gaze a little longer than you would a stranger.

"I think technically it's frowned upon, but hey, I'm up for it. Let's go crazy."

I tucked a strand of hair behind my ear. "You're a Prince fan?" Would he get the reference? Or would he think I had lost it?

He smiled and his tongue darted out of his mouth as he wet his lips. "Of course, aren't you?"

I laughed. "Isn't everyone?"

His phone buzzed on the table between us, but he ignored it and held my gaze.

"So your previous girlfriend, did she find out you were an axe murderer?"

"No, that's a secret I hope to take to my grave."

I wasn't sure joking about killing people was such a smart move on a first date but I let it slide.

"We were just going in different directions. We're still friends, though."

"Still friends? Really? Is that possible?" I couldn't imagine being *just friends* with Joel after we'd been so much to each other.

"Well, we didn't cheat on each other. I can't say we didn't *hurt* each other, but we got out before it got too bad." That sounded . . . I wasn't sure, healthy or something. I didn't know if it was a trick or if he was lying to me. Maybe he wanted her back and Internet dating was just a distraction, but from the glass house where I sat, I wasn't about to start throwing stones.

We continued to swap stories until our glasses were drained dry.

"Do you want another bottle?" Will asked.

"Wow, has the whole bottle gone already?"

"Time flies."

"It's true, it does and I did—have fun, that is—but let's quit while we're ahead." I pulled my bag onto my lap. I'd really enjoyed the evening. But I was ready to go home.

"Does this mean I failed your tests?"

"No, it means I have an early morning." He'd passed every item on my checklist that I could recall. I liked him. There was nothing to dislike. So why didn't I want to stay?

"Can I take you to dinner another time to discuss my results?"

Date two had been my goal for the evening. That was another tick. "You can take me to dinner another time—"

"Is the weekend too soon?"

I shook my head, the wine making the action more exaggerated than it needed to be. "I can do Sunday night."

I smiled all the way home. Will was nice. Suitable. And because I didn't have to worry about the possibility of him being a real prospect—someone I could fall in love with— the evening had gone as well as I could have expected. I could fake this. With him. For a while.

He'd never make my stomach swoop or my thighs shake. He'd never have me dreaming of a life together. But he was decent. And that was the standard. Eight years of being on my own was evidence that the bar had been set too high for too long.

I TOOK advantage of a quiet spell at work, and the week I had to get over Joel, and crammed in three more dates before the weekend rolled around. I shouldn't have bothered. Andrew had been okay—if I could forgive the fact his voice made David Beckham sound like a baritone. And then there was that part of the evening when he spoke to my chest. Meaning the *entire* evening. I may have great boobs, but I liked a man to look at my face for at least *part* of our first conversation.

Then there'd been David . . . who lived with his mother. I wanted to be open-minded, I really did, but to live with your mother at thirty-five? He explained it was only temporary while he found a place to buy, but they'd clearly been living together for years. Come on. *Your mother?*

But my date with Bruce would go down in history as an all-time bad date. When I first arrived, I didn't immediately see him. Well, I saw him, I just didn't recognize him. He'd lost a lot of hair since his profile picture had been taken. Some men could carry that off, but Bruce wasn't one of them. He'd clearly not gotten the universal memo sent out to all men annually since 1990 explaining that if you suffered from hair loss, you had to cut the remainder very, very short. That, combined with the fact that an hour in I'd not found a sense of humor, meant Bruce wasn't the date of the century.

How long did I have to stay?

"Aves?" Bruce asked. What had he been talking about? My mind had wandered. And why was he calling me Aves?

"Sorry?"

"Am I boring you? Not clever enough for you?" My cheeks heated. *Nobody wanted to fuck Hermione*, as Jules would so eloquently explain my singledom. I hadn't meant to make him feel bad.

"No, sorry, I'm just distracted. It's been a difficult day."

He scoffed. "Yeah, being a lawyer is so much more stressful than being a salesman."

Was I being rude, or was he? "I wasn't trying to imply anything."

"I thought you were going to be one of those girls—all about books and no sex appeal. But you're quite pretty."

Images of Joel flashed into my head. We'd been so different. Even now I couldn't understand why he'd picked me.

"I need to loosen you up. Let's get another drink inside you." He snapped his fingers to get the attention of a waitress and that was my cue—dull was acceptable, and he could always cut his hair, but a man who snapped his fingers at anyone wasn't the man for me.

"I'm afraid I can't stay, Bruce. I'm going to have to head off."

"Jesus. What a waste of a night. You're a bitch. No wonder you're single. And don't think I'm paying for that glass of wine you had." He was making this way too easy for me.

"It's been a pleasure, Bruce." I fished out a twenty pound note from my purse, laid it on the table, and walked out.

I might be too clever sometimes. I might not be the beautiful girl men make fools of themselves over. Or the charming, polished social butterfly everyone wants at their party. But I'd learned enough since college that I knew I deserved to spend time with someone who was nicer to me than Bruce.

SIX

The ten-minute post-kiss walk to the library seemed to be over in about ten seconds. I had to hold myself back from reaching across to touch Joel. I had so many questions. Was the kiss a one-off? He could have any woman, why me? What were his inappropriate thoughts?

I wanted to fast forward and find out what happened next.

We found our desk and set up our laptops as usual. I couldn't risk a glance in Joel's direction. I was sure my confusion was written all over my face. I just had to concentrate on studying—I could handle that. It took me ages to settle down, but eventually I focused on my thesis.

Hours later, I genuinely jumped when a scrunched-up piece of paper hit my keyboard. Joel was grinning at me when I looked up. He pointed at my computer and mouthed, *Email*. My stomach flipped at his smile. My body tightened under his attention.

J: You wanna grab lunch?

He'd written it over an hour ago. I looked back at him, trying desperately to suppress my grin. I half nodded and shrugged. I could hardly say no. But lunch would mean talking. Were we going to discuss the kiss and what it meant? Would things shift between us? Joel started typing and another email popped up.

J: *Is that a yes?*

A: *Yes, that's a yes. You want it in writing?*

J: *I thought lawyers liked everything in writing.*

A: *Yes, but I'm the lawyer.*

J: *Good point. You're going to be an excellent one. Let's go.*

I glanced up from under my eyelashes and found him still looking like that cat who got the cream. I rolled my eyes and collected my things for lunch.

I had to assume the kiss was a one-off, right? Things would just be the same as they were. We were friends and were spending a lot of time together, so lines got crossed sometimes. Nothing to get excited about, please move along. At least it wasn't going to be weird. He'd asked me to lunch, so we were still friends. I took a deep breath and we headed out.

The library cafeteria was crammed. We fought our way through the crowds, and Joel spotted a table in the corner by the windows where we set down our trays.

"Wow, it's busy." Were we going to talk about what had happened? I didn't want him to think I was freaking out. Which I completely was.

Joel nodded, his mouth full of lasagna.

"Hey, Joel."

I glanced up to find a rugby player hovering over our table. While Joel was friends with everyone, my world was more restricted. I might have coffee with one or two of the people who took the same courses as I did and I'd wave in the corridors to a few others. The people I lived with were the only people I considered friends. After various discussions of what the plan was for a party later in the week, the nameless rugby player said goodbye to Joel and left as if I were invisible—as if I hadn't been sitting there the whole time. I guessed that's why Joel never introduced me. He understood how different we were and how I didn't fit in his world.

Joel turned back to the table and began to eat again; his full attention seemed to be directed at me. He took a sip of his drink without taking his eyes off me.

"So, I enjoyed kissing you this morning," he said just as I'd taken a bite of my apple.

God, I was going to choke. He enjoyed kissing me this morning? I raised my eyebrows and gave a half nod, unable to speak—and not only because my mouth was full. I had no idea how to respond.

Joel grinned. "Was that 'I enjoyed kissing you, too,' in Ava-speak?"

I swallowed and grinned back at him; his teasing brought me back to our easy friendship. "You want it in writing?"

Joel tipped his head back and gave a full, throaty laugh. During all the conversations Joel had with all the people who had interrupted our lunches over the last few weeks, I'd never seen him laugh so freely and genuinely. I could reach a part of him those other friends couldn't. And it felt great.

THE NEXT MORNING, Joel didn't pick me up, which

was normal for a Tuesday—something about the Modern History of European Macroeconomics—but I was still disappointed. Part of me had hoped he would skip lectures this morning, stop by and kiss me again. He'd left the library the previous afternoon for hockey practice, and other than joking about how he enjoyed kissing me, it was almost as if it hadn't happened. Which was good but . . . I wanted something more.

I secured our normal table, slung my jumper on the desk opposite mine and, without Joel to distract me, I quickly buried myself in work.

I felt him before I saw him. The air seemed to thicken, the scent of his familiar body wash surrounded me and my skin tightened all over. A second later, his bag landed on the desk opposite. I fought a smile and looked up under my lashes at him. He was grinning at me as if pleased to see me. He had my favorite blue T-shirt on and his hair was particularly scruffy. His hair always took the brunt of his focus when he'd been thinking too hard. As Joel unpacked his backpack, I kept trying to suppress my smile, but it kept popping back up. Out of the corner of my eye, I saw Joel grinning to himself as well.

It took all my energy to refocus on my work, but knowing where Joel was settled me. Somehow, I felt better when he was around. Even if we weren't talking, him being close by felt right—as if all my pieces fit together properly.

At various times throughout the day, we would wander away from our desks—for books or the loo. But we'd never be gone for long without telling the other where we were going. I'd noticed Joel leave about twenty minutes ago and I was beginning to wonder where he'd disappeared to.

"Hey . . ." Joel whispered against my ear, appearing behind me out of nowhere, his arms laden with books. His voice combined with his proximity and his clean, warm scent overwhelmed me. I closed my eyes. It took everything I had not to groan, to reach out and pull him close to me.

Oh my God, what is he doing to me?

"Hey, you," I whispered back. When I opened my eyes, he had returned to his side of the table, setting down his books while looking straight at me. I felt myself blush all over. This man was under my skin.

He pointed down at his laptop—his way of telling me he was going to email me. I was researching background on one of the cases I was working on, going through Hansard, when an email popped up. I resisted looking at it for at least two seconds.

J: You look like you're working hard.

A: Yes, that's what the library's for. Stop distracting me with inane observations.

Of course I loved that he emailed me. And he distracted me just by being alive.

J: You started it.

A: You emailed me!

J: Only because you're so distracting.

Oh my. He was cute.

A: That, I can't help you with.

J: Oh, but I think you can.

A: I can?

J: What are you up to after this?

My heart began to thump against my chest. Why was he asking?

A: Sleep?

J: I can think of something way better.

Flirty Joel Wentworth might just kill me.

A: I love to sleep.

J: Waaaaay better.

A: Chocolate?

J: Waaaaaaaay better.

A: Better than sleep or chocolate . . . vodka?

J: You're really going to make me work this hard?

A: I don't know what you mean.

I wasn't sure if he was suggesting a drink, a date, sex? Or just a stroll back from the library. He was definitely being flirtatious but I wasn't about to assume anything. He was Joel Wentworth and I was just Ava.

J: Let me cook dinner for you tonight. At my place.

Was I ready for just the two of us? We'd only kissed once. I knew I liked him, but was "dinner" code for sex for a man as handsome as Joel? I wasn't sure I could sleep with him. If I crossed that line, I might not survive. It would be so much more of a big deal for me than for him. I couldn't handle being a notch on Joel's bedpost. But I was excited, and I knew I wouldn't say no. I wanted to spend time with him. I wanted him to kiss me again.

A: What are you cooking?

J: Chicken.

A: Chicken? Just chicken? Sounds delicious . . .

I loved to tease him. Pretend I was inoculated against his charm.

J: It is delicious. It's my mom's recipe. I can't give too much away. We can go straight from here.

A: Okay.

J: Please stop being so enthusiastic. It's overwhelming, really.

A: Okay.

He peered over his laptop screen and we exchanged grins. There was no hope that the rest of this study session was going to be productive. My mind was whirring and my stomach was in knots. Was he *really* going to cook? Would the conversation between us dry up when we were off campus, and holy moly, what underwear was I wearing?

JOEL LIVED *JUST* OFF CAMPUS, less than a ten-minute walk, but it somehow seemed more grownup than living in student accommodation. I'd been here once, but not since our first year—the very beginning of the first semester—for a punch party during Freshers week.

"This house is nicer than I remember," I said as I put my bag down in the hallway. Joel came up behind me and helped me off with my coat.

"Well, last time you were here you were one of a hundred people." I hadn't expected him to recall I'd been at that party. Joel hung our jackets up and walked toward me.

"I guess." Nerves stole my words. We were talking as if everything was normal, but my knees were weak from his stare and my heart was pounding. He looked at me as if he wanted to rip my clothes from my body. He was so close, but not touching me. My breath hitched. *Why* wasn't he touching me? Finally, he pushed my hair behind my shoulders and bent to kiss my exposed neck. My skin burst into flames and my head fell back, urging him on, but he pulled away.

"Are you going to help me with the chicken?"

"The chicken?" Was he serious?

"Yes, the chicken. Do you listen to anything I say?" I'd expected him to jump me as soon as we got through the door, and he *had* kissed my neck, so what was the fascination with eating? Did he want to prove to me he hadn't invited me around just to get naked? Was he *trying* to hold back?

I followed him through to the kitchen—my skin still singing—totally confused and more than a little frustrated. I wanted to be kissed.

"Grab the mushrooms and onions from the fridge and start chopping, my little sous chef."

I sighed exaggeratedly. "I wouldn't have accepted your invitation if I'd known I was going to have to cook my own dinner."

"You so would have." His raised his eyebrows in a pulse and grinned. I couldn't argue with him. He was right. "Either way, I'm glad you're here," he said as he passed behind me, his hand skirting my waist as if he couldn't bear to be near me and not touch me.

Joel busied himself with chicken and spices and God knew what, but he really seemed to know what he was doing. I stole glances at him at every opportunity. He padded around his kitchen barefoot and comfortable, his muscles flexing beneath his worn T-shirt. I had to concentrate so I didn't instinctively reach out to touch him.

"How are you getting on?" He stepped in behind me, pushing his stomach into my back, rubbing his cheek against mine. "You smell good."

"You like the smell of onions?"

"You don't smell of onions. You smell of you."

"I have a smell?"

"You do. It's . . . sexy."

I pushed back against him, unable to stop myself. I wanted to feel more of him. He snaked his hands around my waist. I dropped the knife and ran my hands down his arms. His breath slid down my neck and he kissed me lightly, his skin on mine. My T-shirt rode up and his fingers trailed over my belly, sending shockwaves to my groin. Right then I'd happily become another notch on Joel's bedpost.

I was affecting him, too. His hardness pressed against my back. My underwear dampened at the thought of his dick and how it would feel in my hands, between my thighs. As if he knew, he spun me around and buried his hands in my hair and pushed his lips to mine. His mouth was urgent, like he couldn't hold back. I couldn't—didn't want to—stop. I savored the thick, broad muscles moving beneath my hands.

"We should stop. We have dinner to make," he whispered. Abruptly, he pulled away, and I stumbled against the counter, my head light from his touch, trying to get my thoughts together. He'd turned and was again consumed with cooking, as if nothing had happened. What was going on with him?

I found my balance and turned my back to him and began again on the onions.

"So, how's the thesis going?" he asked lightly as he rinsed whatever was in the colander under the tap.

"Okay, I suppose. I'm just not sure I'm that interested in the result. I'm just going through the motions."

"That doesn't sound good." He set the pan down and leaned on the counter next to me. "You have to love what you do." He slid his hand down my back and I turned to him. He was focused on me as if what I was saying was the most important thing he'd ever heard.

"You think so? Don't people just get by?" I shrugged.

"You want to just get by?" He drew his brows together. "You don't want passion in your life? You don't want to love what you do and who you're with when you do it?" He made it sound so simple. And it probably would be for him.

"I'm not saying that's not what I want." I studied his face—his smooth skin, those high cheekbones, his full mouth. He looked so handsome when he was earnest. "But is it realistic to expect it? Isn't life easier if you accept that it won't be perfect?"

"I think we should totally accept life as *gloriously* imperfect, but I think we should at least *strive* for passion in what we do."

I leaned against the counter. "I guess."

"You guess?" His face relaxed and he broke into a wide grin. "That's a convincing rebuttal. What are your grades like in Advocacy?" he asked, the smile ringing through his voice.

I giggled and threw a mushroom at him. I loved his teasing. It was who we were. "I told you, I'm not sure I'm passionate about this legal stuff. Maybe I've not found anything to be passionate about. Yet." I glanced up at him, and he was looking at me but didn't reply. Did I sound stupid? Did people feel passionate about anything except alcohol at university? I turned back to the counter. "Here, I've done your chopping. Do you have placemats?" He pointed to the cabinet next to the fridge and I began setting the table. "So what's your deal?" I asked.

"My deal?" he responded from behind me.

"Yeah. Your deal." I wanted to know why he seemed to be so many people rolled into one. He was popular but had time for everyone, including me. He was a good student but knew how to have fun. He seemed too good to be true.

"I'm not sure I have a deal."

"We all have a deal. You seem to be this domestic god slash study freak by day, man-whore, party animal by night."

"Wow, man-whore?" His back stiffened.

"God, I'm sorry." I'd been trying to be funny and casual and got it all wrong. "I just open my mouth and whatever's in my head just falls out." I abandoned the silverware and made my way over to him. I pushed myself up onto the counter to sit next to where he was stirring the onions in the saucepan on the hob.

"Yeah, I'm learning that about you," he said, though he wouldn't look at me.

I dipped my head, wanting to catch his eye but his gaze was downcast and fixed on the pan. "I'm sorry. I really am. I was trying to say you seem to be perfect."

He sighed. "I'm sorry that's how you see me."

"They're not bad things to be."

He turned to look at me finally. "Are you actually high? How can 'man-whore' be anything but a bad thing? Jesus, Ava." He threw the wooden spoon into the pan.

He moved away, but I took hold of his T-shirt at the waist and he paused as the material tensed. "Joel." Holy fuck, I'd really upset him. What was I thinking, calling him that? He just seemed so relaxed and confident all the time that it hadn't occurred to me I could affect him. I tugged at the shirt and reluctantly, he turned to face me. I reached out to stroke his arm. How could I make this better?

"I'm really sorry. It's just you have a constant stream of girls following you around, and Adam is always talking about his conquests when he's out with you. We get extreme detail, which is quite frankly disgusting. I don't like the way he treats women—like if he shags enough of them it somehow makes him a better guy." I was trying to explain but the more I talked the worse it sounded.

"I'm not Adam, and just because there are women talking to me doesn't mean I'm shagging them."

"I know. I didn't think." I reached across and pulled at him until he stood between my legs. Face-to-face, I traced his eyebrows with my fingers. He closed his eyes as I made my way across his cheekbones and down to brush his mouth. Such perfectly full lips. I leaned in and licked the seam where they joined together, then pressed my mouth against his. Our mouths parted and then his tongue met mine. His arms snaked up my back and I felt forgiveness.

He pulled back at the unmistakable smell of burning food. "Shit, the rice is totaled."

"I'll do another batch." I pushed myself off the counter and took the pan of burnt rice over to the sink.

Joel stood beside me, his thigh resting against mine. The last thing I ever wanted to do was upset this man next to me. I needed to stop trying to find out who he was and let him show me. And from what I'd seen so far, he was a guy who deserved my trust.

Dinner was quiet. I thought I was forgiven, but Joel wasn't saying much. While washing up, I used every opportunity to touch him, to graze past him, to remind him I wanted him. Eventually, when we'd finished cleaning up, I put my arms around his waist and my head on his chest. We stood wrapped around each other for long moments, his lips pressed against my head.

"I need to get you home before things get out of hand," he said.

"I thought . . ." How embarrassing. I'd assumed there'd be more. That *I'd* have to put a stop to things if I didn't want things to go further. And I wasn't sure I would have stopped anything. I pulled out of his embrace and headed toward the hallway.

"You thought what? That I was going to take advantage of you? You shouldn't believe everything you hear, Ava." His singsong voice had an edge to it.

I turned to face him, desperate for him to understand. I was getting everything wrong. I didn't think Joel was a man-whoring monster. I just didn't get why he would want me.

"That's not what I meant at all—I'd never think that. I thought you were attracted to me." I felt so stupid. I couldn't believe what I was saying. Why would Joel like me when he could have his pick of girls? My dad had always told me my brain was a bigger asset than my beauty. "I thought you were—*we* were going to sleep together."

He reached out and grabbed my waist, pulling me to him so there was no space between us. "Look at me, Ava." His eyes softened when I did. "I'm beyond attracted to you. I think you know that." He rolled his hips, pressing his erection into my stomach. "But I'm not that guy—the one people talk about. I'm not saying I'm a saint, but it's not always just about sex."

But wasn't it always about sex with guys like Joel?

"Okay," I mumbled, unsure what to say.

"You don't sound convinced."

"I'm not sure what you want me convinced of. I just thought . . . I just thought you wanted . . . *I* just wanted . . ."

"No. Not yet. I want you to trust me completely. I'm a patient man and I need you to be ready, really ready, so ready that every inch of you is begging for me." He ran his fingers up my spine and I melted against him.

I wasn't sure if it was Joel I didn't trust or myself. But as long as he was holding me, kissing me, touching me, then life wasn't so bad.

SEVEN

Present

I looked around the busy café. Every table was full and all the customers were wearing black or navy. A typical lunch in the City. I'd make a bet eighty percent of people at the tables were lawyers or accountants.

Jules and I had agreed to meet, but she was running late. I hoped she'd get here soon. I'd had an email from Hanna about a welcome-home dinner for Joel and I couldn't stop thinking about how it would be to see him, to touch him, to watch him smile and him not be mine. I needed Jules to distract me.

I looked around, desperate to empty my head of Joel. There were a couple of good-looking men in the place. Had I not been noticing men for the last eight years? One guy by the window was sitting by himself, reading the paper. He looked up, found me watching him, and smiled. I glanced away, embarrassed to be caught ogling people in the middle of the day.

"Hey, there." Jules burst in, a tornado of red and pink in

a sea of dull. "Sorry I'm late. My bitch-faced boss wanted to tell me all about how great she was, again."

"No worries," I said, still distracted by my stranger at the window, who'd gone back to reading his paper.

"You look relaxed. Was Will a good shag?" She collapsed in her seat and beckoned a waitress.

I didn't need to answer. Jules knew me well enough to know I hadn't slept with Will. I didn't do one-night stands, no matter how much Jules promised me it would help my stress levels.

We placed our order with the waitress and Jules poured water for us both.

"But it's good you're seeing him again," she continued without missing a beat. "You must like him."

I did, and I'd forgotten how good it could feel to meet someone new. Even my girlfriends had been in my life for years. The problem was the moment I started to think about Joel, everything else disappeared.

"Yes, he seems nice." I took a sip of my drink.

"But Bruce the baldy, not so much."

I hadn't told her about Andrew or David. Four dates in a week sounded kind of desperate, and maybe I was, but I didn't need Jules to know that. I couldn't risk her wondering what the sudden urgency was and figuring out the only thing that was different was Joel was on his way back.

"Definitely not. Will's funny and confident. He reminds me of . . ." I caught myself, just before I mentioned Joel. I'd hate to give away my feelings for him now, after all this time. I smiled and looked away from Jules, catching the eye of the stranger in the window. We held each other's glance for a second too long, but were interrupted by the waitress delivering our usual lunch.

"So you seem to be really into it—the Internet dating

thing. I thought you'd wimp out when it came to actually going through with meeting a man."

"Well, like you say, it's hard to meet people in London. And I've not dated in a while, so . . ."

"You've never dated. And it's not like you're not attractive. You've given Hermione a little twist since university. It's high time you fell in love."

It was high time I fell *out of* love.

"Have you loved any of the guys you've been out with since Miles?" We rarely spoke about Miles, or their affair. It had all been so messy.

Jules swallowed and put down her chicken wrap. "Nope, but I'm out there, hoping it will happen. And having some pretty good sex and plenty of very mediocre sex in the meantime. Speaking of, did you get Hanna's email about Joel's dinner?"

"Yes, this morning. What do you mean, speaking of good sex?" Had she and Joel hooked up before? On one of his trips back to London? If she had, it might just kill me. I couldn't bear the thought of Joel being intimate with anyone, let alone my friend.

"You know, all the good sex I'm going to be having with Joel when he's back in town."

"Oh right. Are you seriously interested?" *Please say no. Please say you've decided to become a lesbian, a nun, to marry the guy behind the counter.*

"Of course. He's single, rich, good-looking, tall, funny. Why wouldn't I be?" Right, why wouldn't she be? And Jules was single, pretty, funny. Why wouldn't he be similarly interested? Holy fuck. Trying to get over Joel was hard enough, but doing it while he dated one of my best friends would be impossible.

I'd read Hanna's email regarding the welcome-back

dinner set for Saturday night about eighty-seven times. She'd arranged a private room at a gastropub on Marylebone High Street, near where Joel was staying or living or whatever. The invitation list included Hanna, Matt, Leah, Daniel, Jules, Adam, Joel, and me.

Could this be any more excruciating? Hanna had called everyone to check if we were all free, so I couldn't pretend I had other plans, which left me with work or food poisoning as the potential excuses. Neither one was looking like a strong contender. Work was the obvious excuse, but then everyone would give me a really hard time about it. And did anyone believe you when you said you had food poisoning? Even if I did find an excuse, wasn't I just putting off the inevitable? I was going to have to see Joel at some point. A welcome-back dinner would at least mean I knew exactly when we were going to see each other. I wouldn't be caught off guard if I ran into him in the street or at Hanna and Matt's. It also meant I could spend the next week getting prepared, mentally and physically. If I could do nothing else, I could look as good as possible when he first saw me. I wanted him to know that I'd survived. I wanted him to want me like I wanted him. I wanted him to feel what I felt every time I thought about him.

"Do you want to help me shop on Saturday for a date outfit for Sunday?" I had a hundred things I could wear on Sunday. I was more interested in getting something for the following weekend.

"I'm happy to assist you in spending your money. I have none, though, so you must make sure I don't like *anything*." It was an empty request. We both knew Jules would outspend me two to one—she had little self-control.

"COME THE FUCK ON!" Jules screamed from the sofa. She'd clearly finished her drink and was ready to get going. I was doing everything to delay leaving for the welcome-back dinner.

"Coming," I said, taking a final look in the mirror. I looked as good as I could look. My hair was in shiny, soft brown waves falling loosely across my shoulders, which were exposed with a fifties-style, black-satin, fitted top with a wide neckline. It showed some skin, but no cleavage. My red pencil skirt hit me just below the knee.

Perfect.

Jules burst through my bedroom door. "Wow, you look great."

"Don't sound so surprised."

"I'm not. But . . . I mean you look really good. Sexy even."

"Yes, you said. The shock in your voice isn't flattering."

"You know, sometimes I still think of you as university Ava. I forget you grew up into this . . . " She narrowed her eyes a little. "Confident bombshell. You should date more. It gives you a glow." But I was sure it was the thought of Joel that gave me a glow. Although part of me was terrified and dreading seeing him, part of me was excited. I'd missed him. I wanted to catch up on all his news. I wanted to share my news with him. I wanted to smell him. Dear God, I missed his smell—that clean warm scent that told me I was home.

"Let's go, crazy girl," I said.

"Okay, glowy girl."

We clambered into a cab and set off for Marylebone High Street, my heart rate rising with every mile.

"So, how's Will?" Jules asked. "Did you shag like bunnies?"

"Yes, Jules, that's exactly what happened." I didn't want

to think about Will when I was steeling myself to see Joel again. It was almost as if I were being unfaithful to Joel, which was, of course, ridiculous.

"All right, no need to be snippy."

"Sorry," I said. "We didn't shag like bunnies, but we had a good time. He's funny. Good company." Jules didn't respond as she touched up her lip gloss. "I like him." Which was true, but Will didn't give me butterflies. I didn't fantasize about him naked . . . but I did *like* him.

She twisted closed the top of her lip gloss and snapped her bag shut. "Good."

"Good? That's all you've got? No lewd comments? No piss-taking?"

She shifted in her seat so her body was turned to mine. "It's nice to see you putting yourself out there and having some fun." She patted my hand. "I want to see you happy, Ava," she said, rarely so serious.

"And what about you?" I asked.

"What about me?"

"You haven't slept with your boss' boss, have you?"

"No, you're right. I shouldn't even be thinking about him. I really like my job. I don't want to have to resign because I've seen my boss naked."

"Houston, we have a breakthrough."

"And there are plenty of hot, single guys out there for me—Joel included."

Jules was relentless and rarely failed when she set her mind to something, so I really hoped she was joking about making a play for Joel. Joel wouldn't do that to me, would he? Even a one-night stand between them would potentially kill me.

"Are you even listening to me?" she asked.

"Sorry, I'm distracted."

"Thinking about Will naked?" she asked.

I smiled at Jules. This was what I'd wanted, right? To be dating someone by the time Joel was back so he wouldn't think I was a sad spinster. It was just that now that I was actually going to see Joel, it seemed kind of wrong. I belonged to him. I had from the moment he'd first kissed me back in my bedroom all those years ago. And despite not having seen him, spoken to him, touched him for so long, nothing had changed. For me.

EIGHT

Sitting across from Joel in the library, I couldn't think of anything but touching him or him kissing me. I'd only had sex once before Joel—a one-time thing with a boy from school. I'd manipulated the situation so I was completely in charge, or so I'd thought. I didn't want to go to university a virgin, so I'd decided to find an opportunity to make sure that didn't happen. And that's what I did. It wasn't about lust. It was about control. It was an item on my task list. The experience wasn't unpleasant. I wasn't one of those girls who were damaged by their first time, but it hadn't rocked my world, either. It had been practical and over quickly. Job done.

My desire for Joel was something I'd not experienced before. My whole body was attuned to him. I could tell when he was close, even if I couldn't see him. My skin tightened; a warmth spread through me when he was near. Every now and then, he would look at me in a certain way and instantly my legs would weaken and dampness would rush to my sex.

He looked up at me and caught me staring. It was late and I was done studying. I'd had lectures all morning and he'd had lectures most of the afternoon. I hadn't seen him all day, and I didn't want to be working now that he was in front of me. I wanted his mouth all over me.

My lips parted involuntarily, and he smiled and pointed toward my laptop.

J: You're gorgeous.

My breath caught in my throat. How could he say that about me? But right now, I didn't want to question it. I just wanted to sink into it. Enjoy his attention.

A: Shall we grab some food at yours?

J: Sure.

A: Can we go now? I'm done studying.

J: You're going to have to give me a minute.

A: Are you in the middle of something?

J: Kinda.

It wasn't like Joel to be evasive.

A: Kinda?

J: Kinda. I can't move for a bit.

A: How come? Hockey injury?

J: You're wearing a skirt.

I reread the message, trying to understand what he was saying.

A: Way to change the subject.

J: It's short and I have visions of my hand up it, feeling you, touching you. It's making me hard and if I stand up, I'm going to embarrass myself.

I flushed. He felt this heady desire too. It continued to surprise me—him wanting me. I just wasn't that girl. As Jules always reminded me, I was Hermione. I didn't get the guy. That was Jules. That was Hanna. I wasn't the heroine of my story.

It had been over a week since I first had dinner at his house. I'd been over twice since, and there had been kissing —lots more kissing—but I wondered if, despite his reassurances, the reason he was delaying sleeping with me was that he really didn't want me physically.

A: I wore it for you.

I felt more feminine with Joel, wanted him to desire me. When I'd put on the skirt this morning, I hoped he'd like it. I couldn't remember ever dressing to make a man notice me before.

J: Are you trying to lead me astray?

A: I want you to do the things you said.

J: You want my hand up your skirt?

A: I do.

J: What else?

A: What else?

J: What else do you want me to do to you?

My breath hitched. I'd had a million fantasies, but I couldn't share those with him . . . could I?

A: I want to feel your hands everywhere. I want my hands on you. All over.

Heat flushed across my face and my heartbeat pounded in my ears. I glanced around. Could anyone tell what was going on between us across the table?

J: And my mouth, where do you want that? Do you want me to kiss you everywhere?

A: Yes. Everywhere.

I took a deep breath, trying to steady my breathing.

J: Even where you are warm and wet for me, slick with desire for me?

He heard me gasp and our eyes locked across our

laptops. Before I had time to formulate a response, he'd emailed again.

J: *Tell me what you like.*

A: *I like you.*

J: *What do you like in bed? What makes you come? Tell me?*

Oh God. How could he ask me such intimate questions?

A: *I don't know.*

J: *What do you mean you don't know?*

Didn't he realize how inexperienced I was?

A: *Please don't embarrass me.*

J: *Baby, I'm sorry. I'm not trying to embarrass you. Talk to me. Are you a virgin?*

Baby? He'd never called me that, but I liked it. It made me feel like I was his, which I was. I might doubt his feelings but I was sure of my own.

A: *Not quite. I've had sex.*

J: *You don't sound sure.*

How did I admit to him I was so inexperienced? I had to trust him.

A: *Once.*

I heard the groan from across the desk.

J: *Just as I thought you couldn't get any hotter. Don't be scared. I won't rush you. We don't have to do anything you don't want to do.*

A: *I'm not scared. I want you. I want to be with you.*

J: *We need to get out of here. Right. Now.*

Joel grabbed his hockey jacket and put it on while he was sitting down. It was cute to see him fumbling around. He was always so nonchalant about everything. I followed his lead and began packing up my books and my laptop. Was this it? Were we going back to his place to have sex?

Joel grabbed my backpack from my desk and slung it across his shoulder as he normally did, then took my hand in his. It caught me off guard and I pulled away without thinking. He frowned, but didn't say anything. I was surprised by him wanting to be public about our . . . what was it? Fling? Friendship? Kissing arrangement? I didn't want to be another one of those girls who lusted after Joel Wentworth and made a fool of themselves. I didn't want people gossiping about me, wondering what Joel was doing with me, judging me.

By the time we got to his place, I was nervous. We dumped our bags in the hallway, pulled off our shoes and I followed him into the kitchen.

"So, my little sous chef, what are we going to have for dinner?"

Apparently, dirty-talking Joel was clearly confined to email.

"I don't mind," I said.

"You'll let me choose?"

"I'll let you take the lead."

"What happens if I choose something you don't like?"

"It's good to try new things. It broadens my horizons," I said, obviously no longer talking about food.

He tilted his head as he looked at me, taking his time before he responded. How far would he push this? What did he want? "I wouldn't want to scare you off. What happens if I offer you something disgusting, like sheep's brain? You'd never forgive me."

"I could never not forgive you for anything. Do you even like sheep's brain?"

"No, but I'm just saying . . ."

"Well, if you want to try sheep's brain, I'll trust you." I reached for him and linked our fingers together.

"Now is okay, but not in the library?" he asked, watching our hands.

I nodded and met his gaze as he looked up. "When it's us, it's okay."

"Just us?" He narrowed his eyes.

"I like just us. In a bubble."

He squeezed my hand and kissed my forehead.

"Like we're the only two people on the planet," I said. It was the only way we made sense together—if we had no interruptions, no commentary from anyone else.

"Do you want some wine?" he asked, moving toward the fridge.

"You don't have to get me drunk to take advantage of me."

"Ava. Don't say that." He frowned. "I don't want to take advantage of you."

"Hey, I was joking. I know you don't." I stood in front of him as he placed two wine glasses on the countertop. He wouldn't look me in the eye. "Hey." I reached up and tilted his head so his eyes were forced up. "I want you. You're not taking advantage of me if I want you." I stroked my hands down his chest to the waistband of his jeans. He caught them before I could reach for the buckle and pulled my arms around my back, pulling me in close against him. He was beginning to harden.

"You're driving me crazy." His mouth parted and his gaze darted from my eyes to my lips and back again. With my arms still pinned behind my back, he walked me backward until my bottom hit the cupboard.

"When I release you," he whispered, "I want you to grab onto the work counter and don't let go."

What? I thought he was going to kiss me. Undress me. Make love to me.

"Did you hear me, Ava?"

"Yes," I replied breathily. Immediately, he released my hands and I grabbed the counter as instructed.

"Good girl." He stepped back and surveyed me, his eyes sweeping up my body. "You are so beautiful."

I squirmed under his inspection. Why didn't he kiss me? Instead, he busied himself on the other side of the kitchen, pulling out a bottle of red from the wine rack and placing it next to the glasses, and then started opening and closing drawers. His arms flexed under his T-shirt, and the semi-scowl on his face was so enticing. Just looking at him, watching him, was intensely sexy.

"Joel?" I wanted to touch him.

"Stay there, Ava." He didn't look at me.

I wanted to know he wasn't angry at me for pushing slightly. He'd said he wanted to wait until I was ready. I was just trying to tell him how ready I was.

"Are you punishing me?" That got his attention. He whipped around and raised an eyebrow. God, he was sexy when he did that. I didn't move, but I became more desperate to touch him, for him to touch me. As if his withdrawal of affection fed my need for him. He grinned to himself. He didn't look angry at all.

He found what he was looking for, opened the bottle, and poured equal amounts into two glasses. He paused before he picked up our drinks and took a deep breath, as if he were gearing up to say something. As he walked over to me, he took a sip from one glass and then offered me mine. "Keep your hands where they are," he instructed. He brought the glass to my lips and I took a sip, keeping my eyes locked with his. He pulled away and leaned against the cupboard opposite me.

"So," he said, looking at me with a half-smile.

"So?"

"So, you started telling me in the library what you wanted me to do to you. Remind me what you said."

I blushed and looked at my feet. When it was over email, it was safe. It was a fantasy. But here? With his gaze burning me up, my knees already weakened by him, I wasn't sure I could be so brazen.

"Ava? I think you said something about me touching you. All over. Remind me. Am I right?"

I nodded without looking up. I was afraid he'd see my desire for him, that he'd peek inside my head and see just how much I wanted him.

"Where should I start, Ava?" *Was he asking me to tell him where to touch me?* I peeked out from under my lashes and in a single stride, he was as close as he could be without touching me. I moved forward and he stepped back, avoiding contact.

"My lips," I mumbled. I could do this. He was Joel. I trusted him.

He brought his finger up and stroked the seam of my mouth. I opened my lips, trying to pull in more air.

"Down," I whispered. He trailed his finger under my chin and along my neck.

"Talk to me. Tell me where."

"Your hands on my breasts, Joel, please," I whimpered. He grasped me firmly. I arched into him, my head falling back.

"You like this?"

"Yes," I gasped. "I want to feel your hands."

"You have to tell me, Ava."

"Joel, please, undo my shirt. I want your skin against mine." I wanted to be closer to him in every possible way. And that was all that mattered.

Finally, he brought his mouth to my neck and pressed his lips against my skin. "Like this?"

"Yes. More." His fingers found my buttons as he kissed down my neck and across my collarbone, then followed the buttons down. Finally, Joel pushed my shirt down over my shoulders. I moved instinctively.

"No, Ava. Hands stay where they are."

My stomach flipped as I moved my hands back to where they were. I liked that he was calling all the shots. He was in control and it took the pressure off me.

He kissed between my breasts, bringing his hands over the cups of my bra, then delving inside, finding my nipples as they pebbled beneath his fingers. "Is this what you wanted to feel, Ava? Me touching you?" He rolled my nipple between his thumb and forefinger, the pressure just on the brink of being painful. His stare bore into my soul, but I couldn't look at him. Afraid that he'd see my need for him reflected back. Pleasure built deep in my belly. "Do you want to feel my mouth on your breasts, Ava?"

He knew I did.

"Talk to me. Tell me what you want."

"Joel . . . please." As if that was the signal he needed, his tongue wrapped around my nipple, his fingers still on the other one. As he alternated between tongue and teeth, I wanted to thread my hands in his hair, but I also wanted to do as I was told. He was torturing me. I moaned loudly as his teeth caught my skin. It hurt so good. "Please!" I cried out. "Let me touch you."

His lips crashed into mine, the force of the kiss taking me by surprise. He pushed his tongue into my mouth as if he just couldn't wait a second longer. His hands found my waist and then one slid lower, under the hem of my skirt to dip between my thighs.

"What about here, Ava? Do you want to feel me here?" he asked, his lips hovering over mine. I thrust my pelvis into his hand. "Is that a yes?"

"Yes, Joel."

"I can feel how much you want me. You're all wet for me." Oh, that mouth of his. My body had betrayed me, but he was so clearly enjoying it, I couldn't be embarrassed. He was chasing my reticence away with each touch.

He scratched his thumbnail back and forth across my underwear, sending tiny vibrations right to my clitoris. My lips parted, and I tried to concentrate on breathing. I felt so exposed to him, but he didn't leave me time to think. He just created need. I wanted more. I wanted to feel his skin on mine.

"More, Joel."

"Can you handle more, baby?" He thrust his hand down the front of my underwear. I cried out as the pleasure reached a new level as his fingers found my nub. "Oh God, Ava, do you see how you respond to me? I love seeing how much you want me." He buried his head in my neck as he continued to circle my clitoris. Within seconds, the beginnings of my orgasm started to build.

"Joel, stop!"

His hand stopped and he pulled back to look at me. "Are you okay?"

"Yes, I was going to come."

"That's the idea," he said, his fingers picking up their rhythm as he continued to watch me.

"Joel, seriously."

"You don't want to come?"

"Yes, but what about you?" I could barely breathe.

"I want to make you come. I want to watch while I make you come." His fingers sped up and there it was, the beginning of an orgasm I didn't have the power to stop. "Look at me, Ava. Do you have any idea how you look right now? Your cheeks flushed, your lips all red, gasping for breath because of what I'm doing to you?"

I was *gone*. I arched into him, my climax barreling down my spine. He caught me just as my legs collapsed.

He kissed me gently. "Follow me."

I staggered after him, my hand in his, to his bedroom.

"You should lie down." He guided me to his bed and I lay down willingly.

"Do you want a drink?" he asked softly.

"I don't need anything. Please stay with me." I wanted his arms around me.

Joel did as I asked and lay down next to me. I scooted closer and he pulled me into the crook of his shoulder.

"You're amazing," I said quietly. He'd only been concerned with me, how I felt, that I came. He'd put me first. And I wasn't used to being at the beginning of anyone's list.

He turned toward me and kissed the top of my head. "*You're* amazing."

I shifted my hips toward him and felt his hardness against me. My hand delved toward his jeans.

"Ava, no."

I withdrew my hand. "No?" He didn't want me?

"This was about you." He was worried he was being selfish, but I wanted him. I wanted his orgasm. Didn't he see that?

"Can't it be about us?" I asked, stroking him through the denim. "I want you to show me what to do." He twitched and thickened, so I was on the right track, but I wasn't sure what went next. I went tentatively toward his fly and unbuttoned it, using both hands to push down his jeans and briefs. He sprang loose and I swallowed. *What next?*

He put his hand over mine, curling my fingers around him, and guided me up his shaft. "You can be rougher than you think you can." He released my hand and I continued the same path. I found a rhythm, then I looked up to him for signs I was doing the right thing. His eyes were glazed and he wet his lips. Watching his face and the effect I was having on him was so erotic. A wave of desire ran through me, and I closed my eyes in a long blink to try to focus on him. Pre-come dewed at his tip and instinctively I dipped my head and licked it off.

"Jesus, Ava." He bucked his hips. Grabbing my face with both hands, he coaxed me up and kissed me. I kept my hand on him as his tongue probed my mouth and he thrust into my fist, my movement unnecessary.

I squeezed my hand slightly. "Oh God, yes, like that," he choked.

His forehead rested on mine and his breath was hot against my lips. "Ava, I'm going to come."

He thrust again and his come released on my hand as he groaned. Him coming apart like that—because of me and what I was doing to him—was something I'd never experienced. I got why he liked watching me now. Seeing him was amazing. Making him come was addictive. Powerful. Hot.

His forehead still on mine, his breathing slowed, and he kissed me gently. We'd crossed some kind of invisible boundary where I could no longer wonder whether he was *really* flirting with me. No longer worry if we were *just* study buddies who made out. Joel Wentworth and I had done stuff. Seen each other when we were most vulnerable. Looked into each other's eyes as we came. No doubt about it, we were a thing.

He scooted across the bed and returned with tissues. I couldn't pull my eyes from him as he started to wipe away the traces of his pleasure. Before he could clean my hand, I brought it to my lips and sucked my finger. He watched me intently. He tasted of salt and Joel.

"Jesus, Ava, you're going to get me hard again." He took my hand and wiped it clean.

I leaned in to kiss him. "I like you hard."

"You're perfect."

"Not so bad yourself. Now are you going to make me some dinner or what?" I asked, grinning from ear to ear. For tonight I was going to let myself enjoy him—this amazing man in front of me. I was going to push all my doubts and fears to one side and for a few hours just bask in the afterglow.

NINE

I'd wondered if my body's reaction to Joel would be the same. Sure enough, it was like a homing device. Before I'd even stepped through the doors of the pub where we were having his welcome-home dinner, my skin started singing. He was here.

"Is that Adam? What is he wearing?" Jules asked, gesturing at a blond-haired figure dressed in bright green coming toward us from across the road. "He looks like Kermit the Frog." She waved and he waved back.

"Hey, girls. You both look lovely." He kissed each of us on our cheeks. "Let's get in. It's freezing."

"Are you okay? You look terrible," I said as we made our way up to the stairs above the pub. Normally he was excited about an evening out—like a newly adopted puppy being taken out on his first walk—but he seemed subdued.

"Thanks, Ava. You can be a bitch sometimes."

It took a few seconds to realize he wasn't joking. "Wow. Sorry. I was just concerned. You look a bit down."

"You don't sound concerned. You sound like you're being a bitch."

I really wasn't trying to be nasty. He knew me better than that. "Jesus, Adam. There's no need to bite my head off!" What a great start to the evening.

"Will you two stop fighting and just have sex already?" Jules said as we walked into the private dining room. Hanna, Matt, Daniel, and Joel turned their heads.

"Who's fighting?" Hanna asked.

"Who's having sex is the real question," Daniel said.

"Who do you think?" Jules replied. "These two freaks of nature."

"You're having sex?" Hanna asked with a concerned look on her face.

"No, no one is having sex," I said, watching as Jules wrapped her arms around Joel.

There he was.

My Joel.

He looked no different. Perhaps his hair was a little darker and a little shorter, but other than that, he was just how I remembered him. Tall, strong, mine.

I blinked and took a deep breath. But he wasn't mine.

"Well, I am. I'll take Leah whenever I can get her," Daniel responded, interrupting my internal drama. "She's fucking amazing."

"Enough, Daniel. We don't want to hear about your perfect life all the time," Jules said. She had managed to pry her arms from Joel, and he was helping her off with her coat.

He hadn't met my eyes, but frankly I'd been avoiding looking directly at him until the last possible moment. I wouldn't be able to bear it if there was still anger there—he'd been the most important person in my whole life, and in many ways he still was. I couldn't handle it if he hated me. I tried to take a deep breath, but his presence pulled all the oxygen from the room. Anxiety rose in my chest and I moved toward the door. I had to get out of there. I found the bathroom and locked myself in a stall.

Eight years. It was ridiculous that this was so difficult. I had a successful career and my own flat, but Joel Wentworth could still throw me into disarray. Jules throwing herself at him made it all clear. We weren't a couple. As much as I might still be in love with him, I was just some girl he used to know. He could fuck Jules all he wanted. He wasn't mine. It made the relationship I still had with him in my head all the more ridiculous. I finally understood how I had been waiting for him all this time and how utterly pathetic that really was.

"You stupid bitch." Saying it aloud made me feel better. I could get through tonight. I had to. I couldn't spend the rest of my life broken.

As I went back into our dining room, Joel's back was to me and the group was listening to him intently. "I didn't recognize her. She seems so different, older."

Hearing him talk about me like that felt like a punch to the stomach. The sound of the door closing behind me caught the attention of the group and he turned, and I couldn't pull my eyes away. This was it. And there he was, achingly familiar, but also a stranger. "Hey," I said and I moved toward him, but Adam interrupted our reunion as he pulled me into a hug.

"Sorry for being a moody bastard. Are you upset with me?"

"No, it's fine," I replied as I looked over Adam's shoulder. My eyes hadn't left Joel's.

Joel mouthed back, *Hey.* There was no anger I could see, but I wasn't sure what was there instead. I'd always been so good at reading him, and I was disappointed I couldn't see what he was thinking.

"Really?" Adam asked. "Good." I was forgotten as Adam went to find his seat at the table.

Awkwardly, Joel moved toward me. *Do we hug or wave or shake hands?* I'd not thought this through. The others were exchanging banter, and I could hear them arguing about where Joel should sit. I reached out and self-consciously rested my hands on his upper arms as he cupped my elbows, and we exchanged kisses on each cheek. I was aware of every part of him that was touching me. Of us being so close. He smelled just like the boy I fell in love with.

Joel ended up at the head of the table, and I was on the left at the other end next to Hanna and opposite Matt. Jules and Adam grabbed seats on either side of Joel.

"Are you still banging that supermodel?" Adam asked Joel and my stomach knotted.

"Grow up, Adam. You're like a horny fifteen-year-old," Jules spat.

"You're just jealous. He's way out of your league, Jules." Their to-and-fro continued like that for much of the evening. Joel seemed to avoid getting involved, laughing at their banter but not commenting, talking directly over them at times to discuss business with Daniel. I talked a little to Hanna about work, but I didn't have to say much at all. Joel was the center of attention, and my reaction to him went unnoticed.

He didn't look at me again, not even fleetingly, and I found it easier and easier to watch him knowing his eyes weren't going to meet mine. He seemed a little older, but not in any specific way. It wasn't that he had developed laugh lines, time had been kind to him in that way. It was just in the way he carried himself. It wasn't confidence; he'd always had plenty of that. Perhaps it was wisdom.

"So, what brought you back if you're doing all this great stuff in Africa and the US?" Daniel asked.

"Nothing will change. I can run things here as well as anywhere else, and my parents are getting older. My mum has to have a hip replacement, so I'm going to look more closely at some opportunities I've got in London."

"So you've not left anyone special behind?" Hanna asked.

My insides churned, and I twisted the napkin that rested in my lap.

"We're his special people, Hanna," Jules said.

"You keep in touch with special people, wherever they are," he replied. I felt like I'd been punched in the stomach again. I was supposed to be his special person. But he was right. How could I be when I'd not seen or spoken to him for all this time? It was his way of telling me whatever affection he may have had for me had long since disappeared. And although I knew that to be true, hearing it cut like a knife.

I'd planned to make an excuse about a morning gym session and leave Joel's dinner early, but I surprised myself by staying for the entire evening. I was still drawn to Joel, even if he wasn't to me. Maybe that's what made me feel so uncomfortable. He was indifferent, which was unexpected, and brought another kind of pain. I'd been prepared for his anger to still be there. Even if I'd tried to tell myself I wasn't, I'd been hoping to see some remnants of love. But indifference?

"Shall we go for drinks?" Jules asked, clearly wanting to make it a big night.

"Yeah, let's go to that bar behind Bond Street," Adam piped in.

"Leah's away, so yeah, sure," Daniel said.

"Daniel, you are so fucking pussy whipped. Thank God I've got a real man to hang out with now," Adam sneered.

"Cheers, Adam," Matt said, clearly put out that he'd just been ignored as a potential drinking partner. Fact was, we all knew Matt was under Hanna's thumb.

"I'm not pussy whipped. I've got a hot girlfriend who I'm in love with. Of course I'd prefer to spend time with her instead of you. But if she's not here, then you'll do. It's that simple." Daniel was always so clear about things. I guess that was what had made him the richest man in England.

"You guys are great, but I have to get back," Joel said, slapping Adam on the back as disappointment spread across his face. "We'll catch up again soon enough. I'm seeing you on Tuesday for squash, right?" he asked and Adam nodded.

"We'll have to go to dinner and have a proper catch-up," Jules said. "Maybe I can cook for you at my place?"

I watched carefully for Joel's response. Was he up for a slice of Jules? I couldn't tell.

Damn it. He used to be so easy to read.

"We'll definitely do something," he said as he kissed her cheek.

And just like that we were filing out of the restaurant and waving down cabs, having said our goodbyes, and the only person who I hadn't kissed good night—the only person who I'd not made eye contact with since the beginning of the evening—was Joel.

I took a cab home on my own. Normally, Jules and I would have shared, but I couldn't bear to hear her talk about Joel and her plans for him this summer, so I hopped in one and drove off before she could ask to share.

My phone buzzed with a text from Hanna.

H: Are you okay? You seemed quiet tonight.

A: All good. Just tired. You okay?

H: Fine. Come to dinner Tuesday night. x

A: Great, thanks. Let me know what to bring. x

What I really wanted to do was run away—from everything. I ached from seeing Joel again. After all this time, it seemed ridiculous that I could still feel as strongly for him, but at the same time entirely normal. Tonight had just confirmed my feelings. Seeing him again, being close to him, hearing him laugh and joke—there was no denying he was the man I loved. Now and forever. And it was all the more painful because he wasn't mine. I couldn't reach out and touch him or look forward to later in the evening when I would be in his arms. It had been torturous.

He'd made it clear his feelings had long since passed. Pain hit me in the gut as I remembered him saying how changed I was—how much older I looked. He might be the man I'd always known. But the feeling wasn't mutual.

Surely the worst was over now. He was back. We'd seen each other. Hopefully the pain would ease. I couldn't avoid him now he was back in London, so I needed to distract myself. I should fill up my time so there was no room in my head for thoughts of Joel.

I would date Will.

And get over Joel.

It had to be possible.

TEN

Sunday night was officially date three with Will, and I wasn't sure how this worked. Would he be expecting me to sleep with him? I wasn't ready for that, but maybe it would be the right thing to do. Perhaps it would get me over Joel more quickly. I scrambled about in my underwear drawer trying to find something nice. I was running late. Will was picking me up and we were walking to a place on the high street that he liked. I'd never been—it was Turkish. Oh God, did that mean we'd be sitting on the floor? Maybe the dress I'd picked out wasn't the right thing to wear.

The doorbell rang. Going to the door in a robe was going to give him entirely the wrong idea, but holy hell, I didn't have a choice.

"Hey, I'm so sorry. I'm not dressed yet," I said.

"You look beautiful just like that," he said, a bouquet of pink roses in his hands. "Don't bother getting changed." He raised his eyebrows and grinned at me. Instantly I felt more relaxed. When I wasn't with Will, I somehow imagined him differently from how he was in person. I was always more comfortable with him than I expected to be. I smiled at him as he held out the roses.

"They're beautiful, thank you. Can you help yourself to a glass of wine while I put these in water?" I asked, moving into the kitchen to look for a vase.

"Sure, can I get you one?"

"No, I'm good. How's work?"

Will stood next to me, leaning on the counter as I started cutting down the stems of the roses. He reached out and stroked my back through my robe. I could only think about how I wasn't wearing much and how uncomfortable I was.

"It wiped out my weekend, but it was worth it. We really made progress." The fact that Will was so involved with his work was one of the things I liked about him. "You look totally stunning, Ava." His voice softened as he ran his hands up my back to my neck. He wore a serious expression. "Incredible."

He pulled me toward him, bending to kiss my neck. I tilted my head to give him better access and he laid kiss after kiss from my neck to the edge of my robe, which he softly moved off my shoulder. Releasing his hands from my waist, he slowly circled me, moving his lips around to my back as he continued his parade of kisses across my shoulder up to my neck. I sighed and heard him groan. He was good at this. Maybe I could sleep with him. I really wanted to want to.

"You feel good," I whispered.

"I do?"

"You do."

"Good to know." His lips curled into a grin against my skin. "You are spectacular."

I reached back above my head and dug my fingers into his hair. It tipped him over the edge; he spun me around and pressed his lips onto mine. As I closed my eyes, an image of Joel flashed in my head.

As his tongue pushed against mine, I pulled away. Something didn't feel right. I shouldn't be thinking about Joel while I was kissing someone else. "Come on. We have plans, don't we?"

"Well, all was going according to *my* plan." He circled his hands around my waist, but I braced my arms against his, holding him away. I was happy to flirt but I didn't want things to get too . . . physical.

"I need to get dressed."

"We could stay in."

When I looked away from him without responding, he released me and I went to get changed.

DINNER WAS tense and made worse by the fact the music was so loud we could barely exchange a sentence. Will liked flashy, expensive restaurants or seemed to. That was probably what a lot of girls expected when they dated —the newest restaurant, plenty of money spent, and if it was good enough, they were prepared to give up the goods. It seemed to be the game, but I wasn't convinced it was the way to find love. But then again, was it love I was looking for? Love hadn't been enough for Joel and me. Perhaps it shouldn't be my goal. I should just focus on getting over Joel.

After a bit of wrestling over the bill, Will paid and we headed outside to get a cab. Just as we hit fresh air, Will stopped.

"Are you okay?" I glanced behind me to find him staring at his feet.

"I feel like I fucked up. I shouldn't have pushed," he said, bringing his eyes to mine. "I want you to give me a second chance."

"It's fine." I smiled. "You haven't fucked anything up. I'm just not ready for an evening of Netflix and chill."

"I'm sorry." He looked serious.

"Seriously, Will. It's my fault. I just want to take things slow."

"Can we go for a drink? Somewhere we don't have to shout to have a conversation?"

More time with Will was the last thing I wanted. Joel was too in my head tonight. "It's late, and I have a really busy week. I need to go home." I stroked his arm to try to reassure him. It was all true. I did have a busy week, but I *always* had a busy week. He moved toward me, and I let him cup my head in his hands.

"I'm sorry."

"It's honestly fine." That word again. But it *was* fine. I didn't want him to think it wasn't. Because I didn't want to have to find someone else to get over Joel with. Will was a nice guy. "Let's see each other after work this week. Wednesday?" I asked, trying to make him feel better. He hadn't really done anything wrong. He nodded, and I kissed him briefly on the lips then stuck my arm out at a passing cab.

"Thanks for dinner, Will. See you Wednesday."

Everything seemed to bring back a memory of Joel. Tonight was no exception. I had never felt pressure from Joel in the way I had from Will, but it was just being with a man. One I knew wanted me. It brought back so many memories. I kept seeing Joel in front of me instead of Will.

But now Joel was indifferent to me. He no longer wanted me. There was no comparison to make.

"HELLO, I'm here to burgle your house," I announced, walking into Hanna's for dinner. No answer, but I could hear music and the sounds of pots and pans in the kitchen. I kicked my shoes off, hung my coat, and wandered into the back of their house toward the living space. She liked to cook, so we almost always ate at her place, particularly if it was just me. It also meant Matt could disappear and watch football and we were left by ourselves to chat.

"Hey," I said. Jules wasn't coming and although I wish I wasn't, I was relieved. It was too exhausting to be around her at the moment.

Hanna twisted to look at me. "Hey, you. I didn't hear you come in." She was dicing something on the counter in front of her.

I went over and gave her a big hug and the bottle of wine I'd brought.

"It's definitely not in the guest room wardrobe!" Matt shouted from somewhere upstairs.

"Fucking hell, Ava. I feel like his mother sometimes."

I grinned and started hunting about for a corkscrew. I knew Hanna loved taking care of him.

She tilted her head to the ceiling as she yelled back, "Well, I haven't touched it."

"Should I ask what he's looking for?" I poured three glasses of wine, not quite sure why there weren't half-drunk glasses already strewn about the kitchen as there usually were. "Has he lost his penis?"

"I can only hope." We giggled. "It's his squash racket.

He can't find it because he only uses it once every three years."

"Got it!" Matt shouted and thundered down the stairs. He came into the room in very short shorts and a fleece top.

"Why are you wearing Jimmy Connor's shorts?" I asked as he gave me a kiss on the cheek.

"Ha-ha. Don't you start. I've already had abuse from Hanna. This is what you wear to play squash!"

"It's not what I wear, ever, and I don't think anyone has worn anything close to that since 1983," I replied. Hanna and I were still giggling when the doorbell rang.

"Ava, can you get that?" Matt asked as he crouched, his head in one of the kitchen cupboards.

"Sure. Are you expecting someone?" I slid off my stool and headed toward the door.

"It'll be Joel."

I stopped stock-still. *Joel?* I couldn't answer the door! I hadn't prepared myself. I wasn't ready. Why was he here? Was he coming to dinner? *Fuckety-fuck.* No, he must be going out with Matt. I couldn't refuse to let him in, especially since I was already on my way.

I took a big gulp of wine and headed down the hallway.

"Hi!" I said, breezily as I could manage, as I pulled the door open and stood aside to allow him in. His eyes grew wide and I looked away, ignoring the buzz across my skin.

"Er, hi. I . . ."

"Matt's still getting ready. Come in." I think I sounded normal, but I wasn't convinced.

I led him down the hallway. Matt's shouting canceled out the silence between us. "Hey, mate. Give me a minute. I've lost my shoes."

Joel went over to kiss Hanna on the cheek.

"Do you want a snack before you go?" Hanna asked. "A

glass of wine?" She was always ready with food and drink, no matter what time of day or night.

"I think wine before squash could be dangerous." Joel smiled at her with affection in his eyes.

"I think it sounds a lot more fun than sober squash," Hanna said. She had a point. "What have you been up to this week? Do you feel like a Londoner yet?" I was desperate to hear his answers, to hear anything from him now he was here in front of me.

"All good, settling in and meeting contacts . . ."

"Hey, Joel, come and look at this," Matt said, interrupting Joel's vague answer and indicating something on his laptop.

"I hope it's not porn," Hanna muttered.

"Yes, I'm showing Joel porn in front of my wife and Ava. That's exactly what I'm doing."

I giggled, relaxing even though Joel was so close. Hanna ignored him. They both hunched over the laptop, laughing at whatever they were looking at.

Joel was more Joel in casual clothes. More *my* Joel. The Joel I'd have crept up behind and pushed my hands up under his sweatshirt, feeling his broad back, smelling the familiar Joel smell.

"Can you take over chopping while I do the salmon?" Hanna asked, interrupting my fantasy. I moved my stool over so I could sit and chop. "You can be my sous chef."

I looked up, and Joel and I locked eyes. The reference wasn't lost on him. My cheeks heated before he quickly looked away, and I went back to chopping.

"How did it go?" Hanna asked.

"What?"

"Date three with Will, silly."

"Oh, right. It was okay." And not a subject I wanted to

discuss at the moment. Not in front of Joel. Apart from being awkward, it seemed wrong.

"I need more detail than that. I have to live vicariously through my single, beautiful friends." Hanna was always mock-complaining about the fact she'd been in a couple for a decade and that she had a boring life, but we all knew it was just a front. "Was he huge?"

"You're moaning about me showing Joel porn when you're over there objectifying Ava's poor boyfriend?" Matt asked as Adam crashed into the room, clearly having let himself in just as I had.

"What boyfriend?" Adam asked.

I wished I could curl up and die. The last thing I wanted was to have my dating life dissected in front of Joel. I blushed, looked deep into my wine glass, and stayed quiet. Part of me was desperate to know whether Joel was interested in my new boyfriend. Did he have any feelings left for me? I couldn't risk a glance in his direction. I didn't know what kind of reaction I would be hoping for.

"We're not objectifying anyone. I'm asking factual questions about Ava's boyfriend's penis."

"He's not my boyfriend, and we are not discussing penises—penii—whatever."

"Who's not your boyfriend?" Adam barked. "You're not actually dating someone, are you?" I looked up and saw Joel concentrating on the laptop, totally ignoring the whole situation.

"Is that a green-eyed monster I see?" Matt teased.

"Shut up, Matt. You can't start with the banter when you're wearing those shorts," Adam shot back.

"Fucking hell, can we go back to talking about porn?" I pushed off my stool and went to refill my glass.

"Can you boys piss off and go play squash and leave us alone to talk about penises and porn?" Hanna asked.

"Yeah, come on, guys, we're booked for eight. Let's get a move on," Joel said. He completely avoided looking in my direction and acted as if I wasn't even in the room—as if the questions about Will hadn't been asked. I watched him as he strode out into the hallway first. He still had the same confident gait, the same broad shoulders. Would he still feel the same under my fingers?

"So, we were talking about Will's penis . . ." Hanna turned to me as the front door slammed.

"No, we weren't." I sounded resigned even to my own ears. "You know as much about his penis as I do."

"So you're not that keen?"

"Honestly, I don't know." I sighed. I desperately wanted to feel more than I did for Will. I wanted what I'd felt . . . for Joel. "I know I'm not dying to tell him about my day. I know I don't have to hold myself back from touching him. I know my skin doesn't buzz when I'm within a hundred yards of him." I glanced up and found Hanna looking at me, her brows drawn together as if I'd confused her.

"That doesn't mean you two can't work. It's early days and love isn't like fairytales, Ava." I knew different. Life with Joel had been exactly like that. "Well, at least you're getting out there. You'll find someone, even if it's not Will," she said. I kept my smile in place.

But I *had* found someone. I'd also managed to lose him.

ELEVEN

Making dinner had been a waste of time. Joel was a good cook, but I'd lost any appetite with my first orgasm. I couldn't concentrate on anything but Joel and his strong hands and smooth skin—his perfect jaw and messy hair.

I couldn't stop grinning at him, and Joel couldn't stop looking at me as though he wanted to devour me, which was the biggest turn-on. That a man who knew me as well as Joel did and wanted me was nothing I expected. He was everything I never thought I'd find in a man.

Eventually we abandoned our plates and went about what was now becoming a routine of clearing up the kitchen. I used every opportunity I had to accidentally brush his arm or place my hands on his hips so I could squeeze past him. I was practically panting by the time we finished, waiting for the next installment of my physical education. However, to my surprise and disappointment, Joel offered to walk me back to campus instead of taking me to bed.

He didn't try to hold my hand. Part of me was relieved because I'd told him I wanted to keep us private, but part of me wished he had. When we got back to my place, he pecked me on the cheek and left. Just like that. He didn't invite me to stay with him another night, didn't suggest he stay with me.

He just . . . left.

I didn't sleep a minute that night.

The next morning, exhausted and pale, I went to meet a classmate who had some research that overlapped with my thesis. Normally, on Wednesdays I'd be in the library all morning and Joel would meet me there after his 9 a.m. lecture. The change in our routine gave me a moment to breathe. Last night had been so confusing—one minute he'd seemed like he couldn't get enough of me and then he'd just gone cold. Things had been going so well, I didn't understand why he'd put an end to things or why he hadn't wanted me to stay. But maybe all he wanted from me was his release. Perhaps I'd been kidding myself and I'd just been another conquest to Joel. My stomach churned. Had I been a complete fool?

Walking back to the library, I wondered if Joel would be there already. Normally he'd arrive by mid-morning. It was past noon now. If he was trying to avoid me, then he probably wouldn't come to the library at all. My heart was racing by the time I entered through the turnstiles. I made my way up the stairs to the third floor, anxiety thrumming through me, making my steps unsteady and my head swim.

I went the long way around, prolonging the agony, trying to muster up some more courage. But there he was, in his usual seat, his jacket slung over my chair opposite him. I couldn't help but pause and grin at the sight of him. I realized a girl was crouched at his feet whispering to him. He was tilting his head to hear what she was saying and she had her hand on his knee. My vision blurred for a split second. I wanted to punch her. Hard. In the face.

I made my way over and, without acknowledging either of them, unpacked my rucksack, sat down, and powered up my laptop. After a minute or so, the girl stood up and left. I deliberately kept my eyes firmly affixed on my notebook—I could feel Joel's eyes on me. A ball of paper landed just by my hand. I couldn't have *not* seen it, but I pretended it hadn't happened.

"Ava!" Joel stage-whispered.

I ignored him. His chair scraped against the floor as he got up, and he headed over to my side of the desk.

"Hey." He sat on my notebook, almost crushing my hand in the process. "Are you ignoring me?"

Of course I was. "No," I said curtly.

"Can I kiss you?"

He wanted to kiss me? "No," I said. *Please kiss me.*

"Oh, I see," he said as if he'd had an epiphany, but he didn't elaborate. He just sat there. I tried to ignore him and opened my thesis. I was typing gibberish, but I was typing. From the corner of my eye I saw him acknowledge various passersby. Why was he sitting on my notepad, smelling so good? His thigh was almost touching my arm, inviting me to stroke it through the denim. Teasing me, the muscles tensed and relaxed as he swung his leg back and forth. We stayed like that for about ten minutes before he pushed himself off the desk.

"Come on. It's lunchtime," he said brightly.

I sighed, a little exasperated by the whole situation. "I need to get through this, Joel. If you want lunch, go on your own," I said as quietly as I could.

"I want to have lunch with you. If you want to fight

with me, then let's have it. If you want to try to break up with me, then let's hear it. But don't sulk. I can't bear it when you look sad."

He was right—I was sulking, but only because I thought he didn't want me. But if he was talking about me breaking up with him, that must mean that from Joel's point of view, we were together. Was that how he saw us? He was assuming things about us, and I wanted to dip inside his brain and see it all.

I followed him to the cafeteria. He kept falling back to walk with me. I concentrated on looking straight ahead. When we arrived, it wasn't too busy. Instead of grabbing us both trays, which was what he normally did, Joel went to the fridge that stored the take-out lunches and selected two sandwiches and some drinks, then headed over to pay. I stood still and waited. I was unsure where we were going or what we were going to do.

Joel headed toward me with our lunch in a bag and, without looking at me, roughly grabbed my elbow. "Come on."

I twisted my arm from his hand and pulled away. "Oh right, yes. God forbid anyone was to see us touching, Ava," he sneered.

I followed him out of the cafeteria and around the back toward the outdoor tennis courts. It had been raining, and it was the wrong time of year, so the place was deserted. We made our way to the benches set into the hill opposite the courts and Joel took a seat. "Sit, Ava."

I did as I was told.

"What the fuck is going on?" he asked.

I shrugged. I felt small and stupid and I didn't want him to be angry with me. I wanted him to pull me onto his lap and bury his head in my neck. "You look sick, baby. Are you sick?" His voice softened and I shook my head.

"I didn't sleep." My eyes slid to his and back to my lap. He looked concerned.

"Why? Are you worried about something?"

Everything was so confusing. Last night had been so weird but now he seemed back to normal. "I wanted you to stay. Last night, I mean. But you went cold on me." I sighed. "I don't know what's going on with you, Joel Wentworth. With us."

He didn't say anything for a long moment, then exhaled. "I wanted to stay. I just don't want this to . . . I don't want to rush you, or me, or . . ."

Relief rolled off me. "So, you're not bored with me?" I asked, looking up at him under my lashes.

"How could I ever be bored with you? All I think about is you. I just want it to last. I don't want it to burn out. I went home last night because we have plenty of time."

"You think about me?" I asked.

"Yeah. All the time. How do you not get that?"

I shrugged. It didn't seem possible. Didn't he see how mismatched we were? "Me too."

He chuckled. "You too?"

"You're on my mind. A lot. Like all the time, I mean. And I don't want us to burn out either."

He nodded and I reached for his hand and linked my fingers with his.

We ate our sandwiches one-handed.

TWELVE

Will and I were on date four, discussing work, a possible pre-emptive bid on a pharma company. I liked the fact he was interested in my world. He knew a lot of lawyers, so he understood when I talked business. We were at another flashy restaurant. It was quieter this time, though. We could talk, and I remembered I enjoyed his company without having to try too hard.

"Do you think that will work?" Will asked. He seemed genuinely interested in our strategy.

It was Friday night and we'd met straight from work. I felt less pressure that way. I didn't have to worry so much that he would suggest we stay in.

"We're not sure. It's a bit unusual, and the client isn't 100 percent comfortable, but I think they recognize it's probably the only realistic option," I replied.

Since our last date, we'd had a few phone calls that'd lasted into the night. It had relaxed me, and despite having canceled our mid-week date, I'd agreed to reschedule.

"Should I order another bottle of wine?"

"Sure," I said, slightly too fast. I was nervous and aware Will would probably want to take things further tonight. I was ready. Well, I had picked out my best underwear, at least.

"Do you think you'll always want to work?" Will asked, catching the waiter's attention as he did. It gave me a beat to think about what he'd said.

"As opposed to what?"

"You know, when you have kids. Do you think you'll want to still work?"

I laughed. "Do you think you'll still want to work when *you* have kids?" I asked him right back.

"Touché, Miss Elliot."

I wasn't sure whether it had been a question off the top of his head or if I was being interviewed as potential wife and mother material. I'd never really thought about my sudden frenzied entry into Internet dating as anything but a means to get over Joel. I certainly hadn't thought it would be the path to marriage or children. I couldn't ever imagine being married and sharing a life with anyone but Joel.

The second bottle of wine arrived and we fell silent as the waiter went through the ritual of presenting the bottle, uncorking it, pouring a small amount to taste, and then filling our glasses. Will caught my eye. I smiled and looked down to my glass.

"So how are your gang of friends?" he asked. We'd spoken on Tuesday night, right after I'd gotten back from Hanna's, and I'd given him the rundown on my "gang." It felt a bit juvenile when he said it like that. But they were important to me. They were family.

"Good. I'm going shopping with Jules and Hanna tomorrow."

"Hanna's the married one and Jules is in PR, right?" He grinned as if he knew he'd just aced a test. But I didn't like it. He wasn't part of that world.

"Well remembered."

"Hanna's married to Matt and Jules and Adam are single. Daniel is with Leah but Leah is not from university."

"Er, yes. Thanks for the recap."

Will laughed. "I just want to make sure I remember who they all are. I'm looking forward to meeting them."

What? I'd never suggested he meet my friends. "Oh right." I didn't know what to say. It wasn't unreasonable for him to assume I might introduce him to my friends at some point a long way off in the future.

"In fact, a friend of mine gave me a bunch of tickets to opening night of that new Simon Russell Beale thing at the National Theatre. We could all go, if you'd like. It's next Thursday." Will was sweet and sincere and trying so hard to please me.

"That's really nice of you, but this week at work is going to be a nightmare for me. Another time, though."

He didn't respond but regarded me as if he were trying to decide if I was telling the truth.

"Maybe the week after?" I offered. "We could all have dinner together or something." I was between a rock and a hard place. I didn't want him near my friends, near Joel. He didn't fit into that world. Bringing him into it would mean things were serious between us and they weren't. But at the same time, I didn't want to offend him. I wanted to keep dating him—going to dinner and drinks with him. But I was happy the way things were. I didn't need to take the next step with him. Going out with Will hadn't expedited my getting over Joel as quickly as I'd hoped it would. I just had to give Will and me more time. Away from Joel.

My dinner suggestion seemed to settle him, and he took another sip of wine. At least I'd put him off. For now.

THIRTEEN

Lost in thought about the evening, about Will, I fumbled in my bag for my keys, my head a little hazy from the wine. Would Will hold me to my suggestion of dinner with *my gang*? Hopefully I could delay things for a while.

I hated my handbag. It was so big and had too many pockets—I could never find anything. Fuck. I emptied it onto my front step, every so often shaking it to see if I could hear a jingle that would give me a clue where to search. No jingle. No keys.

Double fuck.

It was well after midnight. Hanna and Matt would be asleep. The only other person who had a spare set of keys was Adam. He wasn't likely to be in bed by now, but if he was I wouldn't feel bad about waking him. He regularly inconvenienced me. Trying to focus on my mobile, I squinted as I scrolled through my contacts, looking for Adam. I was drunker than I'd thought. That wasn't going to incentivize me to get to my early morning Pilates class.

His number went to voicemail. Jesus, this wasn't going well. I called back, hoping he just hadn't heard it the first time.

"Ava?" Adam sounded like he'd just woken up.

"Hey, sorry if I woke you. I've had a disastrous evening —can we skip the banter and arguing? Can you bring my spare keys over? I'm locked out."

"Ava, it's Joel. Adam forgot his phone when he left my place earlier. Are you okay?"

Oh. Holy. Fuck. Joel was the last person I needed to be talking to right at this moment.

"Oh God. Don't worry about it. Sorry to bother you." I didn't want to speak to him after my date. It seemed wrong. As if I'd been cheating. And I certainly didn't want him to hear me slur my words. I wanted him to experience capable, confident Ava. Not slurring, forgot-her-keys Ava.

"You're not bothering me. Where are you?" He sounded stern, and I didn't remember him that way. I shuddered.

"Don't worry. I'll think of something."

"Ava, answer me."

"I'm outside my flat. It's fine, though—"

"Give me your address."

I paused, not knowing how to respond. "Look, I'm going to go. I'm sorry if I woke you."

"Ava Elliot, give me your address."

I sighed. I could never argue with him when he used that tone with me, and he knew it. I did as he asked.

"Are you safe to wait there?"

"Yeah," I mumbled into the phone and hung up. Was he calling a locksmith or going to Adam's to get my keys?

Fifteen minutes later, a cab pulled up and Joel stepped

out, squinting into the darkness. I moved into the streetlight and my breath hitched. Here, in the half light, when it was just the two of us, I had a flash of how it would have been if we'd stayed together.

"Hey, come and get in."

I didn't argue. I didn't want to. I wanted a few stolen moments with him, just the two of us.

Joel held the door open for me, and I clambered into the cab far less elegantly than I would have liked. I scooted over to the other side and tried to make myself as small as possible.

Joel got in beside me, as unselfconscious as always. His long legs stretched out in front of him. He had no problem taking up space in this world, unlike me. I looked away from him and out of the cab window. His familiar smell engulfed me. I wanted to put my head on his chest and drink it in.

"Where are we going?" I asked quietly. I could touch him if I just moved a couple of inches.

"My flat," he replied.

Oh.

"Sorry to do this," I said.

"It's fine, Ava. You can stay tonight and get your keys tomorrow."

If we were just old university friends, he'd be right, it would be fine. But we *weren't* just old friends, and staying at his place *didn't* feel fine. Not to me. It felt wrong. He wasn't mine, and if I had a whole night of pretending he could be, I wasn't sure there was any chance I'd ever get over him.

"I could just get a hotel," I offered.

He exhaled but didn't respond and the rest of the cab journey was spent in silence, the air thick with awkwardness. If things were different, he'd be holding me now. If we were still together, I'd be able to tell what he was thinking. I closed my eyes and tried to remember happier times. The wine allowed me to block out how much I hated that I didn't know him anymore, that he didn't love me any longer.

I grabbed my wallet as we pulled up. Joel stepped out of the cab first, and before I had a chance, he paid the fare.

"Please let me pay, Joel," I said, pushing some cash toward him. He ignored me, greeted the concierge with a nod, and headed to the lift. I followed a couple of steps behind.

"Thanks . . . for this and the cab," I mumbled as the doors closed.

"It's no bother."

"You keep saying that."

"What would you prefer?"

"What about 'How the fuck did you lose your keys?' and 'You're a pain in the arse'?"

"You mean I should react like Adam would react."

That wasn't what I meant, but he was right—that was what Adam would have said. I followed him out of the elevator and to the only door in sight. Was his the only flat on this floor?

We entered a hallway as big as my bedroom—and way too large for London. Joel slung his keys into a bowl on a console table and strode through an archway into darkness.

"Do you want another glass of wine?" he called. I quickly slipped off my shoes and followed his voice into a huge living space. Joel stood with the fridge door open.

"Another?"

"Are you suggesting for one moment that this one might be your first?"

I gave in to a small laugh. "Sure, I'll have *another* glass of wine."

He brought two glasses out of an overhead cupboard and poured chilled wine into each of them, sliding one across the granite toward me.

"Did you have a good evening? Before you got locked out, that is?" he asked as he took a seat in the sitting area.

"I guess," I said, following him and sitting on the sofa opposite him.

"With Will?"

I gulped my wine. He'd obviously been listening to the conversation at Hanna and Matt's. "Er, yup." I adjusted the cushion behind me, trying to find an excuse not to look at him when we were talking about Will.

He nodded, his focus on his glass of wine.

"How's work?" I asked, wanting to change the subject. Joel would be able to see through me. He'd be able to tell that Will was nothing to me. Not compared to him.

"Good. Busy. Things are kicking off."

I nodded, my eyes on my glass. Was he waiting for me to say something? Something about eight years ago?

"So you've not had much time to just hang out and socialize?" I asked, trying to force lightness into my voice.

"No, not really. Just with the guys a bit."

"And Jules, of course."

For the first time since we got into the flat, he looked directly at me. He pulled his brows together. I shouldn't have said it—I was fishing for information or reaction or something. No doubt he'd smell it a mile away.

"I thought you'd said you had dinner with Jules or something," I mumbled.

"Oh right, yes. Next week."

I'd been deliberately dodging Jules' phone calls, so I

hadn't realized that she and Joel hadn't caught up. Had he cancelled or had she? I could only hope it would never happen.

"Do you mind if I get to bed?" He shifted to the edge of the sofa. "I have a conference call first thing with Beijing, and I need to be on good form. I can show you a guest room, but feel free to stay up."

God, I was keeping him awake. This evening was just getting worse. "Of course. I've got an early start tomorrow, so I'll head to bed, too."

"The bathroom is through there," he said, showing me into a bedroom. "And I think there are some toiletries in there. Toothbrushes and robes and stuff. The housekeeper stocked everything up yesterday."

For a second I forgot all the uncomfortableness and grinned at him. "Housekeeper?" The words didn't seem to sound right coming out of his mouth.

He chuckled. "I know. We're grown-ups now."

His smile quickly disappeared, as if he remembered himself, remembered his indifference toward me. A sharp pain sliced through my stomach. I wanted to reach out and touch him. To run my fingers through his hair, feel his breath against my skin.

Why had I thrown him away?

"Joel. I'm so very sorry," I whispered, trying to keep my voice steady.

He nodded, sharply. He knew I wasn't talking about inconveniencing him this evening. He knew.

"Good night, Ava."

"Good night, Joel."

He closed the door behind him, and I burst into tears. Through my sobs, I fished about and came up with a hair tie, which I put to use, and padded into the bathroom to wash my face. The tears slowed but kept falling. When I'd finished brushing my teeth, I headed over to the bed, undressed to my bra and panties, and slipped beneath the covers.

A second later, I heard a knock at my door.

"Come in," I said, holding my voice steady.

He opened the door and stood in the doorway.

"Hey, I thought you might want a T-shirt to sleep in."

"Thanks." I looked down as he stepped forward, trying to conceal my tears.

"Are you okay?" he asked.

I nodded and tears spilled over my cheeks. I was so clearly not okay.

I lay back down on my side, tried to control my breathing, and closed my eyes and put my hands over my face. Embarrassed that he'd seen me cry, and no doubt understood my upset was all about him, I hoped he'd just leave the T-shirt and go.

The bed sank behind me. Oh God, he was still here.

He lay down next to me, his head on the pillow behind mine, his breath on my neck. My body shuddered with sobs. I couldn't handle the tidal wave of emotions that crashed over me. I'd always known, but being here, so close to him but not *with* him, it was so clear to me.

I still loved him.

I would always love him.

I was so, *so* sorry.

How had I been so stupid to have missed the last eight years of his life, and the rest of our lives together? He slipped his arm across my waist over the duvet.

"Shh," he whispered and stroked my hand.

I reached for him and linked my fingers with his.

We lay like that, neither of us speaking, for what

seemed like hours. His presence soothed me. I was finally back in his arms, even if it was just for this moment.

I WOKE the next morning to the sounds of horns. Living in central London did have some downsides. As the events of last night filtered into my conscious brain, I remembered I wasn't at home. The unfamiliar smell of the bedlinen reinforced my realization. I shot upright to see if Joel was still beside me. There was no sign of him.

Shit, shit, shit. How would I handle this?

I rushed to the bathroom, and despite my intention to leave as soon as possible, I was seduced by an amazing shower and an array of super-expensive shampoos, washes, and scrubs. I had to get myself a housekeeper.

Properly washing my face, which was still swollen from the previous night's tears, was a relief. Last night I'd been reckless, just pouring out my emotions. Even though his presence had created them, I wished he hadn't seen me like that.

I found a hair dryer and pulled an eyeliner and some lip gloss out of my bag. I wanted to look a bit more put together than when Joel had last seen me. Would he be more than indifferent with me this morning?

I gathered my things, took a deep breath, and headed out to the living area. I didn't hear any noises. There were no signs of Joel.

Oh.

Should I go? It felt rude to just leave. I should write a note. Looking around for a pen and notepad, I spotted a piece of paper on the counter.

A,

Help yourself to breakfast. I've gone to the office for the day. The door will lock behind you.

J.

The fact he'd left me this morning felt horribly familiar. It reminded me of the feeling of abandonment I'd had when he went to America. The universe had a way of twisting its knife into my stomach.

FOURTEEN

Past

"Only two weeks until the end of term," Joel said on our way back from the library.

"Yeah, it's gone so fast." I usually loved Christmas, but four weeks without Joel might be the worst of all worlds. I was going to miss him.

"Have you got plans?" he asked.

"I have my thesis to work on, and we always spend Christmas Day and Boxing Day with my grandparents. So I guess I'll be doing that."

"And New Year's Eve?"

"I don't know." I hadn't wanted to think about the holidays. I didn't want to dwell on the fact I'd have weeks without Joel. As much as I loved my family, I wanted to be right here with him.

"You want to come to mine?" he asked.

"I can't tonight—Hanna, Jules, and I have that girls' night out."

"I don't mean tonight. I was thinking for New Year's Eve."

I stopped dead in the middle of the path and tried not to split my face in two with my grin. "To your parents' place?"

"Yeah. They'll be away, cruising."

"So, we'll be alone?" I started walking again. The idea of being away from campus, away from everyone who knew us, had my hands shaking and my heart beating out of my chest. I didn't have to be the badly dressed geek who didn't know what to do with liquid eyeliner somewhere else. Perhaps we'd make more sense together *somewhere else.*

"Yeah, my brother is going up to see his girlfriend, so I thought you might come and see me. Why, are you scared to be alone with me?" Joel laughed.

It wasn't that I was scared, but I understood it would be a test. As much as things might be better between us, they might not be. Would we survive outside the containment of campus? Would it be the same together? I couldn't wait to find out.

"Sure, okay. Let's do it."

"Okay. So, good."

"Okay." I bumped him with my hip.

"Okay, loser," he said.

Neither of us could stop grinning.

"Hey, Joel!" Adam shouted out of his bedroom window. Joel raised a hand at him, and we went inside. I took my rucksack from Joel and deliberately brushed my hand against his arm. He glanced back at me, and I gave him a shy smile.

"Joel!" Adam sang from somewhere upstairs.

"Coming." Joel headed up to Adam's room on the floor above mine.

Part of me desperately wanted to kiss him goodbye, but

I knew I couldn't. I had to keep him, us, about him and us. I didn't want to bring it out into the open where it could decay and die under people's scrutiny and expectations. I didn't want to be told I didn't deserve him and listen as people told Joel he could do so much better.

Jules tumbled into my room with her hair rollers and a romper on while I was lying on my bed, contemplating what Joel and I looked like outside campus.

"What are you wearing?" I asked as she slumped on my bed.

"My nightclothes. I like them!"

"Tonight, Jules. What are you wearing *tonight*?" I rolled my eyes.

"Oh, that red dress I have." I knew that dress—it always got Jules plenty of attention, that was for sure. "What are you wearing?"

I shrugged. "Jeans, I think?"

"Jeans? You are not wearing jeans. You are never going to get *laid* wearing jeans." She adjusted herself and sat cross-legged facing me.

Unlike Jules, I wasn't man-hunting tonight. I had my man, but of course, she didn't know that. I liked it that way. She'd tease me mercilessly if she knew about Joel and me. I wouldn't be able to move for Hermione jokes. "They're comfortable, and I don't really have anything else."

"Well, I'm going to make you wear that strapless black dress I have. It will look fantastic on you."

"Don't be ridiculous. My boobs will never fit in that thing," I said, peering down at my chest.

"There's no need to show off because you have a humongous chest, and yes they will, because the material is stretchy. Hang on, I'll go and get it." She scooted off my bed.

Nights like this were an endurance test for me. I didn't

enjoy being in noisy bars surrounded by pounding music and drunk guys. I was used to all three individually, but all together it was just too much. I didn't expect to have fun, but we were going to cheer up Hanna, who'd had a huge argument with Matt. So I forced myself into the shower and then into Jules' black dress.

About an hour later, we were running late, but ready to go.

"Holy fuck, girls," Adam snarked as we stumbled out of my bedroom, dressed to the nines. He was in the corridor talking to Joel. "You look half decent for once. You might not die old maids."

I left Jules to retaliate. I was too busy staring at Joel to engage with Adam. His eyes widened as he took me in.

Jules and Adam started to bicker, and Joel and I just grinned at each other.

Joel cocked his head. "Seriously?" he said.

I scrunched my eyebrows in confusion. What did he mean? Didn't he approve of my dress?

"Come on, Ava. I'm not listening to this small-dicked weasel a moment longer," Jules said, dragging me by the arm out into the evening. On my way across the quad, I briefly turned to look back at Joel, who was watching me leave.

What had he meant? Maybe I looked ridiculous.

As we got out of the cab, someone asked for Jules' number. We hadn't even gotten to the bar yet. But it was pretty much how nights like this went. I'd be left in a corner somewhere while Jules surrounded herself with panting men. I would always be a wallflower in comparison. She swatted her admirer away, and we found Hanna inside being chatted up by the bartender.

"How's Matt?" I shouted, pressing a kiss to her cheek.

The music was ear-splittingly loud and the way my shoes stuck to the spilt beer confirmed this was a place for students.

"Annoying."

"So ditch him. We're going to find ourselves some hotties tonight." Jules leaned over the bar, all her assets on show, and ordered six shots. I was definitely going to pay for this tomorrow.

My phone buzzed against my hip, and I grabbed it from my purse.

J: *Seriously?*

My stomach flipped. What did he mean?

A: *Seriously, what?*

Why did he keep saying that?

J: *Seriously, you're going to dress like that and then not spend the evening with me? Seriously, you're going to look like that and not let me touch you? Seriously, you're going to look at me like that and then leave me and my hard-on to spend the evening with Adam? Seriously?*

I giggled.

"What are you laughing about? Who are you texting?" Jules shouted over at me, pouting. All our attention was supposed to be on her. I wasn't sure how she'd even seen me; this place was so dark.

"No one. Just watching that guy crash and burn over there with that girl," I said. Jules was easy to distract with gossip.

I liked the fact that Joel wanted me to spend the evening with him, wanted to touch me. I wanted to be with him now. I went to the restrooms and texted back.

A: *Ahhhh, I see. Yes, I'm deadly serious . . .*

J: *You are enough to drive an economist wild.*

A: *Wow, the mother of all compliments.*

J: Know it. <3

I couldn't wipe the smile off my face. The fact that Joel would be thinking of me all night, the fact that he made me feel like I looked good, the fact that I had a plan to be with him later, even if he didn't know it yet—it all made the evening almost bearable. I relaxed, and instead of pretending to have fun, I realized I actually was having fun. When Hanna came back with shots five and six, it struck me that I was going to have to be creative if I was going to get to see Joel again tonight.

"Jules, it's your song!" I shouted through the opening bars of "Don't Cha."

"I *love* this song! Let's dance!" she yelled back.

"You two dance. I'll stay here with our drinks," I said, watching as Jules and Hanna headed off to the dance floor, followed by most of the male eyes in the place. Plenty of them were clearly wishing they had girlfriends who were that hot.

Seeing Jules and Hanna with those guys made me realize I didn't want to dance with strangers at all tonight. I pulled my phone out.

A: Text me when you're back at your place?

My phone buzzed. Hanna and Jules were giving the club a show—Jules grinding her way around the dance floor, writhing suggestively around Hanna.

J: Heading there now. We're done here. You okay?

I looked at my watch. A little past eleven. I loved my girls, but I wanted to be with Joel—in his arms. In his bed.

Checking that someone else had Jules' and Hanna's attention, I surreptitiously poured my two shots into the champagne bucket on the table next to us and put the empty glasses down in front of me.

Sia gave way to Madonna, and Hanna and Jules kept

dancing. One guy in particular was trying to impress Jules and he was half succeeding. He was a good dancer, and although he wasn't dancing with her, he took several opportunities to talk to her, which of course meant his mouth got very close to her ear. She rewarded him intermittently with a giggle or a flirtatious look but kept dancing with Hanna, who had her own admirers. Eventually, Jules grabbed Hanna's hand and pulled her off the dance floor back toward me.

"You girls were showing them how it's done!" I yelled.

"Your turn next, babe." Hanna smiled. Jules sat and, without saying anything, did the two shots in front of her, one straight after the other. "Come on, Hanna. You're the only one with a drink. These boys need to feel useful, help them out," she said.

Jules' good dancer was wandering in our direction with a couple of friends in tow. Hanna dutifully downed her shots and by the time Good Dancer and his friends arrived at our table to offer to buy us drinks, we were able to accept without looking like we were too interested. It was also the perfect opportunity for me to leave before Jules lost interest in Good Dancer and Hanna started to worry about getting home to Matt.

"Girls, I'm going to head off. Those drinks went straight to my head."

"Don't go!" they yelled simultaneously and started pawing at me as I stood up. "We don't get to do this very often, Ava. Stay, please," Hanna persisted. Normally, Hanna saying *please* in her oh-so-sweet voice would work on me. I'd give in and take another shot. But not tonight.

Tonight, I had other plans.

FIFTEEN

My eyes were glued to the index of the recipe book as I sat on one of Hanna and Matt's bar stools by their kitchen counter. Hanna wanted to make coulibiac. She had her head buried in a cupboard looking for ingredients while I listened to Adam, Matt, and Joel talk as they played Xbox. I wanted to figure out if Joel had said anything to anyone about me staying at his last night.

"You know Ava locked herself out last night?" Matt said.

"Shit," Adam said. "I have a set of keys, but I left my phone at Joel's."

"Yeah, she came around this morning to get our spare set," Matt continued.

So far Joel was quiet.

"Wait," Adam said. "Where did she stay last night?" Joel's eyes flicked to mine and I went back to the recipe book.

"A *friend's*, according to her," Matt said, raising his eyebrows at a confused Adam.

"Did you finally get laid last night?" Adam bellowed at me across the kitchen.

Hanna stopped talking and looked back at the boys, but I kept my head in the book as I died inside. Laid was the exact last thing I got last night.

"Adam, you pig, who are you screeching at?" Jules yelled as she wandered into the room holding a bottle of wine.

"Ava got laid last night," Adam said.

I wished Adam and Matt could keep out of my love life.

"She did not. Did you, Ava?" asked Jules. I met Joel's eyes again. Nothing had happened last night. Joel had just helped out a friend. So should I just say I stayed at his? The thing was, I didn't want to dismiss anything he did for me as *nothing*. Was he going to say something? I didn't know anything anymore.

"No, I didn't get laid last night."

"You see?" Jules said, obviously happy to be right about my lack of sex life, again. "I told you."

"So where did you stay?" Adam asked.

"Ask Matt. Apparently, he knows everything." I slipped off my stool and went to the loo. Jesus, I hoped they were over this by the time I came back.

When I returned, everyone was ensconced around the Xbox again and Jules was lying on the back of the sofa behind—and far too close to—Joel. She kept asking questions about the game, giggling and generally annoying the shit out of me. Could she be any more obvious? "I'm off," I announced. This situation was torturous. And anyway, Hanna and Matt were having Matt's boss and his wife over for supper, so I knew Hanna was stressed—it gave me the perfect excuse to get the hell out of there.

"Are you out tonight?" Jules asked from her reclining pose on the sofa.

"Yup, dinner with Will," I answered.

"Wanna hang out tomorrow? I need to pick out a sexy date outfit for Tuesday night with this hunk," she said, her hands roaming across Joel's back. Joel didn't seem to react—either to encourage her or discourage her. It was almost as if he hadn't noticed she was there.

"Maybe. I'll text you." I let my eyes wander to Joel, but he was concentrating on the screen in front of him. Should I have said something? He was going to think I was still that girl who hid things from her friends. That I was still scared of everyone else's thoughts and opinions of us. That I didn't care enough about him to overcome my fears.

But he would be wrong. Everything had changed.

Past

I knocked on Joel's door. No answer. He hadn't messaged to say he'd made it home, but his last text said he was heading back, so I'd grabbed a cab and touched up my makeup on the way over. Maybe he'd changed his mind? I knocked again. Joel's silhouette appeared behind the frosted glass in the door, followed by rustling of keys in the lock. My heart began to pound. Was I really about to try to seduce Joel Wentworth?

"Hey, you." I grinned at him, his appearance dissolving my nerves. I had been careful not to drink too much; I wanted to be fully conscious. But a little bit of alcohol to give my confidence an extra boost hadn't hurt.

"This is a nice surprise." He smiled. "I was just texting

you to say I'd got home, but I'd have stayed home all night if I'd known you were coming." He opened the door wide, and I teetered inside on very high heels.

"You say the nicest things." I laced my fingers through his and leaned into him, pressing my body against his. "My shoes are high and my dress is tight." I mock scowled, hoping it would draw his attention to the right things about me.

"I noticed."

The lust in his eyes gave me courage to continue. "Feel how tight it is." I brought his hands to my waist as he walked me backward toward the kitchen.

"It feels perfect," he said as he ran his hands over my bottom to the skirt of the too-short dress, tracing the hem around my thighs, sending tiny shocks of desire through my skin to my belly. Abruptly, he stopped and busied himself in one of the cupboards.

"I think I need to lie down." I sighed and pushed my hands down my body, carving out my silhouette. I wanted him to want me like I wanted him. "This dress."

His eyes flicked toward me but he didn't say anything. He just smiled, found some water glasses, and headed across the hall to his bedroom. I followed and crawled across his bed on my stomach, flicking my feet in the air and crossing my ankles. I wanted him to strip me naked and kiss me everywhere.

"Could you take my shoes off for me?" I asked, my eyes following him around the room. He hadn't lost his smile.

"Are you sure? I rather like them on," he said, coming around behind me and reaching for my foot. He bent and kissed the inside of each ankle. I swivelled onto my back and rested on my elbows, my feet in his hands.

"You do?" I asked.

"Of course I do."

"Did I tell you how this dress is so tight?"

"You mentioned it." He arched his eyebrow.

"Perhaps you could just unzip it a bit—that might make it a little easier to breathe."

"I could do that. Just to make it a *little* easier," he whispered as he straddled my body on the bed. I put my arms over my head, revealing the zipper in the side of the dress.

He trailed his hand up from the bottom of my dress to my waist, then higher, pausing briefly to cup my boob. I arched into him, but he ignored me and moved his hand to the top of the zipper. He pulled it down an inch.

"Is that better?" he asked, his eyes darkening.

"A bit more." I stifled a grin.

"More? That dress must be really tight, baby." Without his eyes leaving mine, he unzipped another inch. "More?"

I nodded.

Slowly, tantalizingly, he pulled the zipper down as far as it would go, then trailed his finger back up the path of my naked skin. I rolled to my side, allowing his fingers better access. He bent toward me and started pressing small, delicate kisses that set my skin alight up the line of exposed flesh. I loved the way his stubble grazed me every now and then, reminding me of his masculinity . . . as if I could ever forget. He stroked my thighs, shifting my dress higher and higher. I moved onto my stomach and he pulled the fabric away from my body, revealing my back.

"Your skin is so soft," he said, bending and pressing his lips to my skin revealed by the opened zipper.

"That feels good."

He brushed my hair away and rained kisses down across my back, tracing the lines of my shoulder blades, right up my neck and then down my spine, lower and lower until he reached the edge of my dress. He didn't try to remove it, just occupied himself with the flesh on display. My entire body shivered with lust. *Did he feel all this pent-up desire in the same way I did?*

I gently twisted under him to lie on my back. His kisses didn't stop. He licked the top of my breasts just above the fabric. I grabbed the back of his head and I urged him lower.

He stopped, and abruptly fell to the bed on his back, his hand finding mine.

"Jesus, Ava."

"Hey. I was enjoying that." I hooked my leg over his, but he shrugged me off and sat upright.

"You're going to have to give me a minute. I need to cool down," he said.

I frowned. That was the last thing I wanted. So why did he? "Do you not want me?"

Joel growled, grabbed both my wrists, flipped me to my back, and pushed my arms above my head.

"I don't want you to cool down. I like you hot," I said.

He was giving me whiplash.

"Seriously?"

"Yes, seriously. I like you hot!"

"Ava, how am I meant to keep things between us on a certain level if you come back to my place, dressed like this, looking like that, saying things like . . ."

"A certain level?"

"Yes, a certain level." Why would he be trying to hold himself back?

"Maybe I want things at a new level."

"Ava . . . I want you so badly," he whispered, stroking my cheekbones with his thumbs. "But I don't want you to feel—"

"Joel, I'm trying pretty hard to seduce you, and I'm

starting to feel silly. I don't know how else to show you that my body is begging for you, that *I* am begging for you."

He crushed his lips to mine, then fell back, pulling me with him until my body lay on top of his. "Can you make this outfit your study uniform?" he growled into my ear, pushing his hands up my thighs, under my skirt, and finding my underwear. "I love how it's so tight on you, how your breasts burst out of the top. But I only want you to wear it for me from now on."

"During private study sessions?" I asked.

"Yup. Like this one." He rolled me to my back and lay on his side facing me, trailing his hand up and down my thigh, stopping just short of my underwear, watching me. I closed my eyes and as his hand travelled up, I wished it higher.

"Look at me, Ava."

I opened my eyes and, without hesitation, reached for the top of the dress, pulling it slowly down my body, revealing my breasts, my stomach, my waist, my underwear, my legs. I tossed the dress away.

"Do you have anything?" I asked, unsure of how to ask. "I mean, I've been tested and I have the pill, but . . ."

"I do and I've been tested, too," Joel said, his gaze roaming over my body. "I'm fine, and I've never—not without something—but with you, it's different. I don't want anything between us."

I nodded. "Me neither."

Joel took a deep breath. I moved his hand from my leg up to my breast.

"You are *so* perfect, Ava." He cupped my breast and inched forward to take my bottom lip between his teeth. He continued to palm my breast, his flesh against mine. I reached for him, but he shifted away from me, dipping his head to my neck and creating a path of kisses between my breasts, then down to my stomach. When he got to my underwear, he licked a line above the hem, leaving my skin hot and desperate. I wanted him to rip them off, to bury himself in me. But Joel was right—he was a patient man.

I threw my head back, and he brought his hands to my hips and dragged my underwear slowly, tantalizingly, down to expose my sex. The coolness of the room mixed with the anticipation of what was to come made me shiver. His breath hit my thighs. He was so close to me, to *that* part of me. He sucked air into his lungs and the thought of him breathing me in, smelling me and my arousal for him, made me moan.

He responded by bending my legs and pushing them apart.

"Joel," I said, suddenly exposed and on display. I moved my knees together.

"No, Ava. I want to see you." He gently parted my legs again and I covered my eyes with my arm, embarrassed. "Do you have any idea how beautiful you are? Don't look away—you should see how much I love looking at you. You're already glistening for me," he said, his words adding to my arousal. "You're right. Your body *is* begging for me. You are so ready."

His fingers rhythmically stroked the insides of my legs, stopping inches away from my sex. It was torture. I wanted to feel him, but Joel was in no rush. He replaced his hand with his tongue, and slowly made his way from my ankle up my leg, stopping to taste the sensitive flesh at the back of my knee, then moving up my inner thigh, and then up, up, up, stopping just before he got where I wanted him, where I needed him, most. I threw my hands onto the mattress in frustration, and I felt him smile against my thigh. He moved his attention to my other leg and repeated the delicious torture. I tried to grab him. I needed him to know what I needed, but just as I thought it would be too much to bear, his breath whispered against my clit and I shivered.

"So beautiful, Ava."

I held my breath, waiting for what was next. Softly, just a fraction heavier than the air, he flicked his tongue against me. I exhaled, sinking against his touch. This was what heaven felt like.

"Oh, Joel." I pushed my hands into his unruly waves. He laid his tongue flat against my clitoris, and I bucked beneath him. He stopped until I stilled, then gently thrust his tongue against me, down, deeper, until the warmness in my belly spread across my stomach, through my limbs, and up my spine. What was he doing to me? I'd never come close to the way I was feeling. My heart felt so full. Yes, it was pleasure, but more than that, this was a connection . . . this was *intimacy*.

I was finally giving myself to Joel and it felt *right*.

Any embarrassment, any shyness had been replaced by sheer desire. His tongue flicked and pushed and circled and the intensity built, quickly becoming too much. I thrust my hips up and he caught my bottom in the air and pulled me forward, his tongue thrusting and pushing, twisting and turning. And his fingers, oh God, his *fingers* were on my clitoris, rubbing, circling. The warmth turned to fiery heat.

"Joel." *Oh yes.* "I'm . . . Joel." His name was all I could manage as my orgasm gripped me. I tore at the sheets beneath me and my body went rigid as the waves washed through me. Finally, I slumped into the bed, and I felt Joel trail his tongue up my stomach.

"You are so sexy when you come. So open, so out of control."

He was right. I let him into every corner of my body and mind. This wasn't about me being in control or getting things done. This was about me wanting him and having no other choice but to give myself to him.

I brought my hands around his back and realized at some point he'd taken his shirt off. I opened my eyes to find him looking in mine. He leaned forward and kissed me briefly, but I held him to me and deepened the kiss. I tasted myself on him—a secret between only us.

I found the waistband of his jeans. I wanted his body next to mine. Skin touching skin. Flesh touching flesh.

"You know this is it for me. *You're* it for me," he said in my ear as I unbuckled his belt. I nodded. I did know. I knew this, what we were about to do, had the power to end it for me, and that he felt it, too.

Maybe that's why he'd held me back for so long. Perhaps it had been as much about him protecting himself as him protecting me. Even before tonight, I'd known I'd never be the same after Joel. It would be forever about him. I didn't want—I *wouldn't* want—anyone else, whatever happened.

Joel kicked his jeans off and we lay side by side, stroking each other's contours, watching each other's fascination with the other. I loved the way his shoulders rounded into his arms. Was mesmerized by his hard chest and how it reminded me of wet, ridged sand at the beach. He trailed his fingers along the valley of my breasts, my nipples pebbling as he continued around my waist and down to my bottom.

I pulled my eyes from him and glanced between us. He shifted toward me, just slightly, but enough for me to know he wanted more. He wanted me.

I grasped him, his flesh thick in my fist. His breath

caught and he grabbed my wrist.

"Let me go," he said. "I have to take this slow or I won't last long."

I did as he asked and brought my hands to his shoulders. He pushed me gently to my back and kissed me, keeping his eyes locked with mine. The anticipation was almost too much when I felt him against my stomach. This may not have been the first time I'd had sex, but it was the first time I'd been intimate with a man, and the first time a man had been intimate with me.

Intimate.

Open.

Raw.

Bound, forever.

With his forearms either side of my head, he lifted himself over me, hovering as I parted my legs, bringing my knees up to lead him where I wanted him to go. He nudged at my entrance and looked at me, his eyes asking me if I was sure, if I was ready. In answer, I lifted my hips to his.

"Oh, baby." He closed his eyes as he pushed inside, just a fraction.

"More, Joel."

"Fuck," he choked out. "I don't know . . ."

"I want you inside me." I grabbed his bottom and pulled him toward me, but he resisted.

"Lie still, Ava," he said. I released his bottom and slid my hands up his back. Then quickly, without warning, he buried himself deep in me, pushing my legs farther apart.

The feeling of fullness that overcame me stole my breath away.

"You're so tight, Ava, so good," he whispered into my neck as he pulled out and thrust again.

His words released a boldness in me and I moved,

swaying my hips deeper into the mattress. Mirroring me, he pulled out and we found our rhythm. Both desperate to be closer.

A vibration grew deep in my belly and I cried out. "Joel, yes." I grabbed at him, and unable to tell him what I felt—I didn't understand it myself—I put my mouth on his shoulder and pushed my teeth into his skin. He moaned out and I bit harder. I felt his fingertips at my hips, pressing into me, into the soft flesh. I hoped they left a mark, a branding on me.

The rumbling in my core spread slowly at first, then gathered pace, pushing into every atom of me. The feel of Joel buried deep inside me, his fingers on me, his breath covering me, my senses were all his. I broke apart in slow motion under him. He bent forward to kiss me and I silently screamed into his mouth, desperate for him to feel what I did right at that moment.

He pulled out and I lay there, loose and boneless.

I closed my eyes and Joel licked the throbbing pulse in my neck as if trying to tame it. It did the opposite. I tried to lift my arm, to stroke his chest, but I had no energy. He moved to my side, pulling my limp body toward him, my back to his torso. He pushed my top knee up, so my legs parted, and he entered me in one thrust.

Right. Up. To. The. Hilt.

Oh, Christ. I twisted so I could watch his face and raked my fingers through his hair. He was right here, in the moment, behind me, pushing into me, taking me. It was oh-so-slow, and oh-so-right.

"You're delicious," he said. "Every beautiful part of you."

He grabbed my breasts, dragging his thumbs across my nipples. What was that? That sensation he found there, with just the right amount of pressure. His hips circled behind me and I pushed back, forcing him deeper.

"Be careful, Ava. I'm close. I want you with me when I go." Almost there, I pulled his arm from my breast down to my stomach.

"Touch me," I whispered. "Please, Joel." I encouraged his hand farther down and his fingers found my clitoris.

"Like this, baby? Is this what you like?"

I nodded.

"Talk to me. Tell me what you like."

"I like your fingers exploring me."

"You do? Do you like me to feel how silky wet you are?"

"Yes." That familiar buzz reverberated across my body.

"What else?"

"You . . . inside me," I gasped.

"Like this?" He held my shoulder as he pushed deeper into me. "You like feeling so full of me?"

Words were beyond me.

He increased the rhythm, and his fingers pressed harder around my nub. A film of sweat coated our bodies, providing a shield between us and the rest of the world. I bucked beneath him but he held tight, keeping me close to him, pulling away only to dive in deeper. Pleasure bloomed in my stomach.

"Joel . . ."

I was there, shuddering around him, clenching him inside me, my climax pulling his from him.

"Ava," he moaned, pouring himself into me.

I lay there, connected to Joel and knowing things had shifted forever.

I wanted to stay right there, in that moment.

Because nothing could ever be that perfect again.

I was sure of it.

SIXTEEN

After a sleepless night wondering what Joel thought about my collapsing into tears on him the night before last, and trying to figure out if there was anything I could do to right all my wrongs, I'd agreed to go to Jules' to look at outfits for an hour if she promised to take me to a boozy brunch.

"You like this one?" Jules twirled in front of the free-standing mirror in her bedroom.

"Sure," I replied.

Did Joel like blue? I couldn't ever remember him saying he didn't. Would he be attracted to Jules in that dress? I reasoned that if I helped Jules pick out an outfit, I could make sure it was something Joel wouldn't like.

Was that entirely selfish? Yup.

Was I entirely okay with that? Yup.

The problem was, I didn't know what he liked or didn't like anymore.

But I'd try anything. Desperate times called for

desperate measures. The thought of the love of my life dating one of my closest friends was just too horrifying.

"I don't think it shows enough skin," she said and began to strip off down to her underwear. "So, how was Will? Did he leave this morning?"

"He canceled dinner, so I spent the night in." I'd cancelled him as soon as I got home. My head was more full of Joel than usual and I hadn't been in the mood for distraction. I'd wanted to spend the evening remembering what it felt like to be held by him.

"Oh, you should have come out with us. We had such a fantastic night!" My heart sank. Had she gone out with Adam and Joel? "We ended up at that karaoke bar in Soho, and oh my God!" She clamped her hands over her mouth. "I just remembered. I snogged that hot guy in Finance." Oh, right, she'd had a work thing last night. I tried to hide my relief.

"What hot guy?"

"You know—the wheatgrass man." Jules had set her sights on Wheatgrass when he'd started six months ago, but when he didn't respond to any of her flirting, she'd convinced herself he was gay. This was a very good thing. It might take the focus off Joel for a bit. Or forever. Wheatgrass might be The One for Jules.

"So, what about the red one I bought last month? Joel hasn't seen it," Jules said, interrupting me mentally planning her wedding. She rummaged about in her wardrobe.

"Oh, so you're still going on Tuesday?" I asked, as she pulled out a tiny red scrap of material on a hanger and held it against her.

"Of course, why wouldn't I be?"

"Oh, I just thought that with you kissing Wheatgrass . . ."

Jules laughed. "Come on. This is Joel Wentworth. I'm not giving up dinner with him because I kissed some guy in Finance."

My stomach churned. She'd think I was an idiot if she knew what I'd given up.

"So?" she asked. "Short and sexy?" She wiggled the dress in front of her body.

"I guess," I said unhelpfully. "Try it on."

It was jersey and she pulled it on as if it were a T-shirt. It only just covered her arse and clung to every inch of her. But she looked incredible—long, slender legs, tiny waist and enough confidence to wear something like that out in public. She was everything I wasn't.

"Is it too much?" she asked. I shouldn't have been surprised. She looked amazing in most things; short and sexy was no exception. What had I been thinking, that I could convince Jules to look hideous when she went to dinner with Joel? I wasn't sure Jules could look hideous if she tried.

"Too much for what? Where are you going?"

"He hasn't said, but it's bound to be nice, right? I mean, he's loaded."

I cringed. Joel had never been about the money.

"I suppose so. Are you serious about this thing with him?" I asked, desperate for her to say no.

"I think this is too much." She turned back to her wardrobe and grabbed a sequined, one-shoulder dress and flung it at me before turning back to the wardrobe, ignoring my question.

"Or what about this?" She pulled on some bright green jeans. I was pretty sure the Joel I knew would hate them, but I wasn't sure about Eight Years Later Joel.

"I don't know if I'm serious about him. I really like him

and he's rich and gorgeous, so we'll have dinner, and I'll see if he's good in bed. I don't have to decide now, do I?"

She would see if he was good in bed? If I told her that Joel and I'd had a thing, would girl code kick in? Was that even how girl code worked? Would she take pity on me and cancel? There were no guarantees.

"No. I guess not," I said, wishing I liked Will more. If I did, I'm sure I wouldn't have been so wrapped up thinking about Joel and Jules. I was going to make more of an effort with Will; perhaps I'd grow to like him. I pulled out my phone from my pocket.

"Who are you texting?" Jules asked while pulling on a blue dress.

"Will."

"You must have it bad. Is he good in bed?"

Maybe she hadn't believed me yesterday when I told her I hadn't gotten laid. Since she'd ignored *my* question earlier, it was only fair I ignored hers now.

A: Sorry about last night. Are you around this evening?

"Were you lying when you said he canceled? Did you actually shag all night? Is that why you're in such a grump today?"

"I'm not in a grump."

"Well, you're not sweetness and light either, are you? I would have thought you'd be in a permanent good mood now you're getting some."

What was with her obsession with my sex life? Was it weird I hadn't slept with Will yet? He'd made it clear that's what he wanted. It was me who was holding back.

"Do you want to meet him?" I asked. Will wanted me to introduce him to my friends. And if Joel was going to dinner with Jules then why shouldn't Will come to dinner with everyone?

She stopped what she was doing and looked at me. "Will?"

"Yes, Will. Who did you think I meant, my window cleaner?"

"Wow." She stood facing me, looking at me as if I'd just taken my head off and I was carrying it under my arm.

"What wow?" Will had acted as though it was no big deal, but the way Jules reacted made me realize what I'd done. I'd never introduced a boyfriend to my group of friends.

"Yes, *of course* we want to meet him. When? Where?" She looked at me expectantly, as if she were trying to pin me down with a response straight away.

"Who is *we*?" I wasn't sure why I asked. I knew the answer. My dating was big news and I was sure the entire group had discussed it when I wasn't around.

"Us. We. You know, your friends."

I'd done it now. There was no taking this back. I'd never hear the end of it. Anyway, dinner was just dinner, right? "Dinner maybe. Next week or something."

She squealed. "Sounds like you are super serious about this guy."

"Jesus, it's dinner, Jules, not a wedding."

I was regretting bringing it up already.

Past

"So I'll see you in a few weeks, I guess," Joel said as we were walking back from the library on the last day of term.

"I'll see you tonight, though, right?" I asked, panicking at the thought of not seeing him every day. What if whatever he saw in me suddenly disappeared when we left campus? Our perfect spell would be broken.

"Yes, of course, it won't be just . . ." He didn't finish his sentence, but I knew what he meant. This was our last time in our bubble, just us. My stomach churned. I didn't say anything. I couldn't look at him.

As we arrived at our block, Joel's fingers brushed mine and instead of flinching as I normally did whenever he touched me in public, I lingered close to him. "I'll see you tonight, Ava, and then again for New Year's Eve, and we can talk on the phone."

I nodded, but it wasn't the same.

That evening, in preparation for the end-of-term party, I wore Jules' dress that I'd worn on our first night together. As I slipped it on, I remembered him peeling it off me, kissing every inch of exposed flesh. I wanted him to have that side of me fresh in his memory.

"Wow, you look great, Ava. That dress looks better on you than it does on me," Jules said, bouncing into my room carrying two plastic glasses containing a clear liquid I didn't think was water, judging by Jules' good mood.

"Thanks, so do you." Jules always looked great—even first thing in the morning after a big night out. Tonight was no different. Her hair salon glossy and her dress fit her perfectly, showing off every curve. She made it look so effortless. Whenever I made an effort with my clothes and makeup I felt like a complete fraud—like I was five years old and playing with my mother's things.

"Thanks. I'm desperate to hook up with someone tonight." She collapsed on my bed as I finished my mascara. "Is Joel shagging anyone at the moment?"

Sirens blared in my head. Joel? Was she kidding? I shrugged. I couldn't think how to respond.

"I've not seen him with anyone in a while. I might make my move tonight," she said.

I didn't say anything. I was sure if I did I'd give myself away.

"Have you got your eye on any boys?" she asked. "It's our last year at uni, Ava. Our last year as irresponsible adults. It all goes downhill after this. You need to make the most of it."

"Thanks, I'll bear that in mind."

"Alright. God, I hope you cheer up." She was right. I just wasn't in a celebratory mood. The last day of term meant the last day I'd spend with Joel for weeks.

ADAM, Daniel, and Matt were already halfway through their drinks when we arrived at the pub to begin our big night out, but where was Joel? We got our drinks and shuffled into the booth next to the boys. I kept glancing at the door waiting for Joel. God, I hoped he hadn't decided to bail.

Daniel was in the middle of making a lewd joke about one of his professors when my smile widened—Joel was here; I could feel him. He came over and scooted in next to me. Every part of his leg touching every part of mine. I felt better instantly.

"I've ordered shots," he said. "They're bringing them over."

"What? Joel Wentworth gets waitress service?" Adam asked, obviously put out. "Did you shag the barmaid?"

Joel just grinned, then turned to me and said quietly so as not to make a big deal about it, "Nice dress."

I smiled back. "Thanks. It has magic powers."

Joel raised his eyebrows. "I can only imagine."

"Do you like *my* dress, Joel?" Jules interrupted.

Joel's eyes flicked to her and he smiled, "Looks great," he said, then turned his attention straight back to me.

"You have a very active imagination," I said, continuing where we left off before Jules piped up. I was feeling brave. I knew he didn't want Jules—it was me he was complimenting, me he was looking at as if he wanted to devour me. At that moment, I didn't care if people saw us flirting. I was enjoying his attention too much.

"You know it." His hand brushed my exposed leg, one finger pushing under the hem of my skirt, just a tiny bit. I held my breath. What was he doing? He moved his hand back to his thigh. "Breathe," he whispered, and then he asked Adam, "What were you talking about?"

It was excruciating, being so close to him, his smell enveloping me, his leg against mine, but not being able to properly touch him like I wanted to.

I downed my shot as soon as it arrived and caught Jules looking quizzically between Joel and me. On the verge of being found out, I excused myself to the bathroom. Sober me knew I didn't want any pressure and scrutiny on what Joel and I had. Whatever we had couldn't survive it. He was Joel Wentworth. I was a nobody. Sober me knew I wanted to keep what we had between us. I didn't want to risk what we had, not for anything, and certainly not because I was feeling hot and horny tonight.

We moved on to our favorite club and Daniel, Matt, Joel, and Adam propped up the bar while Hanna, Jules, and I tore up the dance floor. Joel didn't try to make an excuse to touch me, didn't try to have a conversation with me. I caught his eye a couple of times, but he didn't hold my gaze. It was as if we were just friends on a night out together. He was acting exactly how I wanted him to act. Part of me was relieved, but the other part was, well, disappointed.

Jules and I'd had enough alcohol that it didn't matter what we were dancing to. The dance floor was packed; we were surrounded by sweaty bodies intent on squeezing the last drop of enjoyment from the last night of term. I flung my head back and my arms in the air, the bass thundering through my feet. This had been such a fantastic term. I had fallen in love, had the most amazing sex, and found my best friend.

We were attracting some attention. Jules was in a world of her own, enjoying the chaos, the music. A guy came up behind her and pressed his body against hers, his front to her back, clearly moving in for the kill. She made the most of it and wiggled her bum. She was about to drop me, I could tell.

I looked around to find Hanna, but she must have disappeared to get a drink or grope Matt or something. Arms slid around my waist and for a moment I thought Joel had joined me. But the touch was too clumsy, it didn't know my body in the same way, and he wouldn't be so reckless, would he? I spun around and came face-to-face with a very tall, very handsome member of the rugby team. I knew his face but not his name. *Oh*.

My eyes shot to the bar to see if Joel had seen us and might come and rescue me. He was busy in conversation with Adam and two girls from my Tuesday International Law class. They were pretty, both of them.

"You look hot," the rugby player shouted into my ear, his arms circling my waist as we continued to dance.

"I am. It's boiling in here."

He threw his head back and laughed. "No, *sexy* hot."

Oh. I wasn't used to getting attention from strange men. Not from any men. But it felt weird, alien. Only Joel got to speak to me like that.

"I've seen you around," he shouted over the music. "I thought you might be going out with Joel, but he said you were just friends."

It shouldn't have stung, but it did. "Oh, yes," I said, "we're friends."

"So you're not seeing anyone?" he asked.

My heart was Joel's, there was no mistake about that, but I wasn't prepared to answer questions about my romantic status—I was in love with someone, but who was going to believe that? I shrugged and he ran his hands across my bottom. Holy cow. I looked over at the bar to find Joel scanning the dance floor. I wanted him to interrupt us, to come and punch this guy for touching me like that. The blonde International Lawyer was on tiptoes to reach his ear. He didn't seem to be discouraging her attentions.

I pressed firmly against rugby hunk's biceps to put a bit of distance between us, but he pulled my hips toward him and moved us to the music. Christ, his erection pushed against my stomach. I needed to get out of this situation. Where was Jules?

"I need to grab some water," I said.

"I'll come with you."

"No, you stay here. I'll be back in a minute."

"Don't be long, sexy." He bent to kiss my neck and ground against me for a final time, then released me.

Pulse racing, I made my way to the bar, looking for Joel. I caught his eye and he looked away and back at the blonde, turning his body into her as if he didn't want me to interrupt them. My jealousy ramped up a level. Adam had his arms around the blonde's friend. Where were Matt and Daniel?

I tapped Joel on the shoulder. Without moving his body, he swiveled his head in my direction.

"Hey," I said.

"Hey," he replied sharply and turned back to the blonde.

"Joel?" I half shouted at his back.

"What?" he said without looking at me.

"I'm leaving."

"On your own?" he spat.

I recoiled from his venom. What had got into him?

"Jules is still on the dance floor," I explained, but he didn't respond. It was as if he couldn't wait for me to leave. Why was he being so shitty? I didn't want to leave him with the blonde, but he didn't seem to want me to stay. "See you around," I said and made my way to the exit. I'd just reached the door when someone grabbed me from behind. I twisted around to break free and came face-to-face with Joel.

"What the fuck, Ava?" he yelled and let go of my arm.

Why was he so angry? I wanted to get out of there. I headed out into the car park. Cold air hit me in the face, tightening my skin.

He was following me. "What the fuck!" he shouted again. I shuddered. Joel didn't scream at me. This wasn't who we were.

I knew I wasn't going to see him for two weeks. I knew he had spent the evening talking to some blonde and ignoring me. But I didn't know what his problem was.

I stopped, but didn't turn around, instead folding my arms close around me. I couldn't speak around my tightening throat.

"What are you playing at, Ava?" he said, quieter now, almost as if he were exasperated.

I turned to find him leaning up against the wall, his hands running through his hair. I took a couple of steps toward him, so I was standing a few feet away.

"Do you not want this?" he asked, gesturing between us.

"What?" I choked. *All* I wanted was him. He knew that.

"Us, Ava. Do you want to end things between *us*?"

His words hit me like a bullet to the chest. "What? No. Why—"

"You don't want anyone to know about us. You flinch if I touch you in public. You spend your night writhing around the dance floor, putting on a show for every drunken twat in the place. You start dirty dancing with a guy I know for a fact wants in your underwear . . ." He bowed his head. "Fuck."

When he put it like that . . . I moved closer to him, still hugging my chest, so close my body was touching his. "I'm sorry. I didn't realize how that looked. And that guy was a sleaze. I wanted you to rescue me. I wasn't encouraging him, honestly."

He stayed still. Cold. Hard. I unraveled my arms, slid them around his waist and pressed my face against his chest. He didn't move. "I was dancing for you, thinking about you," I whispered. "How could you think I want anyone but *you*?"

He rested his chin on the top of my head. "Shit, Ava."

"I hated seeing you with that blonde from my class," I said. I'd wanted to rip the hair from her head.

"I was just keeping her occupied while Adam tried to get with her friend."

I looked up at him and raised my eyebrows.

He sighed. "And I suppose I was trying to make you a little jealous."

"It worked." I put my head back on his chest and pulled his arms around me, squeezing closer to him. The air shifted around us. A crack of thunder sounded somewhere off in the distance.

"Good to know." He kissed the top of my head.

We stayed silent, holding each other like that. He couldn't know how much I wanted him. I'd had no comprehension such need existed until I met him. The thought of how much he could hurt me was overwhelming, so much so that I considered running. Going back to my room, packing up, and leaving. Forget visiting him during the holidays. I could distance myself from him. It would be safer that way. I loved him and I was fighting it every inch of the way, making it as difficult as I could because I was afraid I would drown in him if I gave myself up to everything I felt.

But I didn't run.

Instead, I tilted my head and pushed my hands to the back of his neck. "Kiss me." Thunder rumbled, creeping toward us.

He looked at me as if he hadn't heard me right.

"Kiss me," I said again.

Slowly, he bowed his head and lightly brushed his lips against mine. I pulled his bottom lip between my teeth and felt the corners of his mouth turn up.

I pushed my tongue through his lips as his hands cupped my face, holding me in place. At that moment, I didn't care that anyone leaving the club right now would see us. All I wanted was Joel to see inside me, see how much I needed him. I couldn't tell him, didn't have the words, but he had to know. His tongue grew more insistent, as if he were trying to understand, trying to reach a part of me I'd hidden from him.

The thunder cracked again, closer now, louder.

"Joel," I whispered as the first drops of rain hit my face. I needed something more from him, for him to see me the way I saw him. In answer, he spun us, my back grazing the wall.

His eyes were dark, serious. I'd never seen him so full of emotion before. He crashed into me, his whole body pushing me into the wall. I brought my arms to his shoulders. I loved how big he was, how he physically overpowered me. He hitched me up the wall and pulled my legs around him. Burying his head in my neck, he sucked and kissed and I groaned as his erection strained against me. The rain started to fall in big, heavy drops. I licked his jaw, tasting the rain, tasting him.

"Be mine, Ava."

"Always." How could he not know I already was?

I wanted to ask him to be mine, but I knew it was impossible. I only had Joel for a limited time. Happiness like this didn't last for girls like me.

SEVENTEEN

I still had a hangover when I finished work the next day and as the bus lurched its passengers from side to side, I considered whether or not I could last until Leicester Square before throwing up. I'd spent the previous evening obsessing over Jules being out with Joel. And then drinking, trying to dissolve thoughts of the two of them together from my brain. Would he have sex with her? Would he do it to hurt me or because he wanted to? Eight years might be a long time, but my feelings hadn't changed. Maybe if we'd been something else to each other, something less, it would be different. But Joel had been my world and eight years or eight minutes, it didn't matter. I still loved him.

Out of guilt and confusion, and wanting to be free of thoughts of Joel, I'd texted Will and asked him if he wanted to catch up tonight. I was exhausted, I still hadn't heard from Jules, and the last thing I wanted to do was meet Will, but I couldn't cancel on him again.

At least we were meeting in Leicester Square and not

going to see anything remotely art-housey. I couldn't cope with subtitles, not on a day like today. Instead he'd suggested a blockbuster, and that was okay with me. Anything that involved Hugh Jackman could never be bad.

"Hey, beautiful." Despite the rain, he greeted me outside with a kiss on my cheek, and I found myself smiling without having to force it. He was a really nice guy.

"Hey, how was work?" Work was always a safe topic. I didn't have to discuss what I'd done the night before or what was happening between us. I didn't want to think. I wanted to press pause on anything difficult.

"Great, because I had a date with you to look forward to all day."

I laughed. "You smoothie."

"I mean it. You're incredible company."

I tilted my head and smiled at him. "You're a really good guy, Will. And I'm really looking forward to our date tonight too." I was. Will was uncomplicated. He didn't know the Ava from university. He only knew the capable lawyer who owned matching underwear. I didn't have to ask myself why he was with me. We were equals. No one looking at us queuing for popcorn would think we were a mismatch.

Once we were in our seats with our drinks and snacks, Will reached over and took my hand, and I let him. I exhaled. This was where I was meant to be right now. Next to this nice, uncomplicated man who seemed to like me. Not obsessing over my first love and friend. I had to look to the future, not the past.

EIGHTEEN

Past

As I got through the barriers at the station, pulling my case, I scanned the concourse but I couldn't find him. It had been two weeks since I'd last seen Joel, and I didn't want to wait a moment longer. The train was over half an hour late. I hoped he stuck around.

Before anything else, I saw his grin. Fifty feet away, Joel stood stock-still, hands in his pockets, looking right at me as people rushed past either side of him. I couldn't help but stop, take in his beautiful face, and smile back. His hair had grown and somehow it looked lighter than usual. My stomach churned at the thought of so much time without him. I ran at him, pulling my case behind me. As I reached him, I released my case and it fell with a crash to the floor. I jumped up and wrapped my legs around him. He caught me and laughed into my neck as I hugged him as hard as I could.

"Anyone would think you were pleased to see me," he said.

I kissed his forehead, his nose, his cheeks, and finally his lips.

"I am very pleased to see you, and unless you want us arrested for public indecency, I suggest you take me home and get me naked." Two weeks had seemed like an eternity. I knew I was in deep, but being separated made me realize how deep. I'd hurt when we'd parted. Pined. It felt as though a part of me was missing when I wasn't with him.

"Hmmm, about that . . ."

I jumped down, he picked up my case, and we headed to the car, my arms wrapped around his middle, his free arm slung across my shoulder. "About what?"

"The naked thing. I don't want you to freak out, but things have kind of shifted on my end."

My stomach hit the floor. Didn't he want me here? Was it his feelings for me that had changed?

"My parents' flight was canceled this morning—bad weather. They're on another plane tomorrow and will be gone before you wake up."

It took me a few seconds to digest what he was saying. "So your parents are at your house?"

"Yes." He leaned over and kissed me on the top of my head.

"And we are heading to your house now . . . me and you?" Was he telling me I was about to meet his parents?

"Yes." He seemed very relaxed, but this was a huge deal. I'd not prepared myself at all.

Panic began to course through me. "Your parents' house, where your parents are going to be?"

"Yes." He really wasn't giving me much here. Should I have delayed my journey? Was he freaking out on the inside like I was?

"So I'm going to meet your parents?" Why was he acting so calm?

"Yes."

"Okay." I had the facts. I just wasn't sure what I was going to do with them yet. "Are they expecting me?" Why hadn't he said? I could have delayed my trip.

"Yes."

"Who are they expecting? Who am I?" What had he said to them about me? And how did they feel about some stranger coming to stay?

"You."

"You know what I mean. Who am I *to them*?" I dipped my head, trying to see his facial expression. His responses weren't giving anything away. He turned and grinned at me as if I were ridiculous or something. We arrived at his car and he put my case in the boot.

"Oh, just some girl. You're not the first one who's stayed this holiday. No pressure."

I bumped his leg with my hip.

"*My girlfriend*. To them, to me."

I bit down hard on my lip to stop myself from squealing. "Okay." My reply was careful, suspicious almost. Was it possible I was Joel Wentworth's girlfriend?

"Okay," he mimicked.

I rolled my eyes. "Okay, loser."

"Okay, girlfriend."

I liked the sound of that. But . . . "Oh my God, so no nakedness?"

"Anticipation is the ultimate aphrodisiac." As we stood by the car, he cupped my face in one hand and brushed his thumb over my cheekbone. His touch and attention weakened my knees and I reached for him to steady myself. "It is so good to see you, to have you here," he whispered.

"It's good to be here."

He bent to kiss me briefly on the lips. "That last night of term was crazy. I wasn't sure we'd still be us after, you know?"

I nodded and pulled at the collar of his shirt, bringing his mouth to mine again.

We had spoken every day while we'd been away from uni, but I knew what he meant. That last night had been desperate between us, almost like an ending. It wasn't until now that I realized it so easily could have been. Jealousy, secrets, and unspoken feelings—they brought out the worst in us both. But when it was just Joel and me, like now, it was easy.

"I wish we didn't have to wait." He kissed me again on the lips and then began to work on my neck.

"It's only a few hours." I said as I sighed and pushed my fingers through his hair. We were taking turns to convince ourselves we had the strength to resist each other. I wasn't sure how long it would last.

We'd waited this long, another night wasn't going to kill us.

Probably.

NINETEEN

Three and a half freaking days since Jules' and Joel's date, and every night since, I'd drunk myself to sleep. It was the only way I could get any rest. Today I faced a day at the spa, which for most girls was heavenly, but not me. I completely hated the spa. I couldn't bear the fact that most of the time was spent sitting, waiting between appointments. It felt inefficient. But Hanna loved it, and it was her birthday, so she, Jules, and I were going. After a day spent in robes we were all having dinner and Will was coming. I wasn't sure how tonight had come around so quickly.

It would be the first time I'd spoken to Jules properly after her date with Joel. We had chatted briefly about today and exchanged texts and emails, but Jules hadn't mentioned her date, and despite being desperate to hear about it, I hadn't brought it up in case it was too painful to handle.

"You look terrible," Jules said as I kissed her on her cheek. I was late, and I was never late. She and Hanna were getting hand massages in reception, their allocated robes and slippers already on their laps. Communal clothing. Gross.

God, I *really* hated the spa.

"Thanks," I muttered, but she was right. I did look terrible. And exhausted. Alcohol was not my friend. Could she just get to the bit where she told us about Joel?

It wasn't until after my massage, which was actually quite nice as it had stopped my brain whizzing for a few minutes, that I finally got what I wanted.

"What are you two giggling about?" I asked, a little dazed and feeling more relaxed than I had in days.

"Joel's penis," Jules replied.

My stomach dropped thirty thousand feet. Oh. My. God. This was it. I couldn't speak.

"We were just trying to figure out what it is that makes him so confident," Hanna said.

"I'm sure it's his penis," Jules said.

I nodded. I needed to get out of here. The air was stifling. I was prepared for the date to have gone well, but not for them to have had sex.

"It's bound to be huge. Everything else about him is perfect," Jules said.

Wait . . . that didn't sound like firsthand experience. "Oh, yes, the date." As if I could have possibly forgotten. "How was it?" I asked, trying hard to be nonchalant.

"Fine."

Interesting. Jules never underplayed anything. What did *fine* mean?

"But you didn't see his penis?" I asked. On that point, I had to have absolute clarity.

"Unfortunately not this time. He had a late-night call

with the US or something, so he had to run off. But it was a great night. He's such a flirt. He knows how to make a girl feel good and that was just what I needed."

It was just what I needed, too.

But he hadn't slept with her. My heart warmed at the thought. Jules was gorgeous, and if he was still angry with me, it would have been easy to wound me by sleeping with her. Maybe there would be a next time for him and Jules, but maybe there wouldn't. It gave me hope. Though for what, I wasn't sure.

I slumped onto the daybed next to Hanna and picked up a magazine I had no intention of reading. My thoughts were all of Joel.

"So, tonight's the night. How are you feeling?" Hanna asked me. "Daniel called Matt and he and Leah are coming, too." Great. The dinner with Will was turning into a much bigger deal than I'd intended. "Everyone wants to meet the man who's caught your attention. It's nice that we'll all be together."

"Yes, we'll get to meet the man that popped your cherry!" Jules interjected.

Jesus. This was going to be horrifying. Everyone was going to be making jokes at my expense.

"I lost my virginity at school, Jules."

"Yeah, but it's grown back since then. Will's your first proper sexual relationship with a human rather than your vibrator."

If I thought I could get away with it, I'd punch her, hard. I imagined my fist connecting with her cheekbone and then remembered where I was. "Will isn't my first sexual relationship, Jules."

"It's nothing to be ashamed of. I think it's nice that you've waited for *the one*."

She was right. I *was* waiting for the one, but I knew that wasn't Will. I didn't respond. It just wasn't worth it.

I'd suggested the dinner because that was what Will wanted, not because it was important to me that he met my friends. Did *he* think this was a big deal?

"So have you met his friends and family?" Hanna asked.

"No," I said, starting to get a little jumpy. "It's not super-serious. We're just seeing each other." I really wanted everyone to get this in perspective. "I didn't think dinner with you all was such a big deal. We do it all the time."

Jules and Hanna glanced at each other and my heart began to race. I'd been too quick to invite him. I should have continued to delay things.

"I'm going to change," I said as I headed out of the relaxation room. "I'll see you guys up there."

"Okay," Hanna said, her expression concerned. Jules, as usual, was oblivious to any anxiety or irritation on my part.

Back in the changing rooms, I pulled out my phone. Perhaps I could discourage him. I slumped back on my seat. What had I gotten myself into? I was really trying with Will, though I still couldn't have sex with him. I wanted to want him more than I did.

A: Are you sure you want to come tonight? It's no big deal either way.

The more I thought about it, the more I didn't think I was being fair to him. I jumped as my phone buzzed.

W: Of course, I want to come tonight. I can't wait to meet your friends.

My stomach flipped. He was too nice. I needed a drink.

I heard Jules' voice outside the changing rooms and quickly headed to the shower.

WE WERE due to go straight to dinner after the spa, so I'd brought a change of clothes with me. I had brought a simple, black, knee-length wrap dress with silver strappy heels.

Jules, as usual, had gone dressier. She was still working short and sexy.

"You look beautiful," I said and meant it. She was beautiful. I'd always wondered why Joel had chosen me when there were girls like Jules about.

"Thanks. Do you think Joel will like it?" she asked, admiring her back in the mirror.

"He'll love it," Hanna replied.

Did Hanna want them to be together? Was *everyone* rooting for them?

I grabbed my wallet and unzipped the secret pocket buried behind the cardholder. I hooked the necklace chain with my finger and pulled. Hanna and Jules were chattering away. I wasn't listening to what they were saying. They weren't concentrating on me, which was my only concern. Linking the chain was the familiar silver infinity symbol. The necklace was a bit tarnished, so I pulled a tissue from the box on the dressing table and set about polishing it up.

I always had it with me, but I'd not worn it for years.

The bright silver came back quickly, as if it were desperate to be noticed. While Jules and Hanna were still chatting, I fastened it around my neck and pressed the symbol against my skin.

I should never have taken it off.

"Let's go and get some champagne. We've got time," I said. I needed a drink before the boys arrived. I was going to have to make an effort to be a bit more enthusiastic about tonight.

"Great idea," Jules said.

Hanna nodded.

Dinner was set for seven thirty at the Soho Hotel, one of our usual haunts, so we headed to the bar just next door to the spa for our champagne before we met the others. The place was packed but we managed to find a table in the corner. I could do with downing the bottle myself before dinner.

"Cheers!" we chorused and clicked our glasses together.

"Here's to good sex," Jules announced.

I rolled my eyes. I'd have to sit at the other end of the table from her tonight.

"The hot guy from Finance asked me to go to the theater next week," Jules said, referring to Wheatgrass. "It's very nice of him, but . . ."

"But what, Jules?" Hanna asked. "You've liked him for a while, haven't you?"

"And you said he was a good kisser," I added. *Please God, let her date Wheatgrass.*

"Did I?" she asked, frowning.

I wasn't sure she had said that, but I was sure we would have heard about it if he hadn't been.

"I think so." I focused on the cold, zinc table, covered in dents from previous drinkers, so I didn't catch her eye. I was a terrible liar.

Jules shrugged. "But there are so many lovely men out there." She scanned the bar as if she was trying to find some more to add to her list.

"You mean Joel?" Hanna asked.

"Well, yes, but then there's my boss' boss . . ."

"Your *married* boss' boss," I said. Shouldn't I be encouraging her married boss fantasies? Anything to keep her away from Joel.

"I know. I know." She flipped her hair over her shoulder.

"It's one night at the theater. You should go," Hanna said. I wanted to kiss her right then and there.

"I should. I will." Jules nodded resolutely.

"Good," I said. "I think it's the right thing to do." I reached for the bottle of champagne and topped up our glasses. Tonight was looking up. Her evening with Joel couldn't have gone that well if she was going to the theater with other men and still thinking about her boss's boss.

"We might all be married this time next year," Hanna said.

Jules and I looked at each other and burst out laughing. "Not likely. I've never made it past three months, and Ava here is having her first sexual relationship."

"Jesus, Jules, if you say that again I'm going to pour my drink over you. Will and I aren't sleeping together yet, and even if we were it wouldn't be my first sexual experience. I've had a lot of great sex. I just don't tell you about it in minute detail."

"What? I don't even know where to start with all that information," she said. "You've not had sex with Will yet? That guy's balls must be as blue as blue. And you've had *a lot* of great sex? When? And with whom, exactly? And why aren't you telling me about it?"

Now I'd started something. Sometimes I wanted to scream from the rooftops about how much I'd loved Joel and how much he'd loved me back. But I knew there no point. I'd hurt them both if they knew I'd kept it from them. What was in the past wasn't worth dragging up.

"Shit, it's almost time. We have to go," Hanna interrupted.

I slung back the last of my champagne. I'd been saved by the bell.

Jules' drink stayed resolutely in her hand. "I'm not leaving until I get some answers."

"Well you're staying by yourself, then." I stood up and Hanna joined me.

"Come on, Jules," Hanna pleaded.

"You'll tell me in the cab?" she asked, fluttering her eyes at me. Didn't she get that her flirting didn't work on me?

"Come on," I said.

As soon as we got out onto the street we found a taxi.

"So?" Jules asked as our bottoms hit the cab seats.

"Look, it hasn't felt right with Will yet. I'm not sure about him. I like him but I'm not going to feel pressured into doing anything. That's why I don't want you guys making a big song and dance about tonight like it's our fucking engagement party."

"I'm sorry. We're just excited for you. I promise we'll all lay off," Hanna said.

Jules didn't say a word. She wasn't going to let me off the hook.

"And the other thing—I was seeing this guy a while back and the sex was good. Great, in fact." I hated calling Joel just some guy.

"When? When you first came to London and you avoided us? When you said you were busy at work all the time?" Jules pouted.

Before I could answer, Hanna said, "Oh yes, I remember. You went cold on us for a while. I assumed you had new London friends and had traded us in. I didn't realize it was about a guy. I should have guessed though."

"Yes," Jules said. "It makes sense now. You got all glamorous and confident and shit. Good sex will do that to you."

It wasn't good sex that had led to my transformation. More like the absence of it. But my friends had got the timing right. When I'd first arrived in London, I'd realized that my lack of confidence had lost me the love of my life and I no longer had anything left to lose. The worst thing that I could imagine had happened, and I'd survived. But I was determined that my lack of confidence wouldn't destroy anything else in my life. In my first few weeks of being a lawyer, I'd been to a Women in Law conference and one seminar had been all about gaining confidence. Essentially the advice had been, fake it until you make it. So, I'd gone out, bought the wardrobe, had the haircut, and pretended to be the girl that I wanted to be. The girl that Joel ended up with. I wouldn't continue to fuck up my life.

Somewhere along the line, the girl I'd pretended to be seeped into who I was.

I didn't need to say anything to Jules and Hanna. They'd incorrectly filled in the gaps themselves and that suited me.

With perfect timing, the cab pulled up in front of the Soho Hotel.

As we were late, Daniel, Leah, Adam, Matt, and Joel were all sitting at one of the low tables. My fingers went to my necklace and I took a deep breath. I glanced around the bar and spotted Will at the far end. I let Jules and Hanna lead the way toward the group, while I veered off to my date.

"Hey," I said, tapping Will on the shoulder.

He turned and smiled. "Hey. You look beautiful." He put his arm around my waist, pulled me toward him, and kissed me on my cheek. I couldn't help but tense slightly. I wasn't used to PDAs, let alone guys kissing me in front of my friends . . . and Joel.

"Come on," I said, pulling away and leading him over to the table. "We're over here."

I couldn't look at Joel as I approached the table. Didn't want to see a lack of reaction.

TWENTY

Past

As I woke, for just a second I didn't know where I was, but then the unfamiliar pillow under my head and the feeling of arms around me reminded me I wasn't on my own. Joel's chest pressed against my back and I breathed in his delicious, warming scent. I was exactly where I should be.

I stroked his arm and he nuzzled into my neck.

"Hey," he croaked.

"What time is it?" Were his parents still here? Surely not. There were definite signs of light coming through the curtains.

"They left about an hour ago," he said before I could ask.

I turned around in his arms. He still had his eyes shut.

"Why didn't you wake me?" I asked.

"Because you were sleeping. And you're going to need to be rested for what I have in store for you."

My stomach flipped. He opened one eye and grinned at me. I pushed his floppy hair away from his face. He sat up and stripped off his T-shirt, leaving him bare-chested. *Holy fuck.* In just two weeks I'd forgotten how his chest made my heart stop. He caught my wrist as I reached out to him and flipped me to my back, holding both hands above my head, his body over mine, staring into my eyes. Suddenly, he was wide awake.

Finally, it was just the two of us. No parents, no friends, no lectures, no library. Just me and Joel.

"Let's stay like this, just you and me in bed, all day," he said.

There was nothing I'd rather do. I circled my hips beneath him, and he moved his mouth toward mine, gently placing light kisses across my lips.

"It's so good to have you here," he said, trailing kisses down my neck.

"In my town," he said, kissing my collarbone.

"In my bed," he said, pressing a kiss between my breasts.

"In my heart."

I inhaled sharply and grasped his face, pulling him up so his eyes met mine. We'd not slept the whole night together before. I always went home to avoid anyone asking questions. Even on the occasions when I had fallen asleep, I always woke up in the middle of the night and let myself out to creep back to my bed. This seemed . . . real, made *us* seem real.

"It's so good to be here," I replied.

Our lips met, and then our tongues.

There was something different between us. More serious. Like we were both about to cross a line we knew there would be no turning back from.

"I've missed you," I whispered against his mouth.

He trailed his fingers up and down my body. It was half

pleasure, half torture. I reached to the waistband of his boxers to push them down. He helped with the rest. I was already naked and I didn't want anything between us.

He was hard, ready for me, and when I pulled my eyes away from his body I found him watching me drink him in.

"You are so beautiful," he said.

"Joel." I scrunched my nose.

"Ava, please. You are," he whispered.

I tried to cover myself under his scrutiny.

"Don't do that. Don't hide from me. Your body is mine now."

He wasn't saying anything I didn't know already, but hearing it like that . . . from him, was final somehow. He knew it, too.

I slid my hands across his chest, tracing the contours of his muscles.

Slowly he moved above me, his eyes locked on mine as he pushed into me, pulling the air from my lungs.

"Joel," I cried out. I hadn't expected that, but I was wet and ready for him.

He began moving in and out of me, never breaking the connection between our eyes or our bodies. I felt so whole, so understood, so present in that moment. Everything difficult dissolved and only we were left.

Slowly, and in one movement, Joel fell back on his knees, bringing me with him so I was straddling him, my arms around his shoulders. He went deeper like this. Pleasure and sensation built between us. I tuned into the sound of our bodies moving together, his flesh meeting mine. I dug my fingers into his arms, clinging on, and the muscles in his neck flexed. He was concentrating on the rhythm of his body in mine.

His hands were everywhere, covering me, consuming me.

"Joel," I whispered. "Joel. Joel. Joel." He pushed and pulled my hips, the rhythm perfect, gently winding the elastic band in my stomach, tauter and tauter. I pulled back to look at him. He had a sheen of sweat across his brow, and what I felt with him at that moment was . . . everything.

"I love . . . I love making love with you, Ava," he said softly.

My heart stopped. I knew what he meant. We hadn't said it to each other, but I felt it, too.

"I love making love with you, too." I shuddered and arched my back, pushing him deeper and pulling a moan from his mouth. I watched as his orgasm rippled across his face and the elastic band in my stomach snapped. His orgasm traveled across our connection and through every atom of my body.

I made no move to lie down. I just clung to him, wanting to be closer, if that were possible. What we had just shared was different, new. It brought us to a whole other level.

Joel's hands crept up and down my back, soothing and sexy in equal measure. I kissed his shoulder and laid my cheek against him. I never wanted to let him go.

"Wow," he said eventually.

I nodded, my head still resting on him.

"I never . . ." Joel paused. "Never felt anything like this."

"No, me neither," I mumbled.

Joel shifted beneath me until we could both relax against the bed, still connected, my head still on his shoulder.

"Hey, are you okay?" He tried to look at me, but I wouldn't shift to meet his eyes. Along with love came fear.

What happened if he left me? I wasn't sure I could survive. There wasn't much of the university year to go and then what would happen? I wanted to believe we would last forever, but I didn't see how it could be possible for me to be that lucky.

I nodded again.

"Are you going to stay like that forever?"

"Yes," I whispered.

"Suits me."

We lay that way for hours, not saying anything. My grip on him occasionally tightening then loosening, his fingers smoothing my hair down my back.

Finally, I asked, "Was it because we've not seen each other for so long?" I wanted to know what had made it so intense between us.

"I don't think so."

"Because we're away from uni and friends and stuff?" I asked, lifting my head to look at him. I wanted a simple explanation—something that would tell me I didn't need Joel to function the way it felt like I did. Something indicated what we had wasn't so special and wouldn't be such a big deal if I lost it.

He shook his head.

"Then why?"

"I think it's because it's us. Because of how we feel."

Love overtook fear for a moment, and I reached over and kissed him on the lips.

WHAT SEEMED like three days later, even though it was only a few hours, our rumbling stomachs overruled our lust for the first time, and we ventured downstairs. Joel's family's huge, sturdy pine kitchen table was covered in chips and scratches, which I imagined Joel and his brother and sister had created. They must have had a lot of fun sitting around it as a family. Joel dished out toast and cereal although lunchtime had long since passed.

"My mum likes you," Joel said as he swallowed a mouthful of food.

"I like her," I said. Joel's mother had been sweet and welcoming. And the fact it hadn't been planned meant my anxiety had been kept in check. I hadn't had weeks to worry about it.

"I guess that makes life a lot easier all around," he said, though I didn't ask him what he meant. I preferred to imagine he saw us as a long-term thing and if I got on with his family, we could spend holidays and celebrations together without concern.

Joel Wentworth was my boyfriend.

He stood up and put our plates in the dishwasher before turning to me. "I have something for you," he said. He looked at me almost as if he were embarrassed.

I tilted my head. "Is it your penis?"

"Such a dirty mind on such a sweet girl."

I laughed and I stuck my tongue out at him, and he rolled his eyes.

"A gift. I have a Christmas gift for you."

I grinned. I couldn't believe he'd gone out and bought me a gift. I'd bought something for him but not expected anything in return.

"You want it now?" he asked, pulling his eyebrows together in an almost frown.

"Yes, I want it now!"

He nodded and went into the next room. He returned a few minutes later with his hands behind his back.

"Right hand or left?" he asked.

"Both." I put my arms around his neck and kissed him. I was so excited he'd bought me a gift. It didn't matter what it was.

"I'm getting a thank you kiss before you've opened it? What if you hate it?"

"I won't hate it." I couldn't hate anything Joel had picked out for me.

"You might."

"I'll love it."

He smiled sheepishly and brought his hands in front of him, revealing a gift box with a huge red ribbon on it. I took it from him, grabbed his hand, and led him upstairs.

"I have a present for you, too."

"Is it your vagina?"

I raised my eyebrows at him.

"What, so when you say it it's cute, but when I say it, I get the look?"

"There's no look." There was definitely a look. And I loved that he knew it.

"There's a look."

Back in his bedroom, I pulled the gift I'd bought him from my case. He sat on the bed, cross-legged, in just his boxers. He looked so delicious. Rumpled, smiling, mine.

I bounced on the bed opposite him and sat, our knees touching.

Before I could say anything, he was ripping the paper off his gift.

"I didn't know what to get you," I said, suddenly unsure whether I'd done the right thing.

He opened the box and smiled as he took in the leather, plaited friendship bracelet I'd bought him.

"Friendship?" he asked.

Oh God, did he hate it? Was it unromantic?

I nodded. "I mean, we're more but—"

"Put it on me," he said, holding out his arm. "I wanna wear it."

I pulled the black band of leather out of the box and fastened it around his wrist. Before I finished, he pushed me to my back and climbed on top of me, kissing me.

"Is it okay?"

"It's more than okay. I love that I can wear it every day."

I leaned toward him and kissed him back, hard.

"Mine now," I said, feeling for the gift between us.

He rolled to my side, propped his head on his hand, looking up at me. He fingered my hair, pushing it over my shoulders and down my back. I shivered at the feel of his hands and started opening my gift box. It was sealed tight.

Finally, I pulled the top of the box off to reveal a silver chain. I hooked my finger underneath it and pulled it out. Attached to the chain was an elongated, silver figure eight.

"It's the symbol for infinity." He reached across and followed the curves of the symbol. My breath caught. I couldn't speak.

"You know, for you and me." He shrugged and looked at me, trying to gauge my reaction. "You can take it back if you don't li—"

I pushed him to his back and climbed on top of him. "Help me fasten the chain," I said, reaching behind my neck to pull my hair out of the way.

He took the chain from me.

"You like it?" He frowned as if he wasn't sure.

"I love it." I was done holding back. I wanted him to know how I felt. "I love *you*. Forever."

The corners of Joel's mouth twitched and then he took a deep breath. "I love you, Ava. For infinity."

We were promised to each other for infinity. Joel and me together, forever. This was the most perfect present he could have ever given me. It was a symbol of his heart, his love, his commitment to us, forever, and when I was here, with him with no interruptions, no outside forces, or future plans pulling at us, it wasn't difficult to believe we would last until the end of time.

TWENTY-ONE

We had a table in the bar by the window for pre-dinner drinks in the Soho Hotel and I headed toward Hanna as Will and I made our way to join the others. Hanna was a natural hostess, and I was pretty sure she'd take over introducing Will to everyone if I hesitated. Will seemed perfectly relaxed, which only made me all the more nervous. My heart was pounding and I couldn't wait for the evening to be over.

I couldn't look at Joel, and even managed to avoid saying hello to him in the fray. I watched out of the corner of my eye as he shook hands with Will.

I tried to concentrate on catching up with Leah. I shifted in my seat and found myself staring into Joel's furious eyes. I couldn't look away, and as his gaze flicked to my throat and back up to my face, I realized it was my necklace that had provoked his fury.

I grasped the infinity symbol and glanced back at Leah, who was telling me something about Daniel.

I hadn't put it on for ages. Why had I felt the need to wear the necklace tonight? Had I just wanted to provoke a reaction from Joel? Had I wanted to remind him that once he had loved me enough to think we were going to last forever?

I tried desperately to concentrate on what Leah was saying. When Joel got up and went to the bar, I got a brief reprieve from the pressure on my chest.

"You seem really nervous. Are you okay?" Leah asked.

"Sorry, I'm listening. I just . . . you all are making such a big deal about me bringing Will."

Leah nodded. "Don't worry. Once everyone has had a drink it'll be more relaxed."

"Shots!" Joel announced, interrupting us with a tray he placed in the middle of the table.

"Good man," Adam said, picking up a glass.

"Come on, guys!" Joel said after downing his first. His mood improved and he went back to ignoring me.

"Come on, Daniel," Adam said, as Joel picked up a second shot. I'd never known him to be a big drinker. And even at his welcome-home dinner, he'd not drunk anything other than wine.

Reluctantly, Daniel tipped back his glass as Joel reached for a third.

"Come on, stop being such girls," Adam said to Hanna, Jules, and me.

We weren't at university now. Why were we doing shots before dinner for crying out loud? I pushed out of my seat to go to the ladies.

Bringing Will here had been a bad idea. Adam was on a mission to get slaughtered. Joel was, well, I wasn't sure what Joel was being. Nothing about the evening seemed familiar. The dinner was supposed to take the pressure off, meant to put an end to Will pushing to meet my friends. It was designed to show everyone I wasn't a sad old spinster. It was *supposed* to make me feel better about not being with Joel.

I opened the door on my way out of the loo to find Joel leaning against the wall, his head bowed. He glanced up and I looked away as I tried to pass him, but he grabbed my elbow.

"What the fuck do you think you're doing?" he spat.

"Get off me, Joel." I twisted to free myself, but as he released my elbow, he grabbed my shoulders instead.

"What the fuck!" he said in a loud whisper.

"What?" I cried.

"You know what." His eyes went to my throat again, and I covered the infinity symbol with my hand. "You know what," he repeated, calmer this time. He released me and slumped against the wall. "What are you playing at? You're not being fair."

I was rooted to the spot. What could I say? I didn't know what I was doing or why I had worn it.

He shook his head and walked out of the corridor and back into the bar before I could say anything. If I'd been wanting a reaction, it hadn't been anger I'd been hoping for from Joel.

I steeled myself and went back to the table. Before I sat, I took a shot from the tray and downed it. This night was a fucking disaster. I just wanted to leave. If I was going to have to stay, I was going to have to be drunk.

"That's my girl," Adam said, as Joel grabbed another shot.

"I think we'd better get our table. There's an awful lot of alcohol flowing," Hanna said.

Not nearly enough, as far as I was concerned. I needed to be numb to survive tonight.

Things started to settle when we were at the table. Will sat between Hanna and me, and Joel was seated at the other end of the table on my side, so I couldn't see him. My fingers went to my throat again. Will and I were opposite Daniel and Leah. Daniel could always put anyone at ease, so I concentrated as hard as I could on being engaging and delightful. It was exhausting, but eventually the meal was over.

People lingered, but I couldn't wait to get out of there. Joel and Daniel were arguing over the bill. I threw some cash on the table and stood.

"I'm heading off now. I've got to be up early," I said.

Will was right next to me, but I wanted to get away from him, from everyone.

"You stay. I need to go," I said to him.

He frowned. "Ava, I'll get you home."

I didn't want to make a fuss—*more of a fuss*—so I relented. I waved generally, careful to avoid Joel's eyes, and sped away to the door while Will was shaking hands.

The cool night air was sobering, and I was grateful for the space. It didn't last long, though, as I heard Will come through the door behind me.

"Let's get a cab," he said.

"Do you mind if I go alone? I really need a bit of time." For what I wasn't sure.

"Okay." He sounded pissed off, and I couldn't blame him. I'd been distracted and in my own head all night.

"Thanks. It's just, it's a lot, you know."

"No, to be honest, I don't know, Ava. Your friends are nice, and they're happy you have someone, but you don't seem to be."

"Of course I am." God, I hadn't expected him to be angry. He had every right to be. "It's just been a difficult day and I'm having some issues at work that have me distract-ed." I didn't want Will to think this was his fault.

He stuck his hands into his pockets and looked at the ground. "I don't know what your deal is, Ava. You're always running away."

"I don't mean to be. I'm sorry. I really am." This really wasn't fair on him. I was using him and he felt it. I needed to fully commit to him or let him go. "I know you're not going to like this, but can we talk another day. Tomorrow even?" I smoothed out his tie against his chest. "I've had a little too much to drink and what with everything at work . . ."

He shrugged and a taxi with its light on approached.

"Thank you," I said, although he hadn't really agreed. I stuck my hand out and the cab pulled over. "Thank you for being so great. Let's talk tomorrow." I kissed him on the cheek and jumped into my cab, desperate to be away.

BACK IN MY FLAT, I undressed quickly, pulled on a cotton camisole and some pajama bottoms, and then headed to the bathroom to take my makeup off. Facing the mirror, I saw my necklace, the infinity symbol resting on my collar-bone. I pressed it into my skin until it hurt.

I climbed into bed and brought the duvet up to my neck. I was cold and drunk. I hoped I would pass out soon, and then tomorrow would be a new day.

Thirty minutes later, the doorbell rang followed by pounding on my door. Fucking hell, I was going to start getting abuse from my neighbors. Who could that be at this time of night? I dragged myself out of bed and padded toward the front door. Could it be Joel? The thought caught my attention and adrenaline began to swirl through my body. He had been angry with me tonight, for wearing the necklace. He said I'd not been fair. But I didn't understand what he'd meant. Did he mean I was being unfair to Will? We could agree about that.

I took a deep breath before I looked through the peep-hole. Will. I'd been hoping for someone else.

I unchained and unlocked the door.

"What are you doing here?" I whispered.

"I want to know what happened tonight," he said. "I don't want to wait until you decide when we're going to have the conversation."

"What? Come in." I thought we'd agreed we would talk tomorrow. I closed the door. I really didn't want to have this conversation—any conversation—with Will right then.

"We're here now, so what's the deal?" he asked, folding his arms.

"What?" Was he asking about the necklace?

"Stop playing dumb. We both know you're not."

I leaned back on the door as Will stood in front of me, expectantly.

"I don't know what to say," I said, examining my toes.

"I just don't get it. I don't get you. We get on. You think I'm attractive. I make you laugh. You introduce me to your friends . . ."

"I'm sorry." I shouldn't have let him meet everyone. I hadn't been fair.

"Sorry for what, Ava?"

I didn't respond.

"You practically ignored me all evening. I didn't even kiss you tonight. I've barely touched you. We've been seeing each other—"

"I know, I'm sorry." There was no point in denying

what he said. Things hadn't gotten particularly physical with Will and me, and tonight, it wasn't that I'd been ignoring Will, it was more that I'd tried everything I could to blot out Joel.

"You don't talk to me about anything but work. You don't share things with me. It's like you're trying to keep me at arm's length and leading me on at the same time. It's confusing and it's exhausting." He shoved his hands through his hair.

Hoping to ease my own pain, I'd just caused it in someone else. "I'm not . . . I've not been behaving properly—"

"What? I'm not asking you to *behave* properly. I'm asking you how you feel."

He reached out to touch my face. I wanted to be anywhere but there at that moment. He was never going to be the one for me. Not with Joel still in my heart. I quickly moved away and Will slumped.

"Well, I think you just answered my question. I guess we're done."

I could argue with him, try and win him over, but that would just cause him unnecessary upset somewhere down the line. "I'm sorry. You're a great guy."

"It's your loss, Ava." He sighed.

He moved toward the door and I got out of his way. He turned to face me. "Is it Adam? Are you in love with him?"

"No!" I nearly choked. How could anyone think I was in love with Adam?

"It's just you always talk about him and . . ."

"Really, it's not Adam."

He may have gotten it wrong about Adam, but he'd been right that I was in love with someone else.

"But it is someone?" he asked.

I nodded. "I'm sorry. I've been unfair to you." Joel had been right. I wasn't being fair. Not just by wearing the necklace when on a date with Will, but by dating Will in the first place.

"You're right. You have been unfair." He nodded sharply and left. Guilt and relief mixed in my stomach, but at least it was done. I wasn't kidding myself anymore, and I wasn't stringing Will along either.

This was why I didn't date. There would always be someone else.

I locked the door behind Will and climbed back into bed. The alcohol had disappeared, and without it, I was wide awake with my thoughts. I tried to distract myself and reached out and checked my phone. Nothing. Why had I not heard from Jules? Surely she'd want to give me her verdict on Will. Maybe she was still out. With Joel. Joel, who was very drunk and very angry with me. I'd known I didn't like indifferent Joel. But angry Joel? Him, I *really* didn't like.

And I hated the idea he might be out with Jules.

Despite it being late, I called her. I wanted all my bad news all at once.

She answered right away. "Hey."

"Hey. Where are you?" I asked. She sounded like she was alone.

"Just got back. Is Will not with you?" A door slammed in the background and the tap turned on.

"We broke up."

"What? What do you mean you broke up?" Jules was yelling and it was too late and I was too tired to hear it.

"What happened after I left the restaurant?" I asked, ignoring her. I wanted to hear about Joel.

"Apparently, you broke up with Will. What the fuck's going on, Ava?"

"Look, I was a bitch to him. I shouldn't have invited him tonight. I did it because I thought I should, and he was putting a bit of pressure on me to ramp things up. I messed him around and he dumped me." I couldn't blame Will for any of it. If I wasn't such an idiot I would have done everything I could to hold on to him.

"He dumped you?" she asked.

"Yeah, I guess." I didn't care who'd ended it. I was just relieved we weren't dating anymore. I didn't have to pretend.

"You guess?"

"Well, we had a fight and he left. I'm not sure technically who did it, but we are no longer together. Not that we really ever were."

"And that's that?"

"Don't say it like that." I exhaled.

"Like you don't care? Well, do you?"

I couldn't pretend to care when I didn't. "He's a nice guy. I didn't want to hurt his feelings, but I can't pretend I'm all broken up about something I'm not upset about."

"You're so weird. I don't get it at all. He was a great guy. You were lucky to have met him. But it's your life, I guess. So now can we get back to me?"

That was how I preferred things—when all the attention was on Jules.

"That hot waiter gave me his number." She squealed.

"Which waiter?" I'd barely registered we'd eaten, let alone done a survey of the staff. "I thought you were totally into Joel."

"Joel who? Did you see the arse on our waiter? Anyway, Joel behaved like a prick tonight. He was way too drunk and grouchy as hell. No wonder he's friends with Adam. I'm done with him."

"You are?" I bit on my thumbnail in a vain attempt to stop myself from smiling and giving away how delighted I was.

"Well, I am tonight. I have Jackson's number!"

I had a brief reprieve. Jules was so capricious she may well decide she was back trying to land Joel tomorrow. But I might sleep better knowing that for now, she was focused on someone else.

"The waiter's name was Jackson?" I asked.

"That's what I'm calling him. I don't know what his actual name is."

Maybe Jules and Joel would never happen. I couldn't imagine him with someone like her—she was so different to me. But then again, perhaps that's exactly why they would be perfect together.

TWENTY-TWO

After spending New Year's Eve together, Joel and I changed. I didn't change, Joel didn't change, but *we* did. The mutual declaration of our feelings and the time we spent together, just the two of us, shifted something. It made me more confident in his love for me. It was the way I'd catch him smiling at me when he didn't think I could see. The way he had to touch me whenever he got the chance. How he knew what I wanted before I wanted it. Just before I got cold, he brought me a blanket. Just before I got thirsty, he offered me a drink. We were connected. For infinity.

"I can't wait to see you," I said into the phone as I stared into my suitcase. We were heading back to university tomorrow and I wasn't packed yet. I was too busy talking to Joel. We'd been on the phone for hours and it had set me back, so I began to sort through my stuff while we talked.

I'd extended my stay with Joel, but eventually I'd had to go back to my parents' to organize myself for the new term.

We'd spent even more time on the phone than we normally did since I'd gotten back.

"I can't wait to see you, either," he replied.

"It's only been three days," I said. We were being ridiculous.

"I know. But I've missed you. I can't wait to get back to the library where I get to have you nearby all the time."

"I've missed you, too," I said as I opened and closed the drawers of my dresser.

"Only three days. And I'll see you right away because the first night back is Adam's twenty-first birthday," he reminded me.

"Oh, yes. I'd forgotten." Though how, I wasn't sure. Adam had been banging on about his birthday forever. He'd claimed no one ever wanted to celebrate his birthday because it came so soon after Christmas, so this year he was going to make up for all the birthdays he felt hadn't been celebrated properly. *Great.* I just wanted to spend my evening, every evening, with Joel.

"So I'll see you in the union bar at two?" Joel asked.

"In the afternoon? We're starting that early?" Jesus, I was barely going to have time to unpack.

"Yup. Adam's on a mission."

"Holy fuck." I pulled out my underwear and dropped them in the case. Perhaps I should think about upgrading and buy knickers that weren't five for five pounds.

"We're all going to be hammered by four." He paused. "Wear something sexy."

I laughed. "Like what? It will be two in the afternoon in the union bar, where the tables will be unwiped and the floor will be sticky with last term's beer, but you want me in a tight skirt and stilettos? I'll look like the hired stripper."

He hummed. "Sounds perfect. But I always want you,

whatever you wear. Remember that if you don't make it as a lawyer and you're thinking about career choices, stripper could work."

I opened the bottom drawer of my dresser where I kept my jumpers. "You make dirty sound sweet. Or the other way around. Either way you're a big pervert."

Joel laughed. "You make everything sexy. So I'll see you tomorrow."

"Okay." I wasn't ready for him to hang up just yet.

"Okay," he parroted. "I have to pack."

"Okay, loser."

"For infinity," he said

I grinned. "For infinity."

HANNA and I wanted to unpack properly before we started drinking, which I didn't think was so unreasonable. I wanted at least a made up bed to come back to. Even Jules, who was never concerned with being organized, was still rearranging her wardrobe. But Adam wasn't in the mood to be patient.

"I'm not waiting any longer for you. We'll see you up there," Adam said.

"We won't be long. You boys can manage without us for half an hour or so, can't you?" Hanna said, trying to reason with Adam, which never worked. It was best just to ignore him.

"Whatever. I told Joel I'd be there at two, so I'm off." Adam jogged down the stairs, then called, "Are you coming, guys?" Matt and Daniel trailed behind him.

I was as keen as the next person to be up at the union bar, but even I could wait thirty minutes more to see Joel.

"You look nice," Jules said, looking me over as we headed out.

"Thanks," I said, grinning like a crazy person. I'd resisted the short skirt and stilettos, but I had put on some kitten heels with my jeans and put on a low-cut top instead of my favorite, hand-knitted sweater I probably would have worn for anyone else. After we reached the union bar, I stood on tiptoe to look over Jules' shoulder, trying to catch my first glimpse of him.

I found him leaning over the pool table about to make a shot.

I had to chew on my thumb to disguise my smile. I loved the jeans he had on. They were my favorite. They clung in just the right places, and were lower on the hips than some of his others, which meant as he leaned over the pool table there was an exposed inch of flesh above his waistband for me to imagine my fingers running over. I brought my hand to my throat. *Infinity.* I hadn't taken it off since he'd given it to me. I watched as he lined up a shot across the table and saw his leather-wrapped wrist.

As if he sensed me, he grinned, made the shot, then turned straight toward me as if he knew exactly where I'd be standing. He held my gaze until I looked away.

Over Christmas, we hadn't spoken about being more public with our relationship. I hadn't thought about it, but now I wondered if Joel had. What was he expecting?

I waved at Daniel, who was playing pool with Joel, but was interrupted when Matt grabbed me in a hug. Everyone was in such a good mood, including me.

We headed over to the bar, and as we ordered drinks, Joel came up behind me.

"Hey," he whispered in my ear. I turned and put my arms around him, pulling him close.

"I thought I was supposed to be the one who dressed sexy today?" I mumbled.

"You did." His hand slid to my arse. "But I like that you think I did." I wriggled away from him, hoping no one spotted where his hand was and thought we were just having a welcome-back hug.

Joel fingered the infinity symbol and nodded almost imperceptibly.

Jules was hugging everyone and Joel and I got pushed apart in the ruckus. Adam was clearly pleased we had all made it out to celebrate with him, and he wasted no time in getting drinks in.

Hanna and I sat down at a wooden booth with padded seats that had seen better days, close to the boys playing pool. The student union bar was not the most glamorous place in the world, but with all my favorite people in it, it felt like home.

"You seem happy," Hanna said.

I glanced at Joel. "I am. What about you and Matt? You guys seem very together."

"We are. He's my best friend, you know?" she said.

I nodded. I knew what she meant. Joel and I hadn't been seeing each other for as long as she and Matt, but I appreciated the connection they had more than ever before. I was truly delighted she might be as happy as I was.

Jules was flirting with Daniel, who was so focused on the game he didn't seem to notice. Jules had such a thick skin his lack of reciprocation didn't affect her at all. She just moved on to Joel, stroking his arm as he stood waiting for Daniel to take his shot. I wondered how he would respond. Would he flirt back? I thought it might kill me a little if he did, even though I was sure of his feelings for me. But he didn't react, didn't move or brush her off. He didn't do anything. I knew Jules well enough to know that wasn't much of a disincentive to her. She would just up her game.

Daniel made his shot, lost, and as Joel started to circle the table, looking for the right angle, Jules followed him. He squatted down and Jules mirrored him, accidentally-on-purpose losing her balance. She used Joel's body to steady herself.

"Adam, Jules needs some looking after. I think the alcohol is taking its toll already," Joel said as he stood abruptly, and walked away from a slightly shell-shocked Jules. There'd been no doubt that he wasn't interested. He looked over at me and rolled his eyes. I loved him just a little bit more, if that was even possible.

At various points throughout the afternoon, Joel and I managed a few private moments together. He sat next to me at our table for a few minutes when he lost his pool game to Daniel. His arm went around the back of the bench. It felt like a thing a couple would do. His leg brushed against mine and heat rose within me. I was desperate to reach across and breathe him in, to stroke his thigh, to kiss him.

What was stopping me? Joel wanted me. That was enough, wasn't it? Did it matter people would think I wasn't good enough for him? How much pressure could that put on our relationship?

Infinity, right?

I brought my hands to my lap and brushed his knee with my fingers. He stopped mid-flow of whatever he was chatting to Matt about, closed his eyes, turned his head to me, and opened his eyes. They were burning. He wanted me. Right then, I knew if I asked him to take me home, it would be all he wanted to do. With just a slight touch of my hand I'd ignited something in him. It was such a powerful feeling.

"Joel?"

I interrupted our gaze and looked at Matt, who had clearly just asked Joel a question.

"Yeah, I agree, mate."

I wasn't sure what he'd just agreed with. I wasn't sure that Joel knew either, but it broke the spell between us, and Joel excused himself to go to the men's room.

WE FINALLY LEFT the bar late into the evening and managed to make it to our local club. It was packed, which was typical for a first night back. Tonight, I couldn't wait to get to the dance floor, and Jules and Hanna clearly felt the same as we headed to dance as soon as we got inside.

I turned my head to check that Joel was behind us. He nodded in the direction of the bar, letting me know where he'd be when we were done. I didn't want to lose him, in any sense, this evening. Last time we'd been out like this, we'd fought. I didn't want that to happen again. I would make sure no one touched me except Joel tonight.

Dance music throbbed through the floors and walls of the club. It wasn't normally my type of music, but I was desperate to work off the extra energy I had. Jules, Hanna, and I created a tight triangle and started to move to the beat. The monotony allowed me to empty my mind of what was going on around me. I just concentrated on my limbs and the movement. A thin layer of sweat formed over my skin and I lifted my hair to let air caress my neck, never losing the rhythm.

One tune morphed into another and another until Jules brought me back to reality with a hand on my shoulder. She mimed a drink and pointed at the bar. I indicated I was staying put.

Not even a second after the crowd swallowed Jules and Hanna, a hand landed on my waist and I turned, ready to slap someone, but I came face-to-face with Joel. My heart melted and my pulse quickened. He pushed his knee between my thighs and pulled my bottom toward him. He knew exactly how to hold me and how to move. He licked his lips, mesmerizing me. I knew what they could do.

The combination of the alcohol, the music, the tightly packed bodies, and Joel—most importantly Joel—set me alight. I pushed my palms up his chest and circled my hands around his neck, moving up and down on his thigh. He felt so good. I'd missed him. I'd not seen him in far too long. He gazed at me and the rest of the people on the dance floor melted away. It was just us in our bubble.

I slid around in his arms so my back was against his chest. He brought his hands to my waist and I circled my bottom in time to the music, pressing against his denim. He responded by pulling my hips closer, letting me feel his growing desire for me. I wanted to be naked and in private so all the fantasies crowding my head could become a reality. I put my hands over Joel's and we continued to move like that, in perfect time, the tension between us building minute by minute.

Joel's breath caught, stuttering against the back of my neck, then there was the slightest feel of his lips on my shoulder. I gasped as he tried to hold himself back. Knowing he wanted me as much as I wanted him was the biggest turn-on. This beautiful man behind me was mine. The sounds I could elicit from him, the way his eyes begged for my body so his mouth never had to, made me feel powerful, sexy. I didn't care who saw us, who knew. Joel wanted me and I wanted him, and that was enough.

I turned in his arms again and pulled his head down and kissed him, quickly slipping my tongue between his lips. He hesitated for a second before returning my kiss as if a dam had burst. His tongue pushed against mine, delving deeper, wanting more. He reached behind me and pulled me up and I brought my legs around his waist, not breaking our connection. My hair fell like curtains around us, hiding our mouths. Joel moved us through the crowd, but I couldn't move away from our kiss to find out where he was taking us. Joel pressed me against a wall.

"Jesus, I'm going to take you right here if we don't leave now," he growled against my neck and circled his hips, his erection digging into me.

I reached for the cock I could feel between my legs and he moved away sharply.

"Seriously. If you don't want to be fucked against that wall then—"

He didn't finish his sentence, just pulled me through the crowds so quickly I had to run every couple of steps so I kept up with him. He was a man on a mission—a mission to fuck me senseless.

"Joel, what about the others?" We hadn't told anyone we were leaving.

"I don't give a shit about anything but getting inside you."

He practically shoved me into a taxi and clambered on top of me, pushing his hands against my breasts.

"Joel," I said, trying to get him off me. Despite the mixture of alcohol and desire coursing through me, I was embarrassed about the cab driver witnessing our lust. Joel relented and threw himself back in his seat.

"How long until we get there?" he asked the taxi driver, which was ridiculous. He knew it was a five-minute cab ride to his house.

"Five minutes, unless you get your dick out, then I'm taking you straight to the police station," the driver replied.

I giggled and Joel scowled at me before he began to laugh. He pulled me toward him and planted a kiss on my head.

"I forget myself when I'm around you, Ava."

How was it possible that I could do that to a man like Joel? How had he fallen for me as hard as I'd fallen for him?

I fingered my necklace. We were solid. Made for each other. I'd found my soulmate. Nothing so inconsequential such as the end of university could split us up, could it?

TWENTY-THREE

The morning after the disastrous introduce-Will-to-my-friends-and-then-dump-him dinner, I was meeting Hanna and Jules for a girls' brunch at a hotel on Aldwych. I presumed we'd be required to dissect the night before, more particularly my breakup with Will, and as much as it wasn't something I was looking forward to, at least I'd get it over with. But the longer I sat in the restaurant on my own waiting for Hanna and Jules, the less I wanted to be there. Hanna had organized brunch a few days ago. If it had been Jules, I would have cancelled. But no one cancelled on Hanna. She was easygoing in many ways, but she had a strict rule about dropping out on her unless you were in hospital or you'd been murdered.

I felt terrible for leading Will on. He was a lovely guy. A classic case of "It's not you, it's me" but that sounded . . . lame. I should never have let it get so far.

The whole evening had been a mistake.

Joel's outburst had been totally confusing. Was he

angry because he thought I was being unfair to Will? Or
was he just angry with me? Will didn't understand the
significance of the necklace, which didn't make it right, but
it didn't hurt him, either.

That I was dating Will while in love with someone else
—*that* was the problem.

I waved as Hanna and Jules entered the restaurant and
scanned the tables. "So, I heard your news," Hanna said as
she arrived. "Consider this an intervention."

Jules took a seat but didn't say a word.

"And hello to you too." I sighed. "Can I order a drink
first?" I waved at the waiter. "Can I get a mimosa? But hold
the orange juice," I said before the guy could get a notebook
out of his apron.

"You want a glass of champagne?"

I shot him a dirty look. If I was about to face an intervention, then I needed to be day-drinking. And if I was day-
drinking, then I needed to be in denial about it. When I
didn't respond, he scurried away.

"So, what happened?" Hanna asked.

"Nothing happened. Will and I broke up. We were
barely together, so it's no big deal." I concentrated on
my menu.

"Well, I think it *is* a big deal, and I think we should talk
about it," Hanna said.

I said nothing. Jules said nothing.

With no encouragement from either of us, Hanna
continued. "He seemed like a really nice guy, Ava."

"Why are we at such a big table?" I asked, trying to
ignore Hanna's conversational direction.

"And he seemed to really like you," she said.

"We should move to a smaller one," I said.

"I think the boys are coming," Jules said, her nose buried in the menu.

"Fucking hell. I feel like I'm married to them. Can't it ever just be the three of us?" I moaned. The last person in the world I wanted to see right now was Adam. Or God forbid *Joel*. She couldn't have meant *Joel* when she said the boys. She always referred to Matt and Adam like that, and there were only two spare places at the table. I took a deep breath. My hand went to the infinity necklace. I hadn't taken it off. Somehow, I couldn't bring myself to.

Hanna and Jules shot each other a look but stayed quiet. I was being vile. I liked spending time with the boys. I just couldn't handle anyone else trying to give me an intervention.

"Sorry," I mumbled.

Silence.

I might have been the lawyer, but Hanna was a master negotiator and she used the fact I didn't like awkward silences against me. I gave in and spoke. "He's a nice guy, and yes, I think he liked what he knew about me, although that wasn't very much. But please, stop making it such a big deal."

The waiter came back with my glass of champagne. I felt guilty, and I smiled at him in apology. He smiled back. It was more than I deserved. He'd probably spat in my drink.

"Can I take your orders?" he asked.

"We're waiting for a couple of—oh, here they are. Can you give us a few minutes?" Hanna said.

My back was to the entrance and I couldn't bring myself to look away from my menu.

But, of course, it was Joel. With Adam. Fucking hell. This was officially the worst brunch ever.

"Hey, girls," Adam asked, bright and breezy. An apocalypse must be brewing. "What are you lot gossiping about?"

"We are trying to have a serious conversation with Ava about why she dumped Will."

"Honestly, Hanna, I love you, but can we drop this? I don't need an intervention. I just want to enjoy my drink and gossip about someone else."

"Okay, Ava, but I leave you with this: Guys like Will don't come around that often. You shouldn't be so picky."

"Did she drive him away already?" Adam asked.

"I'm ready to order," I said, looking around to see if the waiter was hovering, anything so I didn't have to look at Joel.

"Well, Joel added to the notches on his bedpost last night, even if Ava didn't. That girl was insanely fucking hot. I'm not sure what she saw in a drunken twat like you, though. You were hammered."

And just when I thought brunch couldn't get any worse. Discussing who Joel banged last night might just tip me over the edge.

"Hanna, can you order me eggs Benedict with some carbs the size of Africa?" I asked. "I'm going to the loo."

I had to get out of there. *Fuck. Fuck. Fuck.*

What was I doing? I was turning down perfectly nice, respectable, funny men because I'd been in love with a man for the last eight years who barely knew I was alive, and by all accounts, was out shagging half of London. The "insanely hot" half, apparently.

Fuck.

For the second time in less than twenty-four hours, I walked out of a loo and into Joel. Had he been waiting for me?

I didn't know what to say, so I forced a small, fake smile

and tried to walk past him.

"Are you okay?" he mumbled.

"Why wouldn't I be? Why would I care who you are fucking?"

"I meant about Will."

My cheeks heated and I looked away. Christ, why was my every thought about Joel?

"And I didn't fuck her," he said.

Oh, he didn't fuck her.

I didn't have a response. I was exhausted at feeling so much for this man and trying to hide it.

"I'm sorry I barked at you last night," he said. "I didn't get why you would be wearing the necklace." His gaze dipped to my throat. "It threw me off."

What did he mean the necklace had thrown him off? I wished I knew him like I used to know him. Exasperation rose in my chest and my eyes began to well. I couldn't have him be nice to me. I had to have more distance from him. Not less. "Don't, Joel."

He reached for me as I started to cry.

"God, Ava. Don't cry," he pleaded.

"I'm sorry. I don't know why I'm upset."

I let him stand there, rubbing my back.

"Did you wear the necklace . . . What were you . . ."

"God I'm so sorry, Ava," Hanna said, interrupting us. "I didn't mean to upset you." She wrapped her arms around me, and Joel's hand disappeared from my back.

A coldness enveloped me as Joel left.

"It's not you. I'm just tired and hungover." I extricated myself from Hanna's arms and wiped my eyes. "It's fine. You go to the loo." I smiled, patted her on the arm, and headed back to the table.

Maybe I should speak to Joel and properly talk about

what happened eight years ago. Maybe with closure I would be able to move on. The rate I was going, I was either going to lose all my friends or my mind. Something had to change.

I SHIFTED my weight from one leg to the other while trying to decide whether to press the button to call the lift up to Joel's flat. I was here now. I'd done the hard bit by deciding to come, surely.

As I'd approached Joel's building, someone had been coming out and had held the door open for me. The security guard at the desk had been on the phone and had a courier and someone else surrounding him so, like something out of an eighties spy film, I slipped past unnoticed. I hadn't expected it to be so easy. Maybe it was fate. I was desperate not to feel the way I did about Joel after so long. I wanted a solution to the longing I had in my heart. If at some point he'd have got married or even come back to London with a girlfriend, perhaps things would be easier, but knowing he was single gave me hope when there was none. I had to erase that possibility he and I could ever be anything to each other again.

Talking to him seemed to be my only option. I needed to hear how much he hated me. I had to see in his eyes how he saw me differently now.

At this point, I had nothing to lose but my love for him.

Maybe I should call up? Did it look weird if I just appeared at his door?

Holy hell. I tapped the button. I was irritating myself with my indecision. My temperature rose at least ten degrees as I stepped in and pressed the "P" on the brushed metal panel. I needed closure. I needed to move on.

Nothing to lose. I just had to knock on the door. The rest would happen. The lift was quicker than I remembered, and before I'd taken a breath, the doors pinged open.

Nothing to lose, I reminded myself.

I clutched at my stomach and took the three steps to Joel's door and knocked. Three confident raps to the metal door.

Yup, I was doing it.

I waited. No answer.

I knocked again, then heard movement. My heart pounded through my shirt. *Nothing to lose, nothing to lose.*

The door opened and I discovered there was something to lose after all.

My pride.

My hope.

An insanely hot, gazelle-like woman answered the door in a towel so small it only just covered the tops of her thighs. So Joel had fucked her, after all.

I tried to hold my expression steady as pain coursed through my body.

She gave me a huge grin as though we were old friends who had just bumped into each other at the grocery store.

"Hi," she said.

Fuck, I was going to have to speak.

"Hi," I replied, hoping I'd actually said the words out loud and not just in my head.

"Are you looking for Joel?" she asked in an American accent.

I nodded, not trusting anything else that might come out of my mouth. I don't know what I'd been expecting, but it wasn't meant to hurt like it did.

"He just left. Do you want to wait?" She fiddled with the top of her towel.

"No, no. That's fine. I'll call him later." I began to back away, wanting to be out of sight when my legs gave way.

"Shall I say you stopped by?"

My back hit the wall, and I turned and furiously pressed the down button. I swallowed. The air was thin and I couldn't seem to take a deep enough breath. "No, I'll catch him another time," I managed to choke out.

"He'll have his phone with him, I'm sure," she said, as helpfully as anyone could be in a towel.

"Okay, thanks." I lifted my hand in a semi-wave as I headed into the lift. I needed out. Now.

Just when I'd thought I had nothing to lose, I found out there was further to fall. But perhaps this was it. Maybe now I'd be done.

TWENTY-FOUR

Past

I groaned as the pain in my head coursed through my whole body. I was never drinking again.

"How's your head, baby?" Joel asked from beside me.

After rolling over and attaching myself to him like a limpet, my eyes still closed, I stroked his chest.

"Don't speak, don't ever speak," I croaked.

He chuckled and pulled me closer. He was always so fucking cheerful in the morning. If Joel had one thing that irritated me about him, that was it.

"I'll make you feel better." He grabbed my ass.

"If you put your penis anywhere near me, Joel Wentworth, I will throw up on you."

"You're adorable when you're grouchy and hungover."

"Fuck you."

"Anytime, baby. Shall I get you some juice?"

I shook my head. "Stay." I didn't want him to leave this bed. His bed. I sat bolt upright. "I stayed over."

"Who said you wouldn't make it as a lawyer? You have the ultimate powers of perception."

"I mean I'm not at home."

He chuckled. "Again with the perceptive thing."

I flung a pillow at Joel as he lay there looking perfect, grinning at me.

"How am I going to explain this?" I asked. It wasn't like Jules wandering back into our block in the morning as she often did. I never stayed out, and Hanna and Jules would want to know why.

"I think the questions about us making out on the dance floor will be the first ones you field."

"Oh God." I groaned and fell back on the bed.

"What's the big deal, anyway?" he asked. "This is good, isn't it? Everything out in the open?"

We'd never really discussed my need to keep us a secret. He never pushed me, never wanted an explanation. I assumed he was happy with the arrangement. Or at least not *unhappy* with it.

"I like things just between us." I was being evasive, and I knew it.

Joel turned and propped his head on his elbow, staring at me as I focused on the ceiling.

"But you don't want people knowing about us."

"I don't see how it's anyone else's business."

"It changes how we are together and how often we see each other. I don't understand why we can't just be ourselves—like we were over Christmas."

He wasn't moaning or demanding or whining. He was just raising excellent points. It irritated me. He was just so good at *everything*. Like making me feel good, being a good friend, a great student, handsome without trying. And he was superb at making reasoned and reasonable arguments. He should be the lawyer. I looked at him as he stroked my face. "There's nothing to be scared of."

"I don't want people weighing in on our relationship, telling us what's right and wrong, and how you could do better . . ."

"That's what you're worried about? That people will tell me I could do better, and that I'd have some kind of epiphany and be persuaded that they're right?"

When he said it like that, it sounded ridiculous. I knew he loved me. I pursed my lips. I didn't have a response, at least not one that made any objective sense.

"Jules likes you. I don't want to upset her."

Joel moved so we were nose to nose. He pushed my hair away from my face. I loved the feeling of his weight on top of me.

"You're just grasping at straws now. Jules likes everyone. She doesn't discriminate, and you know she wouldn't be upset we're together."

He was right, as usual. I trailed my fingers down his back.

"Are you trying to distract me?" he asked.

I grinned. "You're the one lying on top of me."

"I just like you waking up in my bed. I can't resist you in the mornings. Or the afternoons. Or the evenings." He always knew just what to say.

"Even when I'm grouchy and unreasonable?" I pouted.

"Especially when you're grouchy and unreasonable."

I shook my head. "You're sick, you know that? Perverted."

"Maybe." He smiled at me and dipped his head to push his lips to mine.

A shiver slid down my spine as he moved his mouth across to my neck, his arms braced on either side of me, and began to nip and lick and suck my neck.

"So, if people saw us together . . ." Distracted by his mouth, I lost my train of thought for a second. "I guess we can just—oh God—tell people we're together." He pushed his erection against my thigh in response and moved to my breasts.

"And if they didn't see . . ." My back arched at the feel of his teeth around my nipple. "We can just—*fuck!*" I screamed as he pushed into me, then brought his eyes back to mine, watching the reaction he had on me.

"I couldn't wait another moment to be inside you, Ava." He started to move and all I could think about was how perfect he was, how good he felt, how much he wanted me. "How does that feel?"

"Perfect," I choked out.

"Perfect?" he asked. "Perfectly hard? Perfectly deep? Tell me."

"Joel." I was so turned on by his words, but I couldn't answer him. I was too embarrassed.

"You are perfect. Perfectly beautiful, perfectly soft, perfectly wet, perfectly mine."

I clenched and pushed my hips toward him, meeting his rhythm. He tightened his jaw, and I could tell he was holding himself back, waiting for me. I gripped his shoulders as he thrust deeper and deeper. I was right on the edge of the most mind-numbingly pleasurable moment and I wanted it to last forever. But in seconds, I was lost. I exploded, waves pulsing across my belly and down my arms and legs as my back arched and I called Joel's name.

Joel's thrusts quickened. "You look fucking amazing

when you come for me," he said, then tensed as he came deep inside me.

I would do anything for this man. Even risk the judgment and criticism. Even if it meant risking losing him.

TWENTY-FIVE

Present

"Don't sweat it about Will, babe," Jules said after we'd been on the phone for about twenty minutes. I couldn't recall anything she'd told me. I just wasn't engaged in what she was saying. "Are you listening to me?" Part of me was watching a muted episode of *Nashville* that I'd seen before, and another part was reliving my encounter with Insanely Hot Girl. And one tiny part of me was wondering how long it would take before my spoon would be able to dig into the cookies and cream ice cream I had defrosting between my knees. That didn't leave much room for me to focus on Jules, and apparently, she'd noticed.

"Sorry, my mind wandered."

"You seem so cut up over the breakup—you must have really liked him. Why don't you give him another chance?"

I rolled my eyes. Will wasn't the fucking problem.

"He wasn't the one."

"Fucking hell, babe. You need Mr. Right Now, not Mr.

Right. Just find someone you can have some fun with. Someone who's good in bed. Did you two even get that far?"

"You know we didn't."

"I bet he had a huge cock. You could see it in the way he walked."

"What?" Jules was officially losing it. "You could tell the size of his penis by his gait?"

"I'm not saying that having it swinging between his legs made him walk differently, just that he was confident."

"Whatever." I rolled my eyes.

"You could have missed out there."

I sighed. "Well, why don't you go and find out since you're so obsessed with his cock? He's single now, from what I've heard."

"No need to get snarky."

"Sorry. I just—I wasn't thinking about Will. I wish we could just drop it."

"So, what were you thinking about?"

I frowned. That wasn't the sort of question I expected from Jules. She normally didn't notice much about anyone's mood.

"That I need a change." I hadn't been thinking that, but as it came out, the statement felt good. Maybe I needed a new job or a hobby. "I might go and work abroad, start a pottery class. Take a year out or something."

"You didn't even take a gap year with the rest of us." Jules didn't need to remind me of that. "So you're really considering stepping out of the rat race? Wonders will never cease."

"I'm not saying I'm going to do it. Just that I'm thinking about it." I was pretty sure I wasn't about to hand in my notice the next day, but things needed to change. I couldn't go on so wrapped up in a man I didn't know anymore.

"Right. But you didn't even think about it after uni, so it counts as personal growth."

If only she knew *how much* I'd thought about it. A wave of regret passed through me and I stood abruptly.

Things could have been very different.

TWENTY-SIX

Joel and I spent the morning in bed and I headed back to campus just before lunch. Joel could tell I was nervous, and offered to come with me, but I reassured him there was no need for him to chaperone me. I was the one freaked out by people knowing about us, and I had to deal with it. And anyway, I would have felt more self-conscious had he been there.

I felt braver on my own.

I had my story prepared. I would simply say that, yes, Joel and I had kissed and left together and I'd stayed at his place. I wasn't going to give away the fact we'd been a couple as long as we had.

People were going to put two and two together, and as much as I'd avoided anyone finding out about us, I wasn't about to blatantly lie.

As I approached our block, I took a deep breath. People often congregated on the stairs at the entrance, so they may have already seen me. It was obvious I was doing the walk of shame—I had heels on, for goodness sake. But I had nothing to be ashamed of, nothing to hide, so I pulled back my shoulders and walked into my block. It was dead quiet. Not a soul to be seen. Every door of the twelve bedrooms was closed. That never happened. What was going on?

I took my time fishing my keys out of my bag, and I kept looking around, waiting, half wanting someone to catch me.

I hung around my room for twenty minutes, but there were still no signs of life in the block, so I gave up and showered. I still had my towel wrapped around me when Jules bust in.

"I feel fucking horrendous." She was still in her PJs and her hair was standing on end. Jules normally wore her hangover better than that.

She slumped on my bed and covered her eyes with her arms.

"How are you showered already? You were pretty hammered last night."

"It's like two in the afternoon. I slept in, believe me." I smiled at the memory of Joel and I doing anything but sleeping this morning.

"Well, you may never sleep again after what I've got to tell you."

But what about what I have to tell you?

"Uh-oh," I said, only half listening. Was Joel right? Would she not care I was seeing him?

"You promise not to tell?" she asked.

Or maybe she'd stop speaking to me and our friendship group would be broken.

"Ava?" she asked.

"What? No, I won't tell. What did you do?"

"Why do you assume I did something?" She scowled at me.

"Well, didn't you?"

"Yes." She grinned but shook her head in mock dismay of herself.

I rolled my eyes. "Go on."

"I shagged Adam, then I freaked and ran away, but I didn't know where to go so I slept on the doorstep of the block."

Adam? I'd never seen those two together. "That is way too much information in one lump. Break it down for me."

She groaned and pulled herself up so she was sitting, ready to give me all the details. "You are such a fucking lawyer."

"You slept with Adam?" I asked.

Jules chuckled. "I did. Oh my God, I did."

"So, do you like him—as in fancy him?"

"What?" She jerked her head back as if I were offering her dog shit to eat. "No."

"Then why did you sleep with him?"

She shrugged. "I'm only supposed to sleep with guys I fancy?"

"Well, it's one way to go." I wasn't a prude, and I wasn't crazy about the guy I lost my virginity to, but sex with Joel was incredible and seemed inextricably linked to our feelings for each other—I couldn't imagine it any other way.

"Okay. And you slept on the doorstep why?"

Jules looked at me as if I were asking the dumbest question in the world. I raised my eyebrows in expectation of her answer.

"To get away from him." She shook her head.

"And you didn't just go to your room?"

"He was *in* my bedroom. *We* were in my bedroom."

"Oh, I see." But why hadn't she just asked him to go?

Jules wasn't backward at asking for what she wanted. I really couldn't follow her logic today.

"So, have you seen him this morning?" I asked.

"Not after I saw him leave early this morning. Now I'm in hiding."

I nodded. And I'd thought my news would split apart our group. Jules and Adam were going to be first past the post on that. And in any event, Jules hadn't even asked about Joel and me. Maybe no one had seen.

Part of me was disappointed. I had worked myself up to the reveal. I was ready, I thought, to take on the world. Now it seemed the world didn't want to be taken on. Not yet anyway. Hanna was bound to have seen us, though. She never drank that much, and she always managed to have all the gossip the next morning. It was the only advantage to staying sober, as far as I could make out.

Jules jumped to her knees and covered her mouth with her hands at a knock on the door.

"Don't answer. It will be Adam," she stage-whispered.

This was ridiculous. I couldn't pretend we weren't in here, the walls were thin, and whoever was at my door would have heard us talking.

I waved at Jules and made my way over to the door. "Who is it?" I asked through the door.

"It's me, Ava, let me in." Hanna said. Thank God for that.

I opened the door. She was also still in her PJs. Had the clocks changed or something?

She joined Jules on my bed as I continued to comb through my hair and busy myself at my dressing table.

"Oh my God, Hanna, what am I going to do? Can you believe it?"

"You didn't, did you?"

Jules nodded. I wasn't sure she didn't love the attention at that moment. She was certainly getting enough of it. Maybe she did like Adam. Or maybe this was all just a ruse to keep the spotlight. As much as I loved Jules, she had an insatiable desire to be at the center of everything. I guess that was why the three of us got on so well. Neither Hanna nor I craved that like Jules did. We were happy for her to take center stage. Still, I'd thought today would go a slightly different way.

"Oh my God, you were so drunk. You just went up to him and that was it," Hanna said.

"I can't really remember," Jules said through her grin.

"We were at the bar, and I think you'd been to the bathroom or something, and you came over and said that you hadn't given him a birthday kiss. Then you just grabbed him and stuck your tongue down his throat."

"I did not."

"You so did," Hanna continued. "And when you came up for air, he said, 'With all the shit you give me, I deserve a birthday blow job,' and you just nodded and said, 'You're on,' took his hand and left. It was hilarious."

Jules guffawed. She wasn't the slightest bit embarrassed. Here I was, ready to be mortified about a kiss on a dance floor with my serious boyfriend, and Jules outdid me without even trying.

No one mentioned that Joel and I had left together the night before.

"So, do you like him?" Hanna asked.

"Who, Adam? Don't you start." Jules cocked her head toward me.

"I think you guys really match," I said.

Jules snorted. "That is such an insult."

"It is not. You're both my friends," I replied. They did go well together in a funny sort of way.

"I'm just going to pretend it didn't happen. I can't remember most of it, anyway, which means it didn't happen, right? Isn't that what quantum physics says or something?"

"Or something," I said.

"Well, I think you should make a go of it. What have you got to lose?" Hanna asked.

I loved that Hanna responded like that. It gave me hope that if and when people found out about Joel and me, I would have at least Hanna batting for us. Unless she assumed I'd get hurt because he was so far out of my league. Oh God, I was driving myself crazy. Should I just tell them, get it over with? Jules would think I was trying to steal her thunder.

No. I would leave it and see if it came up. I loved having Joel to myself in our bubble. That way it was us against the world. And I wouldn't have to hear how naïve I was being by being in love with a man so much better than me. I wouldn't have to worry people would start to tease him about his choice of girlfriend.

Whose business was it, anyway?

TWENTY-SEVEN

I stood outside Hanna and Matt's, trying to muster up the courage to go inside for our semi-regular Sunday lunch. It would be the first with Joel, and no doubt Hanna would pull out all the stops. Was this what it was going to be like now? Was I going to keep turning up with a bottle of wine, on my own, to watch everyone else's life move on? Could I really watch Joel bring a parade of women into our group until he found one he wanted to marry, and then stand aside as they built their lives together? Presumably he was going to bring the insanely hot girl. Would she recognize me? Probably not.

But what if she did?

Christ, I felt pathetic. I plastered on a fake smile and pushed the heavy, Victorian door open. I loved that Hanna still left her door unlocked in the middle of London as if she was living in the 1950s.

There was plenty of noise in the kitchen at the end of the hallway. I could hear Joel. Feel him, as always. I wondered if he ever sensed me in the way I did him. I'd never asked him, but it had always been like that for me. And it had never gone away.

"Hiya," I announced as I entered the room, not looking at anyone in particular and heading straight to the fridge. Alcohol would make things better.

There was a chorus of replies, but I concentrated on Hanna, who was elbow deep in something I hoped, by the looks of it, we weren't going to have to eat.

"What's that?" I asked, suspiciously regarding the rice and egg that covered Hanna's hands.

"It's that coulibiac thing that I made for Matt's boss."

Great, we *were* going to have to eat it.

"Wine?" I asked.

"What, you think I haven't started already?" She sighed and glanced around the kitchen that was littered with half-cooked food and dirty dishes.

"You want me to help with something?"

"No, don't touch a thing. I have everything under control. I think."

I settled on a stool and realized that Matt, Joel, and Adam were, as usual, involved in some video game on the sofa at the other end of the huge open plan area. None of them had stopped what they were doing just because I'd arrived, which was fine with me. Slightly less comforting was that Insanely Hot Girl had joined them. She was so young, but then, of course she was. How could she even breathe in jeans that tight? Apparently, she was an insanely hot alien that didn't require oxygen.

"She's young," Hanna muttered under her breath. "Jules is not going to be happy."

I'd forgotten about Jules chasing Joel in all my drama.

"She's with Joel?" I faked the question.

Hanna nodded. "From New York," she added, and raised her eyebrows.

I felt a punch to my gut. This wasn't just some girl Joel had slept with. This was someone from his life in New York. Someone who liked him enough to visit him in London. Someone he liked enough to have in his flat. Thank God I'd run the other night. I really hoped she didn't recognize me, or that she'd forgotten about me.

There was a disappointed cry across the room from everyone except Adam, who cheered, as their game came to an end.

"I whooped you all," he said, punching the air.

Everyone ignored him.

"More beers?" Matt asked as he got up then came over and kissed me on the cheek, everyone following him.

"Ava, this is Jamie," Hanna said, smiling sweetly as Jamie came toward us.

Her eyes lit up. "Hi again." She hugged me awkwardly and giggled. "I have more clothes on this time."

I smiled tightly and nodded. The heat of Joel's gaze caught my attention, but I didn't dare look at him.

Jamie took two beers from Matt, who was juggling the four he'd taken from the fridge, and went straight back to the sofa and perched on the arm, next to Joel.

"Again?" he whispered as he leaned into her.

Jamie shrugged. "We're old friends." She giggled again. Yup, an insanely hot giggling alien.

Joel looked confused and glanced over his shoulder at me.

I looked away and hopped off my stool. "Shall I set the table?" I asked Hanna.

"Yes, for eight," she replied without looking up from whatever she was doing with her pastry and a rollery, bladey thing that looked like it belonged in a Chinese torture chamber.

Eight? "Is Daniel coming?"

"No, Jules is bringing some guy from the office."

From the table, I listened to the conversation between Joel and his New Yorker. I prayed she wouldn't tell him about my visit.

"What do you mean, you're old friends?" he asked her.

Why couldn't he just drop it?

She didn't answer.

"Tell me," he asked again.

"It's nothing, Joel." She was concentrating on the screen, watching Matt beat Adam.

"Have you met her before?" he whispered. I might not have heard, but I was homed in on their conversation.

"She just dropped by the other day. I answered the door, and she changed her mind or something. I don't know." She shrugged.

Fuck.

How was I going to explain this? What excuse could I use for going to his place? I could say I got locked out again. No, that wouldn't work. It hadn't been late and he knew Hanna and Matt had a key.

"And you were naked?" he asked.

"I was in a towel. I'm not going to open your door naked, am I?"

"I have no idea. You are so irresponsible, I wouldn't put anything past you," he said, his voice clipped and irritated, which soothed me. He was pissed, and I had to bite back a grin. Perhaps they weren't in love. Maybe it was just sex.

"Hey, guys." Jules burst through the door, providing just the distraction I needed.

"Wow, you're hot!" she immediately said to our guest. "Who are you?"

"Jamie," she said and pulled Jules into a hug, too. Jules wasn't much of a hugger, even with the best of her friends, and she looked shocked at the intrusion into her personal space.

"Well, aren't you friendly? American, I presume?"

"My accent gives it away, I guess." She giggled, *again*. "I'm with Joel."

Jules threw a look at Joel, then over to Hanna, who raised her eyebrows.

"She's my business partner's little sister," Joel explained.

"I'm twenty-one and not so little."

"And you're staying in London?" Jules asked.

"I am." She grinned, not realizing that Jules' question was hoping to solicit rather more information than she had given out.

"Well, this is Harvey," Jules said, introducing the man by her side, first to Jamie and then to the rest of us.

Harvey was tall, lithe in a way he would grow out of, and had a generous smile. I hoped he was good to Jules. I wanted her to be happy. But tonight, I wanted it to be just our gang. I wished Joel was back in New York and Harvey had gotten the flu and been unable to make it. I wanted just one evening where I wasn't on edge, watching everything I did and said.

TWENTY-EIGHT

Past

"So, how did it go?" Joel asked. He'd called wanting to know how everyone had reacted to our kiss on the dance floor and my walk of shame. Jules and Hanna were still in my room discussing the aftermath of Jules' and Adam's shagfest, so I'd slipped out into the corridor.

"No one's mentioned anything," I replied, speaking as quietly as I could. "I don't think anyone saw, and then Jules is all full of drama because she had sex with Adam last night."

"So you didn't tell them?"

Why was he focusing on me telling our friends about us when there was a much more interesting scandal going down? We'd gotten a get-out-of-jail-free card.

"Did you just hear me?" I asked. "Jules and Adam!"

"I don't give a shit about Jules and Adam." He was clearly irritated, but it wasn't my fault. Events had taken over. And I was enjoying the Jules and Adam drama, even if it was partly because it deflected from Joel and me.

"Did you want me to tell everyone, even if they didn't see us?" I didn't understand what had Joel so uppity. Everything was just as it always had been with us, same as yesterday, same as last week. "Do you want me to make a big deal about it?"

He sighed. "I thought the issue had resolved itself last night, that's all."

"Is there an issue?" I asked. If people didn't know, why did we have to make a thing about it?

There was silence on the other end of the line.

"Joel?" I asked in a loud whisper. Why wasn't he speaking?

"Whatever, Ava."

My stomach flipped. He was never cross with me. "Are you mad?"

"No, I'm not mad. I just don't get it. Why do you care what they think so much?"

It wasn't just that. I was afraid I'd lose him, afraid what we had would disintegrate under the magnified lens of our friends' scrutiny. Afraid he would wake up and realize he could do better.

I wandered further down the corridor, away from anyone who might be listening. "I'm just trying to protect us." This wasn't a conversation I wanted to have over the phone, and I wasn't explaining myself very well. I wanted Joel to understand.

"By hiding?"

"It's that Observer Effect thing, isn't it?"

"You think we'll change if others are looking at us?"

"I don't know, maybe."

"Look, I love you, Ava. That's not going to change. If you think it will for you, just because people know . . . Well, then I don't know what to think."

I didn't realize this was such an issue for him. The last thing I wanted to do was create tension between us. "Did I ever tell you I applied for Cambridge?" I asked, hoping he might understand if I explained it this way.

"No, I don't think so."

I leaned back against the corridor wall. "Well, I did, and I got through the exam to the interview. And everyone was so excited and the school made an announcement in our assembly, and all my friends were telling me how I was going to ace the interview and my parents were so proud and told their friends and—"

"And . . .?"

"And all I felt was this tremendous pressure, like I was trapped in a vice or something. I forgot to be excited about it and I just concentrated on pleasing everyone. On getting in, because that's what people wanted for me." I exhaled. I'd forgotten how difficult it had been. "I totally bombed the interview. I could barely look at the panel members. It was all too much. Too much expectation, too much pressure, and I crumbled. And part of me knew, and still knows, that if I'd just not told anyone—if it had just been left to me—I'd have done it. I would have gotten in. And I know it's not the same, but I don't want that pressure and expectation on us. Not yet. Just until exams are over, can we leave it between just us?"

"Ava, it's not the same. We're *us*. I love you. You have to trust that."

Jules stuck her head out of my bedroom and mouthed, *Who is it?* Her nosiness overruled her worry over seeing Adam. My instinctive reaction was to lie, but I stopped myself. If it came out, it came out.

"It's Joel," I said, loud enough for Joel to hear me tell the truth.

"What?" Joel said.

"Jules asked who I was on the phone with."

Either satisfied or irritated that my call didn't involve her, Jules headed back into the bedroom without any sort of reaction.

"Oh," he replied. I couldn't tell if he was pleased I'd been up front with Jules, or not. Maybe it was the least he expected. "If it comes up, I'm not going to lie, Ava."

"Okay." What else could I say? "I love you."

"I'll see you later."

He didn't say it back. He'd *always* said it back. I clutched at my stomach, trying to calm the rising panic. "Okay, bye," I said.

"Okay, bye."

My heart sank just a little lower in my chest as I went back in. The girls were both sitting cross-legged on my bed chatting, so I pulled the cushion off my chair and sat down.

"What did he say?" Jules asked.

"What about?"

"Me and Adam."

I was confused for a second, then it dawned on me that Jules must have thought Joel had called me to discuss her and Adam. "Oh, nothing. I don't think he knew."

"Oh." Jules narrowed her eyes and then turned away when she realized she wasn't the center of my conversation with Joel.

"Why was he calling?" Hanna asked.

"Oh, just checking I made it back okay," I said.

To my surprise, my explanation was accepted without further probing.

"You can't just hide in here for the rest of the year," Hanna told Jules. "Do you want me to talk to him?" she asked, trying to be the peacemaker as usual.

Jules grinned. "Only if you make it clear I'm not interested."

I zoned out while Hanna and Jules planned just what to say. Perhaps I should head over to Joel's place, smooth things out between us. We were always completely solid, and I wasn't used to this feeling of uncertainty between us. I wanted to reassure him that I trusted him and that I loved him. And I needed to hear the same back.

A week had passed since Adam's birthday and we hadn't been together as a group until now. We were all sitting around a table in the student union bar. All of us except Joel. He'd texted to say he was coming, but he wasn't here yet and I was scratchy all over. My body needed him. Things seemed fine and back to normal between us. Well, almost. We'd picked up our routine from the previous term —Joel collecting me to go to the library, me trying to concentrate on studying when all I could do was smell him, see him, and almost touch him. We'd gone back to his place twice and made dinner and had fantastic sex.

I sighed at the thought of his beautiful, hard body against mine.

"So are you two together, over it, or what?" Daniel asked, looking between Jules and Adam. A silence descended on the group as everyone waited for a response.

"There's nothing to get over," Jules said matter-of-factly. "I still hate him, think he's annoying and irritating beyond words. He thinks I'm amazing and now knows I'm good in bed. That's it."

I looked at Adam and, for once in his life, he didn't have a riposte to Jules' biting assessment of the situation. He just rolled his eyes. "Whatever, Jules."

I grinned. That was why we all liked Adam so much. As much as he dished it out, he could take it. And when it really mattered, he wasn't going to try to come up with a comeback that might hurt Jules. Deep, deep down, he was a very sweet guy.

My skin buzzed and I looked up, searching for him. Joel had just come through the doors and was making his way over to the table. I smiled, but he was acknowledging someone across the bar.

"What's going on here?" he asked as he reached the table and found us in uncomfortable silence.

"We're just talking about Adam and Jules," Matt filled him in.

Joel took some nuts from the bowl in the middle of the table. "Oh yes, Adam's twenty-first. The night I kissed Ava. It was a good night." He turned and walked to the bar as I choked on my vodka soda. Had I just heard him right? A wave of nausea passed through me. He wanted people to know.

"Ava!" Jules screeched. "You kissed Joel?"

I looked into the bottom of my plastic cup and nodded.

"That fucking bastard. I can't believe it!" she screamed.

What?

"That's it—we're not hanging around with these arse-holes. What a complete shit." Jules threw her phone into her bag and got up. I looked at Hanna, who looked confused —or was it concern I saw? "Come on. Fuck these fucking fuckers."

Hanna and I knew better than to argue, so we scooted after her. Joel was still at the bar, chatting to the bartender as we left.

"Right. Let's go into town," Jules said.

"Why? I don't want a big night," Hanna whined. She wanted to spend the evening with Matt. I wanted to spend the evening with Joel.

So how had we ended up here?

"Don't let that fucker upset you, Ava. You should have told us. I'd have punched him in the balls for you," Jules said once we got to another bar just off campus. It was full of retired men wondering what the hell we were doing there.

"Are you mad at me?" I asked her.

"Why would I be mad at you? I'm mad *for* you!"

I still wasn't quite sure what was going on. Hanna looked at me sympathetically. I stayed silent, hoping things would become clearer. "Well, don't sweat it. You're too good for him anyway. Let's get some shots in," Jules said, storming to the bar.

"You seem to be staying really strong, Ava. Good for you," Hanna said.

"Why wouldn't I be? Is Jules mad? Does she really like him?"

Hanna shrugged. "I don't think so. No more than she likes any fuckable guy on campus. Were you worried?"

I nodded.

"You are so sweet. Fucked over by Joel and you're concerned about Jules." Hanna gave me another sympathetic look and squeezed my hand.

"What do you mean?" I asked.

"Don't take it personally, Ava. It's just boys in general. They think with their dicks."

"I'm not taking anything personally. Joel didn't fuck me over," I said.

Hanna patted my hand again.

Jules came back with our shots. "Come on, girls. Let's forget those freaks."

"Look," I said, my voice louder, "Joel didn't fuck me over. At all."

Jules looked at me and raised her shot glass to her lips.

"Seriously, guys, we're friends. I like him," I said.

"Of course you do," Hanna said. "He's Joel Wentworth." She folded her arms. "I don't understand why he had to do this."

"He's a man. I guess every woman is a potential bedmate. Even Ava," Jules said, rolling her eyes. "No doubt he assumed you'd be desperate for it. He's totally taken advantage."

"What? He didn't take advantage of me." I looked between them. "And what do you mean, 'even Ava'." Of course I knew what they meant. They didn't understand why Joel would have picked someone like me. Someone who wasn't glossy and flirtatious. Someone who had to rely on her brains not her looks. Just as my father had always told me.

"She's crazy for him," Hanna said as if I couldn't hear her.

"Oh, Ava. Whatever you do, don't be that girl." Jules shook her head.

"What girl?" I asked, angry, confused, and blindsided. My phone vibrated in my pocket. Probably Joel, wondering where we got to.

"The girl that pines after the player. Don't be that girl."

"I'm not being 'that girl,' as you put it."

"Then I want you to promise me you'll never kiss him again. That you'll not pine after him, or daydream about him. You won't text him. You'll just ignore him." Jules grabbed my arm and was trying to pin me down with her eyes.

"I don't see what the big deal is," I answered. God, what would they say if they knew the whole truth? They'd think I was the biggest idiot in the world.

"Honey, she doesn't want to see you hurt," Hanna said. "You know Joel, he has all these girls hovering . . . Let's just say he has plenty of choices." She frowned slightly.

"And why would he choose me? Is that what you're saying?" This was exactly what I'd expected them to say, and why wouldn't they? They were right. I had no idea why he chose me, but he had.

Hanna tilted her head in sympathy.

"Whatever. I'm going home." I grabbed my bag and headed out.

"Let her go," Hanna said as I left. "Her pride's been hurt."

Fucking hell. I was pissed at Joel. Why did he have to say anything? And to drop a bomb like that in the way he did. I pulled my phone from my pocket.

J: Where the fuck did you go?

A: I just had to endure lectures on what a shit you are and how, with all the girls on offer, there's no way you'd pick me. Naturally, I feel great about the night. I'm going home.

My heart was pounding and my chest felt tight. I didn't know who I was angrier with—Joel for telling people or Hanna and Jules for reacting exactly how I'd expected them to.

J: God, I'm sorry. I should have warned you. I was just frustrated. Come over. I'll leave the guys here.

A: I need to go home.

They'd said everything I'd been afraid of. They were right. Joel did have a lot of choices. Why *would* he choose me? I wasn't the beauty in our group. I wasn't the vivacious, outgoing girl everyone wanted to be around. I carried a little extra weight on my hips and I had no interest in fashion or makeup. Joel was the guy every girl wanted. He could have anyone. I had no right to love him or to want him to love me.

He deserved someone better. Someone sexy and beautiful and charming. Someone who was the *opposite* of me. This was exactly why I didn't want people to know. This was why I wanted Joel and me to stay in our bubble.

J: Please come by. I miss you. I wanted to spend the evening with you and I feel cheated.

My resolve wavered.

J: Ava, please. I can make it better.

TWENTY MINUTES after his last text, I rang Joel's buzzer. I hated that I'd been right about how all our friends would view us, and I needed to escape their condemnation and judgment. I wanted him to make it better. As soon as he opened the door, he grabbed me and held me tight. We stood there, half in and half out of his house, and my tension drained as if he were sucking it from me.

"I just can't handle it," I choked out. I hated being in a fishbowl, everyone glaring at me, pointing and telling me what I should and shouldn't be feeling. And worse, I hated that it bothered me. I shouldn't care what anyone else thought. Why couldn't I ignore everyone?

"You know I love you, and that I'm not looking at any other girls, don't you?" he asked, his touch stilling for a second, as if to make sure I heard him.

I *did* know that. Apart from anything else, I was with him most of the time when he wasn't in lectures. He didn't have time to cheat on me. I knew he loved me. I loved him. I didn't need to doubt him. I nodded. "It's just with people making comments about how ridiculous it was that we kissed and how you took advantage, I don't know which way is up anymore."

I slid my hands over my face to cover the start of my tears. "I want to concentrate on you and my exams. The rest doesn't matter," I sobbed. "I'm sorry I'm frustrating. I'm so weak." I knew I should be able to shrug everyone's opinions off but somehow they clung to me like ivy, invading every crevice of insecurity I had.

He pulled me inside. "No, I'm sorry. I shouldn't have pushed. I just love you and don't want to hide it."

Joel had done nothing wrong. This was my issue. Perhaps things would be better when there was less pressure. "I get it. But can we delay it until after the exams? Telling people, all their questions and opinions—I just can't handle it."

He tightened his arms around me. "I know, baby. I'm sorry. Let's just leave things how they are."

I glanced up at him. "Are you sure?"

"Yes, I'm sure. I just want to make you happy."

"But I want *you* to be happy," I said, misery in my voice.

"I'm happy if you're happy."

I smiled, my tears drying. "I'm happy when we're together," I said.

He kissed me on my forehead and I sighed. "We're together, Ava. Nothing's going to change that."

I nodded. "Okay."

"Okay." He grinned, tucking my hair behind my ear.

"Okay, you loser," I said as he lifted me up and kissed me hard.

"Sounds like you need some stress relief," he mumbled into my neck.

I gripped him tighter. "Always." I wrapped my legs around his waist as he walked me into his bedroom.

"Well, you know I'm big on stress relief. I'm going to strip every piece of clothing from your perfect body, and then I'm going to lick and suck and tease every inch of you until you come screaming my name." His eyes darkened. My lips parted and my cheeks flushed with desire. He brought us down to the bed and pulled my T-shirt off in one fluid movement. He slid his gaze over my body, then greedily leaned forward and took a lace-covered nipple between his teeth, swirling his tongue around the tip. I arched my back and ran my hands across the top of his back. I loved his mouth on me. I dug my fingers into his hair and exhaled, relaxing into his touch. This was where I belonged.

He explored the waistband to my jeans, unbuttoning and unzipping, delving into the front of my underwear, finding my clit. My body went rigid at the contact, then relaxed as he found his rhythm. The rough pleasure to my breasts contrasted against the sweet sensation from his fingers. I moaned. "Joel. Oh. Yes."

He knew me. Knew this got me out of my head, distracted me, made my world just about him and me and our bodies and what we meant to each other. I was slick between my legs, and I wanted him to taste it. He knew. He fell onto his knees and pulled down my jeans and under-wear and flung them across the room.

"Take it off for me," he said. I reached behind my back and unclasped my bra, pulling it down my arms. I loved the look in his eyes when I first got naked, as though he couldn't believe what he saw. With Joel, I wasn't the Ava I was with my friends. I was desired and sexy. I believed in us, in what we had.

I trailed my fingers across my breasts, my nipples tight. "Oh God, yes," he grunted and pushed himself on top of me, claiming my mouth, delving inside with his tongue and then pulling away, leaving me wanting more. Fully clothed, he clambered off the bed and pulled me to the edge, my legs dangling from the end. He bent my knees back, exposing me. His first breath, just a slight breeze, ignited a fire in me.

"So hot for me, baby," he said, then blew against my sex. "Your sweet pussy is so hot and ready for me, isn't it?" I twisted my hips in response and he asked again, "Isn't it? Tell me, Ava."

"Yes, Joel. Always."

"And before you've even felt my tongue." He licked from my clit down, then plunged into me as if to find out for himself. My hips bucked off the bed, willing him deeper. All the heat in my body shot between my thighs and every sensation was magnified. I slid my fingers into his hair. His tongue found my clit again, circled and pressed, and then slid back in as deep as he could go. I glanced between my legs, and his eyes closed as he moaned against my skin. The vibration of his noises, the sight of him between my thighs, taking pleasure from me, creating pleasure for himself, was too much.

"Joel," I cried out, and he plunged two fingers into me as his tongue continued its work. "Oh, God."

"That's it, Ava." His thumb replaced his tongue for a moment, his fingers never losing their rhythm. "I can feel you. I know your body so well, baby. You're so close, so quick. That's what I do to you." He took my clit with his mouth and I was lost. Nerve endings buzzed across my body until something exploded in my heart.

He trailed up my body and as he looked at me, desire burned in his eyes. He wasn't even nearly done with me.

"Come here," he said as he pulled me to sit up. "On all fours. I've got to get deep in you."

Just seconds after my last orgasm, I wanted him again. Just as he'd described, I moved into position. He rearranged my hips, making sure I was ready for him, then swept his hand down my back in long strokes, each touch raising my temperature.

"You look so beautiful like this, Ava. Your skin is so perfect." He reached my arse and smoothed his palm across my body, around and around, almost deliberately avoiding taking things to the next level. My body was on fire, desperate for his fingers, his tongue, his cock. He blew over my sex, as if he could feel my heat, but it did anything but cool me. The waiting was driving me crazy. I wanted him inside me. I pushed back, urging him to give me more.

"So impatient, Ava. You can't get enough, can you?"

"Joel," I whimpered. "Please."

"Tell me what you want."

"I want you deep inside me."

That admission was all it took. He placed his hands on my hips and nudged at my entrance, throbbing, waiting, and then he pushed in, just the tip, as if he were teasing me, testing my control.

"Please, Joel. I want more of you. I want all of you."

"Oh God, Ava." He thrust into me, as deep as I'd ever felt him, laying his front over my back. It winded me, silenced me. He laced his fingers through mine, then pulled back and slammed into me again. He was right; it was so good like this. He possessed me. I hung my head, unable to find any energy, and groaned. All my concentration was on him and what he was doing to me. He changed position so his hands were braced on my shoulders. His pace picked up, and the wetness from my previous orgasm mixed with the new until it slid down my thighs.

Right there, in that moment, there was nothing he could ask me to do that I would say no to.

"Do you feel me? Moving like this inside you? Can you feel how hard I am for you? I've never been as hard as I am just at this moment." He thrust in again, trying to make me feel what he was saying.

I nodded and let out a breathy "Yes."

"I feel you, too, all wet and tight around my cock."

His words were too much. I collapsed on my elbows, which changed his angle. My orgasm began to build.

"Oh God, Ava, I'm so close," he moaned from behind me. His thrusts became more urgent, and the mounting pleasure in my body told me I'd come with him. His hand left my shoulder and stroked my clit.

In a blinding white light, I was lost to him and he was lost to me.

THE DAY after everyone found out Joel and I had kissed, I expected more interrogation from my friends. But it seemed life had moved on.

As I hovered in my doorway, Jules swirled into the block, deep in conversation with a handsome boy following along behind her. I grinned. How did she manage to live so completely unselfconsciously?

"Anyway, I have to spend time with my friend Ava, so you can't stay," she told the guy. He scowled at me, then left as Jules directed.

I looked at her. "Are we due a girls' date?"

"If there's vodka involved, then of course! I'll grab the Stoli. You get the glasses." Jules headed to our communal freezer. Jesus, it was only four in the afternoon, and I should be studying, but I'd made it to the library when it opened at seven this morning, then spent all afternoon in lectures. I was studied out, and the thought of vodka made my decision final. The books would wait for tomorrow.

"Where's Hanna?" I asked as she came back with the half-full bottle of vodka. She shrugged, so I wandered down the corridor and hammered on the door.

"What?" I heard from inside.

"Hanna?" I opened the door and peered into the darkness.

"I hope you woke me up for something good," she snarled, which wasn't like her.

"Is vodka good enough?" As I stepped into the room, I could vaguely make out a Hanna-shaped lump under her duvet. I plunked myself down on the bed and managed to sit on her foot.

"Ouch! Maybe."

"Why are you asleep, anyway?" I asked.

"Don't judge me," she moaned. "Adam was shagging someone at all hours last night and that fucking squeaking bed of his kept me awake."

I giggled. Joel and I had probably kept the neighbors awake too. I kept waiting for someone to mention him. Or our kiss. Or something. "Bless him, he'll be trying to shag Jules out of his system."

"Who's trying to shag me out of their system?" Jules asked, appearing in the doorway. "What are you doing in bed?" she asked Hanna.

"Fucking hell." Hanna sat up, obviously giving up on getting any more sleep.

Jules set the glasses and the bottle on the desk then began pouring the first drinks of the day.

"Do we drink too much?" I mused aloud to myself.

"We're students. It's part of the curriculum," Jules responded. "Anyway, back to me. Who is shagging me out of their system?"

"Adam," I said.

Jules rolled her eyes. "Oh, right. Like that will ever happen. "

"Trust me, he kept me awake last night, hence the pajamas at four in the afternoon," Hanna said.

"Oh, I believe he was shagging someone. I just don't think he'll get me out of his system," Jules said.

"Because you're so awesome?" I asked. Jules made me laugh, even when she didn't try. How could she have so much confidence in her attractiveness to men? I had a man telling me that he loved me and I found it difficult to believe. Jules just assumed all men were in love with her.

"Well, yes, that and I think I gave him the night of his life. Seriously. Besides, he gets attached really quickly."

She was right. Adam did get attached easily. I hoped he wasn't too bruised by the Jules Experience. Deep down—deep, deep down—Adam was a sweet, sensitive guy.

"Maybe we should take lessons from you," I quipped.

Jules ignored the sarcasm. "Sure. I give awesome blow jobs. I could show you. Do you have a banana in here, Hanna?"

"Eww. I really don't want to see you giving head to a banana," I responded. Hanna slumped back into the mattress, covering her face with her hands.

"Well, I'm sure Adam wouldn't mind me demonstrating on him with you watching. In fact, I'm sure he mentioned that was a fantasy of his. Shall I ask him?" She grinned wickedly.

"You're gross. Next you'll be suggesting we pay per view."

"You're a genius, Ava, anyone ever tell you that?"

I couldn't decide whether or not my friends had just forgotten Joel and I had kissed, didn't care, or didn't want to upset me by mentioning it. Whatever it was, I was grateful.

Everything seemed back to normal and likely to stay that way. Joel and I had agreed to keep our relationship a secret until after finals so I could concentrate on studying. He seemed happy about it and nothing else really mattered. It was almost as if last night hadn't happened.

TWENTY-NINE

Present

I should be making myself more useful, helping Hanna with the Sunday lunch, but as Matt set the table, all I could focus on was ensuring I got a seat at the dining table away from Joel and Jamie.

"Can you all get yourselves drinks and sit down, please?" Hanna asked, trying to herd us all to the table. "Matt, can you make sure everyone has a drink?"

Harvey picked his seat quickly and I put myself down next to him so I couldn't be sandwiched between Joel and Jamie. I pulled Jules into the chair next to me and breathed a sigh of relief. Maybe this wouldn't be so bad.

"So, you work with Jules?" I asked Harvey.

"Yeah. Kinda. I guess I'm her client technically."

I nodded, taking him in. He was dressed casually but was wearing a jacket, which was a little formal for a casual Sunday at Hanna and Matt's, but it showed he wanted to make a good impression and that he knew how to dress.

"Have you known her since uni?" he asked.

"Yes, we know all of each other's dirty secrets." I grinned.

"Really?" Joel said, interrupting us from the other end of the table. "*All* your dirty secrets?" Our eyes met for the first time this evening and my stomach flipped. I wondered if that would ever go away.

"Yes, but not all of my secrets are dirty," I said, looking straight at him. What he and I'd had wasn't dirty. It had been beautiful.

"So, tell me a dirty secret," Harvey said.

I glanced across at Joel who was now talking to Hanna.

I fake-scowled at Harvey. "You first."

"I just got dumped," he said without missing a beat.

"Oh, I'm sorry. Who and when?" I didn't understand his connection with Jules—was she helping him over the breakup?

"And then you'll tell me one of yours?" he asked.

I nodded.

"Daisy. Yesterday."

"Daisy," I said, almost to myself. How long had Jules been sleeping with him?

"You thought Jules and I were together, didn't you?"

"The more important question is, did Daisy?"

Harvey laughed. "No, she knows I'm not a cheater. I'm just ready and she's not."

I half smiled, half scowled. What did that mean? Understanding what was going on in a man's head was never my strong point. "Ready?"

"I want to get married and settle down and have a family, and she isn't ready."

Men often seemed so clinical about relationships. It fascinated me.

"So, it wasn't that she wasn't the one, just that the

timing wasn't right?" I asked. He'd ended things with Daisy because she wouldn't marry him right away and get pregnant. Shouldn't he be more patient?

Harvey took a deep breath, his shoulders rising and falling.

"I don't believe there's 'one' out there for me. I've loved a number of girls over the years and I would have married two or three, had it been the right time."

"Wow," was all I could muster up to say.

"You don't agree?" he asked.

"You feel what you feel." The thought I might be just one of the two or three girls Joel could love, could marry, filled me with pain, rage, and sadness. He was *it* for me. He always would be. I wondered if Joel was listening, but I couldn't bring myself to lift my eyes to him to see. I wanted to ask him if I was just one in a line of girls who had been important to him.

"So, you loved all these women, but you're not with any of them now? Would you go back to them?" I asked.

Harvey shook his head. "No. Life moves on, doesn't it? I don't believe in looking backward."

I'd never moved forward far enough to think that being with Joel would be going back.

"Do you think you were really in love? Like thunderbolt, I-can't-live-without-you love?"

Harvey laughed, then stopped as if he'd just realized what I was asking him. "I've absolutely been in love, and I don't have a problem telling women as much, but sometimes love isn't enough."

My stomach dropped. He was right. Sometimes love *wasn't* enough. I finally glanced across at Joel, but he wasn't listening to our conversation. I looked back at Harvey.

"It's not about being able to tell someone. It's about feeling it," I said.

"So you believe in 'the one,' I take it?"

I nodded. "Yeah, of course."

"And have you found him?"

I took a deep breath. "And lost him."

"So what's the answer?" Harvey asked. "You die old and alone because you lost 'the one'? You're not going to give yourself a second chance?"

I shrugged. "I don't know." Being on my own was better than messing good men like Will around. He deserved someone who loved him like I loved Joel.

"You'll heal, and you'll find someone else." He was trying to comfort me, but I felt sorry for him. He'd never felt what I did for Joel. If he had, he'd never be able to say so confidently that there'd be another.

"I don't think so," I replied. "Men compartmentalize these things in a way I don't think women can. Men can say, 'We've split up, life moves on, I'll find someone else,' and then never think about that person again. Women bruise more deeply and love longer, even after we're long forgotten by the person we love."

I'd never not love Joel and nothing would change that. I had to make peace with those feelings and not try to force myself to get over him. I had to accept that although we weren't together and we never would be, I'd always love him and that wasn't going to change. But I couldn't let my feelings stop me from being the woman I'd become. The capable, confident woman who—had she existed at university— would have understood she was worthy of Joel's love and would never have tried to hide it from her friends. If that woman had existed back then, maybe we still would be together.

I FLOATED BACK TO CONSCIOUSNESS, knowing I'd woken before morning. I'd been in bed by midnight, which after Sunday lunch and a bucket of booze at Hanna and Matt's, wasn't bad. But I couldn't have been asleep long. Had I heard something? There it was again, a banging on my door. It couldn't be Will again, could it? Whoever it was, they weren't stopping and they were going to wake my neighbors. Since I was sleeping in just an old uni T-shirt, I grabbed some underwear and almost tumbled over while trying to step into them.

What the hell time was it? I glanced at the clock beside my bed.

Three in the morning! What the fuck? Was the place on fire?

I threw open the door and came face-to-face with Joel.

His arms were braced against the frame and his eyes flew to mine. His stare was heated. Was he angry? What was he doing here? I was poised to expel expletives at the asshole waking me, but I was suddenly mute.

Neither of us seemed to have any words.

I stood aside, making room for him to come inside.

He had things to say.

We had things to say to each other.

It was time.

THIRTY

Months later, sitting in the pub around our usual table, Joel on one side of the table and me on the other, both of us desperately trying not to touch each other, or look at each other, Jules started talking about her summer plans.

"We're going to start in Rio, but I've heard it doesn't live up to the hype, so we might not stay there for long." She was backpacking through South America with a girl from her class. She'd never mentioned it before, at least not to me.

"How long have you been thinking about this?" I asked. I'd had my job lined up for almost a year and with another year of law school to go, graduation didn't seem like the ending it would be for most people.

"We started talking back in September. But we only just bought the tickets. We've been arguing about where exactly we want to go," she replied.

Since September? That was months. Somehow, I'd forgotten that university was a temporary situation and that we would all be forced into a change of circumstance. I didn't try *not* to think about these things, I just *hadn't* thought about them. Right there, in our world that contained just Joel and me and our faith in each other, I assumed that that was it. We would stay right here, blissfully happy and in love. But things were about to change whether or not we wanted them to. What were Joel's plans? Did they include me?

Daniel began to talk about how he was going to New York to intern at an investment bank. And Matt and Hanna were moving to London—both had graduate jobs lined up, which I remembered hearing about but not paying much attention to.

Joel said nothing and I looked at him, panic strewn across my face and bile rising in my stomach. Surely the only reason he wouldn't mention his plans after graduation was if he knew they would upset me. I pushed myself up from the chair and fled to the bathroom.

We'd never talked about life after university. Ever. We'd never discussed what would happen after all this. Everything for me had been focused on finals. Joel must have plans, right? Didn't we all? I would go to law school in London for a year and then start my training contract at the law firm. All lawyers had their lives planned out for the next decade as soon as their degree started. We didn't need to think about anything. But economists? What did they do after an economics degree? Teach? Win a Nobel Prize or something? I had no clue.

Why hadn't Joel and I discussed this?

Joel was a planner. He wouldn't *not* have thought about it. He must have just decided not to talk to me about it. I guess he didn't want to burst our bubble until the last possible moment. If his plans were good news for us, then he wouldn't have kept them to himself. My heart was racing as reality crashed around me.

I was supposed to go to Joel's tonight, but a huge part of me didn't want to face the inevitable news when I asked him about life after graduation.

The last few months we'd been so connected, so together and now, what? Was this a temporary thing for him? Was I just a university love he'd tell his wife about at some point in the future?

Nausea churned in my stomach. I splashed some water on my face, pulled my shoulders back, and made my way out to the bar. Joel was waiting for me when I opened the door, leaning against the wall.

"Hey," he said.

I managed to pull my lips into a shape that kind of resembled a smile, but even I knew it wasn't very convincing.

"Are you okay? You looked a bit green there for a minute."

I nodded. "Yeah. I'm okay. I think. I don't know." I realized I was still nodding, so I stopped myself.

"You want to talk about it?"

"Later."

Joel frowned, but we couldn't have the conversation now and he seemed to understand that. He didn't push me any further. He reached for my fingers, just for a second, not that anyone would know, and then went into the loo. I rounded the corner back to our table.

I couldn't drink any more. I needed a clear head. I had to think. Around this table, with some of my favorite people in the world, was not where I wanted to be. I needed to be in Joel's arms. I wanted him to tell me he'd found a job in London and he thought we should move in together and start life after university. But if he'd found that job in London, he would have said so, wouldn't he? If he'd wanted to move in together, he would have told me by now, right?

If he wanted our lives together to start in real life, then I would know.

I HEADED to Joel's after everyone was drunk and had dispersed. He opened the door still frowning, his head tilted to one side. As soon as he saw me, he pulled me in for a hug before I'd stepped over the threshold. He knew I was upset. I could fake it with the others, but never with him. He could tell.

He'd agreed to keep our relationship a secret until after graduation because that's what made me happy. I couldn't ask more of him, could I? Hadn't he done everything I'd wanted? My cheek found its familiar spot against his chest and I sighed.

"I'm sorry," I said. I didn't want him upset.

"What are you sorry for?" he asked.

"Worrying you. Spoiling your evening."

"An evening with you is never a spoiled evening, Ava. What's up?"

We made our way to his kitchen in what had become a familiar routine of getting water and turning off lights before we headed to his bedroom. I'd never recognized it as a ritual before; I was always too busy concentrating on what was to come. His body, mine, entangled, writhing, wanting in pleasure and release. But this little dance we did and the fact it *was* routine was comforting, and something we wouldn't be doing too much longer. Well, not here, anyway.

Maybe not anywhere.

Time was running out.

We crawled up his bed and lay fully clothed on our sides facing each other.

"I just . . ." I started. "We've just . . . I was thinking . . ."

Joel laughed. "Spit it out, baby. I want to get to the naked part of the evening."

I pushed his chest.

"We've never talked about what happens after finals. And everyone talking about their plans tonight, it just made me wonder. I've never heard you talk about your plans and I just . . . you know."

Joel grinned at me. "I love you. You know that, right?"

I nodded.

"And you love me, right?" he asked.

I nodded again.

"Good," he said as if something had been resolved. "So, actually, I had some news this week that I hope is exciting for both of us."

My eyes widened. I'd been with him all week. How had he received exciting news without me knowing about it? What else was he keeping from me?

"You know I've not applied for any of these graduate programs. I just can't see myself in some big corporation working my way up the ladder. That's Matt and Adam, but it's not me."

I nodded. He was right. He wouldn't be happy in a job like that.

"I feel I just need to get out there and try a few things. Work with different people, get inspired."

What did that mean for us? I kept my gaze fixed on him in case I missed anything.

"I've been talking to my entrepreneurial economics professor about all sorts of stuff, because you know how I love that class, right?" His speech was picking up; he was getting excited.

"The American guy supervising your thesis?"

"Yeah, that's the guy. And so we were chatting a few weeks ago about new ways of financing start-ups, and he put me in touch with a contact of his in New York who is working in the same area as some of the stuff I've been working on."

"Okay," I said cautiously.

"He's got tons of contacts, right, because he used to work in Silicon Valley and spent years in New York."

"Yes, I remember you telling me that."

"So anyway, I've been talking to this guy in New York over the last few months about some of the things I've been working on, and he offered to fly me out to meet him to go through some aspects of my research that he thinks might work in his business, which is all about matching investors with entrepreneurs."

"Wow," I said, reaching up to cup his face. "That's so exciting. A trip to New York." I was so proud. The guy must have been really impressed with Joel on the phone.

"Well, of course, I told him I couldn't go."

I opened my mouth to ask him why, but before the words came out he said, "I can't, Ava. I mean, it's great and flattering and everything, but I've got finals and I can't just take a couple of weeks out to swan off to New York."

"I guess." It sounded like such an amazing opportunity; it was a pity to have to turn it down. "Are you sure you can't make it work? Things like that don't come up that often."

"I thought maybe after exams. I mentioned that to him this week and out of nowhere he offered me a job. For twelve months. Working with him and his team in New York."

"Oh my God." It was an incredible opportunity. But so far away. "Just like that?"

He nodded.

"Well, that just proves you are the cleverest, most charming man ever." I reached across and stroked his jaw.

"Well, you have to say that." He raised an eyebrow at me.

I smiled, although it took all my energy. "That's true. I do." He grabbed me and pulled me close.

"Can you believe it?" Joel asked, looking at me with amazement in his eyes.

"Of course I believe it." He was leaving me, and I'd always thought he would. "You're amazing and talented, and I think you're going to take life by the balls." *But what about us?*

"I never expected this to happen, you know?"

Was he apologizing? Making his excuses? Saying how under other circumstances things between us might have been different?

He pulled me closer. "So you'll come with me?" he asked. "I don't want to go without you."

My stomach swooped. "To New York?"

"Yes, with me. We can go together."

Tension eased away. So he had thought about us, considered what we'd do after school. How could I have doubted him? But New York?

"For the summer?" I needed clarification. I'd gone from not thinking about what happened after graduation to it being the only thing I could concentrate on and now, Joel dropping this huge news in my lap, there was almost too much to think about.

"For the year. While I'm there."

I grew dizzy. I wasn't sure if it was nerves or excitement.

"Wow." It was all I could manage. What would such a move mean, other than I would be with him?

"But law school . . . my job," I said tentatively. I didn't want to burst his bubble—our bubble. But the reality was that I had at least the next three years of my life planned out in London.

"Could you take a year out? I heard some people postpone those jobs."

"God, Joel. I don't know. I've had three seconds to get used to this." Things started to whir in my head. Maybe I could postpone. I could look into taking the New York Bar.

Why was he springing this on me now? I didn't understand how we hadn't talked about this before.

He reached for my hand and linked his fingers with mine. "I know it's all kinda unplanned and stuff, but I want you with me, Ava. I want us to share this next chapter in our lives. I want to live this adventure with you." He brought my hand to his lips and kissed my knuckles.

"I love that you do." It was true I was relieved his plans included me. I couldn't help wondering why he'd hidden it from me for so long, even if things weren't finalized. Even when it was just a few weeks of study in New York he'd kept it a secret. I was just hearing about this and all of a sudden Joel was expecting me to change my whole life.

"Let me do some research and speak to my firm and stuff. And my parents. God, my parents. You know they're helping me pay for law school. I'm not sure how they'll feel about New York."

He squeezed my hand again, like he was trying to transfer his energy and ambition to me.

I grinned. "I'm so happy for you." I could see how New York was everything Joel had ever wanted. But it was nothing I'd thought about. Nothing I'd planned for. This wasn't the life I'd envisaged for myself.

THE SITTING ROOM IN MY PARENTS' house that had once seemed so familiar felt like someone else's home. I glanced around, taking in the photographs of family holidays, birthdays, and celebrations through the years. I wished Joel was here with me. He'd get a kick out of seeing me with braces.

I'd come home for the weekend because I thought I should get some space from Joel while I tried to get things straight in my head, and I needed to talk to my parents about my potential change in plans. It wasn't just me that Joel's internship had an impact on.

"New York? To do what, exactly?" my father asked. It was precisely the question I'd expected. I may have secretly wanted blind support, but it wasn't realistic.

"To experience life." It even sounded lame to me. "To take some time out. Have a gap year. Live in another country." Yes, that was better. It was half true as well. I did want all those things now that I'd thought about the positives about following Joel to America.

"On your own?" my mother asked. "It's a dangerous city. If you want to take time out, what about going to Australia or New Zealand? Or you could spend the summer in Cornwall." My mother wouldn't want me to go far away. The three-hour drive to university was a big enough adjustment for her.

They didn't understand that the most valuable thing of all would be there—Joel. Joel and me. We would still be together. I'd never mentioned Joel to them. There didn't seem to be any need.

"Australia and New Zealand are no better, as far as I'm concerned. What about law school?" my father said. "Isn't your place confirmed? And you have a job arranged." Since I was a child, my academic progress had been the thing that came first for my father. I didn't get to participate in sport, dance classes, or sleep overs with my friends unless I had top grades.

"It's just a year, Dad. I can postpone my place for that long, I'm sure. Anyway, I'm just thinking about it."

"And what about your job? You can't just defer that. They'll be counting on you."

I'd already secured a job at one of the top law firms in the country. They were paying my tuition for my year at law school and my parents had agreed to pay my living expenses. They didn't have a lot of money. It was incredibly generous of them. I had a suspicion they must have been spending most of their rainy-day savings on me.

My mom was a nurse and my father a middle manager in the hospital she worked in. They had met there and worked most of their careers there. They had both worked hard to get what they had: their slice of suburbia, kids who went to university, a trip to Spain once a year, and a retirement fund that would see them through. It was what they'd aimed for all their lives. It was what I'd grown up with, and yet it seemed a bit empty. Had they ever had something as special as Joel and I had?

"Well, I thought I could call them and at least ask if I could postpone my start date by a year."

"That won't create a very good impression, will it? And you've signed a contract, given them your word."

It wasn't unusual for start dates to get moved forward by

six months or a year, but that wasn't my father's biggest issue. The fact I would be breaking my word would be more of a problem for him. My mother's eyes were in her lap. She wasn't going to fight my corner.

"Well, I could ask," I said softly.

"They might end up giving the job to someone else, Ava. Then what will you do?"

"Won't you be lonely in New York?" my mother asked.

I sighed. "I'm going to get a drink." I pushed up out of my chair and headed to the kitchen. My parents just wanted the best for me. I understood that, but I wanted them to support me on this issue. I wanted to have no reason to say no.

"I wouldn't be going on my own," I called from where I was facing the sink.

"Oh?" my mother asked.

"Yes, there's a guy fr—"

"Is this what this reckless plan is all about?" my father asked. "You're going to throw in your education and the chance for a good life for a man?" He looked up as I came back into the room, his eyes scanning my face as if he were trying to find the girl who'd left home three years ago to go to university. "You're going to give up everything for this boy?"

My heart sank. Maybe I should have told them about Joel before now. They would have met him, seen who he was. They would know how much he loved me. They would know he wasn't just some guy.

But maybe my parents were right. Maybe I should try to find a compromise between us.

"Tell us about this boy, honey," my mum said, patting the sofa next to her.

"Well I've been seeing him—"

"Are you pregnant?" my father asked.

Oh my God. I rolled my eyes.

"Geoff, let her tell us."

"No, Dad, of *course* I'm not pregnant. I've been dating Joel, and he's got this amazing opportunity to work at a start-up in New York. He wants me to go with him."

"He wants you to give up your plans so he can do what he wants to do?" my mother asked.

"Mum, it's not like that." But the more I dwelled on the fact he'd kept this huge thing a secret, the more I wondered. "His opportunity can't be put off for a year like mine."

"You don't know yours can," my father said. "And what if it can for a year? Or two because his year has gone so well he wants to extend it? And then three. Then what?"

"I'm not planning on taking a twenty-year break. It would be for twelve months."

"And what would you say if he asked you to stay another year?" my mum asked quietly, as if she didn't really want to say it. Was she right? Was Joel asking too much? I'd been thrilled he'd asked me. Happy he'd thought about us after university, but maybe he'd just been thinking about himself. He was asking me to give up my arrangements. Okay, just for a year, but what happened after that? Would it be another, then another after that like my mum said? And what else would he spring on me? The fact that Joel had kept his New York plans a secret until they were set had been a shock. I'd thought we'd shared everything. When I was applying for jobs, we'd poured over the firm websites together. We'd decided together which ones would suit me and which ones wouldn't. I'd taken his opinion into account about my future. Why hadn't he done the same with me?

"Are you planning to get married, honey? Is it that serious?" my mum asked.

"No," I spluttered. "I mean, it is serious. But . . ."

"So you're not committed enough to each other to get married. But you want to risk your future on this boy?" she asked.

I chewed the edge of my thumbnail. We were young, far too young to get married. I knew Joel was serious about me and that was enough. But what would happen if I couldn't postpone my job and I asked him to stay? Would he give up his opportunity for me? Was this a two-way street? Of course, I could never ask him. I couldn't live with myself if he stayed and he resented me for it.

"Does he have money?" my father asked, pulling me out of my head.

What was he asking me, whether I was after Joel for the money?

"How are you going to live for the year?" he asked.

"Joel has a job out there and I would find something temporary."

I hadn't thought through the logistics. I'd concentrated on the big problems. Like getting my parents on board and thinking about deferring law school and my job.

"So after a law degree, after working so hard for so many years, you're going to end up working in a bar." He sucked in a breath and shook his head. "I need to get some air."

My parents had always been my biggest cheerleaders—for my little brother and me. But now they were acting as if I were switching teams. I slumped forward in my chair, my head in my hands.

"He just wants the best for you, darling," my mum said. "We both do." And I knew it. "You know we've always wanted you to be independent. To rely on your brain."

"I know, Mum. I know you've never thought I was pretty enough to rely on my looks."

She frowned. "You're a beautiful girl, Ava. I hope you never got the impression that your father or I ever thought otherwise. We just never wanted your beauty to define you. We want your heart and mind—your character—to be the thing you value most in yourself."

I'd always considered myself plain—geeky—the girl who was all about the books. I couldn't ever remember my parents telling me I was pretty and they certainly never said I was beautiful. I'd always assumed it was because I wasn't. Perhaps it was because they were wanting to raise a woman who wasn't defined by what she saw in the mirror so they emphasized other strengths of mine. It was a lot to take in. I pushed my hands through my hair.

Nothing changed the fact that Joel was going to New York. I just wanted them to tell me going with him was the right thing to do, and then I wouldn't have this doubt that cloaked me with dread.

"Maybe I should go back to university tonight," I said.

"Don't be silly. Dinner will be ready soon and your father never misses my Saturday night curry. He'll come back and things will get better, whatever you decide. Don't leave on crossed words."

The last thing I wanted to do was fall out with my parents.

"I might go and have a quick nap before dinner." I really wanted to speak to Joel. I needed his reassurance. I wanted an explanation for why he'd sprung this on me.

"Okay, no longer than half an hour, though."

I plodded upstairs to my old bedroom that seemed so unfamiliar to me now. Like I hadn't slept there for the first eighteen years of my life. I wasn't sure why they'd not turned it into a guest room. I wasn't going to live at home again. It was bigger than my not-so-little brother's room and looked over their small but perfectly formed garden.

I collapsed on the bed and called Joel.

"How did it go? Have you told them?" He hadn't even said hello.

"Of course I've told them. That's why I'm here."

"And?" I wanted him to tell me he loved me, not interrogate me.

"And it went down like a cup of cold puke."

"A delightful image, thanks."

"You're very welcome. It's no more than you deserve."

"What have I done?"

I sighed. "Nothing." Everything. Why couldn't he just find a job in London like the rest of our graduating year? Why did he have to go to New York?

I told him about my parents' reaction. He didn't offer any rebuttal arguments when I told him the concerns my mum and dad had raised.

"You know it's your decision and not your parents', don't you?"

"Joel." Nothing my mum and dad had said had been unreasonable. They'd brought up valid issues, and I'd been hoping he'd have more answers for me.

"I mean it, Ava. You're going to be twenty-one this summer."

"It's not just about how old I am, Joel. This isn't easy. They've worked hard to put me through university and to create this life that I have. To not respect what they are saying now . . . It's just . . ."

"What does that mean?"

"It means that I love that you want me to come, and I need time to figure stuff out."

"You mean you need your parents' permission, just like you need your friends' approval. Jesus, Ava, why don't you just decide what you want? *You*."

"It's not that simple!" This was very different to not telling my friends about our relationship. This was my family wanting the best for me and raising arguments I didn't have a response to.

"And what happens after a year, Joel? Do we come back to London so I can go to law school? Will you promise me now that New York will only be for twelve months?"

"You know I can't promise that."

At least he wasn't lying to me. As if he could read my thoughts, he said, "I can promise you that I'll love you for infinity. I don't want to fight. If you decide not to come with me, then that's okay. I just want you to make the decision and not to be persuaded by what your friends and family say."

"I will love you for infinity too, Joel." I stared up at the ceiling. For the first time since Joel Wentworth kissed me, he felt further away from me than he ever had.

THIRTY-ONE

At three in the morning, I was as awake as I'd ever been. Joel came into my flat, and we moved the short distance to the kitchen. I pulled open the cupboard that held glasses, poured us both a glass of water, and put a wedge of lime and ice in his, just how he liked it. I didn't like lime, but I always kept frozen wedges in case one day I needed them. And today, for the first time, I did.

He accepted the drink, and I took a breath. I was ready for this. Ready for something, at least. Closure. His anger. His indifference. A calm descended on me. The conversation with Harvey had helped bring things into focus. Joel was my thunderbolt and I would love him forever—even if he never loved me back.

I pulled a cushion onto my lap as I sat down so my underwear wasn't on display, then twisted toward Joel, who sat at the other end of my sofa. He placed his glass on the coffee table, then perched on the edge of the seat with his head in his hands and his elbows on his knees.

Here he was in my flat. This was how it was meant to be, but at the same time so different. Elation and pain coursed through my body in equal measure.

Finally, he said, "I just don't get it. I don't know if I'm being paranoid, reading things into situations that shouldn't be there, or if you're playing games. I just . . ." He thrust his hands through his beautiful hair.

I wasn't sure what he meant about paranoia or reading things into situations. But I knew one thing. "I'm not a game player, Joel. You know me better than that."

"Do I?" He looked up at me, his brows pulled together.

He knew me better than anyone. And I'd never played games. I nodded. "You know you do."

He went back to staring at the floor.

"What are you paranoid about? When are you reading what into situations?" I asked. This was the boy I'd once shared everything with. He could tell me anything and I'd share with him whatever he wanted to know. It would always be like that for me.

"The necklace," he said after a few seconds. "Why did you wear it the night you introduced Will to your friends as your boyfriend? Were you trying to hurt me?"

My body ached for him. How could he think that? Couldn't he tell how much I loved him? The thought that I might still be causing him pain was unbearable. I was desperate to reach out and touch him, comfort him, reassure him. "Of course not. I would never try to hurt you."

He turned, head cocked, and raised his eyebrows.

I'd hurt him before. Why would he believe me now? I covered my face with my hands, frustrated I couldn't show him what was inside my head and heart right at that moment. I needed it all out, all at once. "I know I've hurt you before, but not because I wanted to. I would never *try* to hurt you," I repeated.

"Then why the necklace?"

I wanted to smooth my palms over his beautiful face. "The whole truth?"

"And nothing but," he finished. I was sure I saw the beginning of a smile at the corners of his mouth.

"I think there were lots of reasons. It's complicated."

"I want to know, Ava," he said to the floor.

I sucked in my breath. This was it. I really had nothing to lose. "I think it was because I was trying to move on with Will, but I didn't want to. Not really. I needed a piece of you with me. Touching me."

He didn't speak and his head was still bowed.

"It's always—the necklace—it's always with me, but I've not *worn* it since you left. Not until that night. It just felt like I was betraying you by introducing someone else to my friends so easily, and I wanted to show myself, and you, that I hadn't really. That it wasn't the same. It wasn't us."

Still, he had no words for me. Perhaps it was too much truth for him. It showed how messed up I was. How he was still in so much of what I did and didn't do. But it didn't stop me from telling him the whole truth.

"And . . . I think on some level I wanted to remind you that you told me you'd love me for infinity. And that you changed, and it wasn't just me that fucked up eight years ago." He was so easy to forgive, and I was so focused on all my mistakes I'd never dwelled on how Joel contributed to our breakup.

"Me, you think I was the problem? I asked you to come with me. I wanted us to be together."

"But you said yes to that job without even talking to me. You never considered staying for me. You wouldn't even try and do long distance. You let me go. You disappeared and you gave up on me. Gave up on us." Thoughts I'd never really acknowledged came tumbling out. Joel had hurt me as much as I'd hurt him. I had wanted him to stay and fight for me.

"I never considered staying for you?" He snorted as if I was full of shit. "All you had to do was ask."

My chest tightened. "What?" He wasn't prepared to take any responsibility.

"You just had to ask me to stay. I would have got a job in London to be with you."

I gripped the cushion. "No. I couldn't ask you to give up your future for me. You were so excited by the opportunity."

"*You* were my future. I would have stayed in a heartbeat. I hoped you would ask. Prayed you would." He shook his head. "But of course you didn't. And I couldn't spend my life worrying about whether I was enough for you. You wouldn't come with me. You didn't ask me to stay." He turned to me and looked me in the eye. "What was I meant to think other than you didn't think you were good enough or that I wasn't? If you didn't love me enough, then how was it ever going to work out between us?"

I shivered and covered my face with my hands. He'd wanted me to ask him to stay? "You were testing me?" My voice rose as the enormity of what hadn't been said between us took hold. "You saying you were going to New York was a test?"

He sank back against the cushions. "Not consciously. But I suppose I was looking for you to say that you were committed to us, that I was your guy—either by coming with me or by asking me to stay."

A metallic taste hit my tongue and I grabbed my stomach, willing myself not to be sick.

"I guess that's why I didn't mention the opportunity for so long. I must have known as soon as I brought it up that I was effectively putting all my money on red and spinning the wheel."

"I was scared," I said. The loss of him clawed at my soul. What had I done? I'd been the girl he would have stayed for, but I'd not had the faith in him to ask.

"I know," he whispered.

"I'm sorry," I said.

"I know. Me too. It was a stupid thing to have asked of you. Too much. We were both so young. How could we understand what the future was going to hold?"

I nodded. He was right—we'd been too young to make decisions that would impact the rest of our lives. Too immature to know if our feelings would last. "It was all so sudden. And I'd been working toward my legal career for so long."

"I get that. It was selfish of me to think you would change all that for me. And why should you?"

For so long I'd worn the responsibility for Joel and me splitting up. But it hadn't just been about my weakness. Even asking him to stay wouldn't have solved anything. "And if I'd asked you to give up your dreams for me, what kind of pressure would that have put on us?" I asked. Either way, one of us would have had to have made a sacrifice that may have become an albatross around our necks.

Joel let out a deep exhale. "There was no easy answer. But I know I blamed you for a long time when you didn't deserve it. I wish . . ."

"Things had been different?" I asked.

He nodded.

The fact was, things hadn't been different. We'd been trying to figure out the world and done the best we could.

We sat in silence for a few minutes. I tried stopping the flow of thoughts about a life I should have had.

"It still wasn't fair on Will," Joel said, finally.

"You're right. It wasn't, but neither was dating him. The necklace . . . well, he never knew."

The sound of Joel's breathing filled the room and I had the urge to reach out and touch him. Instead I gripped the cushion tighter.

"Jamie said you came 'round the other night," he said.

"I did," I conceded. There was no point in denying it. "Why?"

I shrugged. "Why are you here?" We were both looking for answers.

"You know there's nothing going on. She's just staying because she's my partner's sister. I'm not attracted to her. At all." He was answering the questions that had been swirling in my head all evening.

Relief curled in my stomach. Partly because there was nothing going on with Jamie and partly because he wanted to make sure I knew that. To reassure me. That meant . . . what? Something, surely.

"There are always going to be plenty of women who want a piece of Joel Wentworth," I said almost to myself.

"Maybe, but plenty of women are not the woman I want." Before I had time to make sense of what he said, he stunned me with his next question. "And what about Adam?"

"What about Adam?" I wasn't sure what Adam had to do with any of this.

"Who is he to you?" His words were clipped and cold.

"Are you serious?" Did he think we were romantically involved?

He didn't respond.

"Adam's my friend. A very irritating but lovable friend."

"Lovable?" he asked.

I almost laughed at the pout in his voice. And if tonight hadn't been so damn tragic, I might have. "You know he's just my friend, Joel."

"Can I get that in writing?"

I bit back my grin. "Absolutely."

He sighed and glanced toward me. "You don't have feelings for him? Everyone is teasing the two of you about having sexual tension and—"

"No, Jules teases us so people don't say it about her and Adam. To throw people off the scent. Because there is *definitely* chemistry between them, no matter how hard they try to deny it." I didn't know why he was asking, but I liked that he was. "I've never so much as exchanged a flirtatious glance with Adam." I tilted my head. "I have friendly feelings for him, but not romantic feelings."

He pursed his lips. "Do you think he does for you?"

"What, have romantic feelings?" I jerked back. "No, not at all. We don't have that kind of thing between us. We never did. You know that."

"Maybe I do." He shifted on the sofa, his body twisting slightly toward me. "And tonight . . . the things you were saying to that guy about there only ever being one love and . . ."

So he *had* been listening. Had I wanted him to? Maybe.

I could see it all racing through his head. He scrubbed his hands over his face.

"Can I get a question in now?" I asked.

"Sure, why not," he said, raising his palms to the ceiling.

I had five million questions running through my head, but which one should I ask first? I took a breath as I tried to pick.

"There's too many, right?" Joel said and he turned to look at me. He was in my head.

I nodded. "Maybe booze will help. Do you want a shot?"

Without waiting for an answer, I quickly collected two glasses and vodka from the kitchen and set them down on the coffee table. Leaning forward, I busied myself pouring two small glasses and pushed the one nearest Joel toward him.

He mirrored me and picked up the glass, and we looked at each other as we raised our shots. For a second it was as if we'd never been apart, as if the last eight years had just dissolved into nothingness. He looked at me, not as some girl from university who had been his first love . . . but like he loved me *now*.

I tipped back my shot. Heat trickled down my throat. I closed my eyes and kept them shut—I didn't want to open them and find he'd lost that look.

"Have you thought of one?" he asked. "A question?"

The problem was, I wanted to know everything. About what happened back when we split. About his life since. About how he saw his future. But right now, he was inches away from me. Close enough to touch. "Why are you here?" I'd asked the question rhetorically before but now I wanted an answer.

He shrugged. "To ask you questions. To try to make sense of all this." He gestured in the air between us. "Because I miss you."

I understood that. I missed him so much it hurt, but as he sat beside me, hope crept into my heart for the first time in too long.

"And have you made sense of it?" I asked.

He blew out a breath. "Not yet. You?" he asked.

"I think . . . I know what's . . . Will helped me make sense of *me*." I had few answers but I knew if I couldn't date a guy like Will, I couldn't date anyone.

"Oh." He folded his arms.

"What I mean is, I know me better. What's best for me, I mean."

"And that is?"

"Just what I said before, that dating doesn't really work for me. It's not fair to the guy." I didn't want to be the girl who kept guys dangling. Who misled men. "Not when my heart belongs to someone else."

We were teetering on the brink of something. Of me telling him something and everything.

"Someone else?" Apparently, Joel was behind me, trying to shove me over the edge.

I decided to jump. "I'll always be in love with you, Joel."

I didn't think about the landing. Hadn't thought through what his response would be. I just jumped. And being honest with him was like gliding through the air.

I felt free.

THIRTY-TWO

Past

My heart raced as the train pulled into the station. After a weekend with my parents, I had to get to Joel as soon as possible. We didn't have much of this life left, here in our bubble, whether or not I went to New York, and I wanted to squeeze every last drop out of it before that bubble burst.

I had the cab drop me off at Joel's. I rang the doorbell and shifted my weight from foot to foot.

He opened the door wearing a huge grin and a towel around his waist. Holy moly, it was my favorite look on him.

"How did you know it was me?" I asked.

"How did you know I knew it was you?" he countered.

"Do you greet everyone naked with a grin?"

"Don't sweat it. I could see your shortness through the frosted glass. I don't know many people as short as you."

"Hey." I pushed out my bottom lip like a toddler.

"You know I love your height. It means I can physically overpower you at any opportunity." As if to prove his point he kissed me on the lips, threw me up over his shoulder, and marched into the bedroom. He tossed me on the bed and pinned my wrists against the mattress over my head.

He went straight for my neck and started kissing every inch of it.

"Did you miss me?" I asked.

He hummed against my skin, making my whole body vibrate. Oh God, how could I ever expect to live without this?

"So?" He released my arms and tipped up his head as if he'd just come back to consciousness, remembering where he was and what I was here to talk about.

"So?" I mimicked.

"I wasn't expecting to see you until later."

"I couldn't wait."

He grinned. His lips went back to my neck, his hands pushing up beneath my top and across my stomach. "Did you decide?"

"Are you trying to convince me?"

"If I were trying to convince you, I'd be doing this." His fingers strayed under the waistband of my jeans, then pushed aside my underwear, reaching for my clit. I unbuttoned my trousers, giving him easier access. I wasn't going to object if he was going to try to persuade my mind with his body.

"Just that?" I asked, trying to keep my voice steady.

He brought his eyes to mine and grinned. "You take so much convincing."

I nodded. "You're going to have to work really hard."

"I have an excellent work ethic," he said, pressing himself against my thigh.

I laughed. "But you suck at double entendre."

He smiled for a second then, with both hands, stripped off my top.

"You like it when I suck," he said, and dipped his head and clamped his mouth around my lace-covered nipple.

"Oh God, Joel." I threaded my fingers through his hair and arched my back, pushing my body closer to him.

"I feel like I haven't tasted you for months," he said against my skin, heating my body all over.

He pulled back, glanced up and down my body, and swept his hands up my waist and over my breasts. "Turn over."

I flipped onto my stomach and raised my arms above my head, waiting for his next touch, waiting for him to satiate himself and me. I wasn't sure he ever could.

Joel's tongue rested on the base of my spine. The heat and light pressure was tantalizing as slowly, he began to lick and suck, working his way up my back, deepening my need for him with every movement.

He must have stripped naked while I lay on my front. When another part of his body touched me, his arm, his chest, his hip, heat coursed through me as skin skimmed against skin.

My whole body scattered with goosebumps, not because I was cold but because I was desperate. As he moved higher, I began to tremble. I needed him to feed this desire I had in me.

"Please, Joel," I pleaded. He never made me wait like this.

"You want it, baby? You gotta ask. You never ask."

"Joel, please."

He lifted my hips, pulling me away from the mattress, the cool air against my clit was torture. I puffed out a breath as I waited for him. Joel would soon be inside me, where I needed him so badly.

Joel's hand on my hip adjusted my position slightly and I gasped as the tip of him met my entrance.

"Ask for it," he said. "Tell me what you want from me."

"Joel, please." What was he doing? He'd never made me beg like this. "I want you. I want you inside me. I want you to make love to me."

He shoved in up to the hilt, his hand on my hip, keeping me in place.

I exhaled. Finally.

His familiarity, his size, his scent. Everything about having sex with Joel was home for me. It was how things should be. I could shut off my brain and just enjoy him. Experience him enjoying me. I was at my most relaxed, my most free like this.

He began to move behind me, going deeper with every thrust.

He grunted from behind me. The sounds of his satisfaction unraveled my desire and I pushed against him, urging him to take more of me.

I lifted myself up onto my hands and turned to look at him.

"God, Ava, you're so beautiful, so sexy." His brow furrowed and he gasped but it didn't stop him thrusting, over and over.

He locked his hand over my shoulder, dipping his other hand down to find my clit. I screamed as his thumb swiped over the bundle of nerves and my legs began to tremble. I couldn't take much more.

"Oh yes, you love that. You see how I own this body of yours?"

I closed my eyes in a long blink. It was never a doubt in my mind how Joel owned me body and soul.

He pulled out abruptly.

"Hey," I said.

"I was going to come, Ava. You're too much sometimes."

I shifted to my back and pulled him over me, sliding my hands across his muscular back and snaking my tongue into his mouth. Instead of bringing down the desire between us, our kiss ramped things up.

"I can't stop," he said as he slid his cock inside me again.

"I don't want you too," I whispered, curling my legs around his waist as he rocked into me and we both unraveled together.

"DID I CONVINCE YOU?" He kissed me on the top of my head as I lay on his chest, his arms around me.

"Funny."

"I wasn't trying to be. Did you decide?"

I turned my face into his abs and pressed my lips against his skin. "No. I'm going to speak to law school and my firm and see what's possible. And then . . . and then I'm not going to think about it until after our exams."

Joel exhaled, though I wasn't sure if it was relief or frustration. He ran his hands across my back. "Sounds like a plan. It will give you more time to think. I don't want to put pressure on you, but I want you with me."

"No pressure, then."

"No pressure. Just don't underestimate how I feel."

"I won't. I want to be with you, too. But let's just sit with it for a while, get these exams out of the way, and then discuss it again. Agreed?"

"Agreed. Shall I cook us dinner? You can be my little sous chef again."

"Let's do it."

We pulled ourselves out of bed, and I grabbed his shirt and padded into the kitchen after him. He turned and looked at me, shaking his head. "Oh, no you don't." He put his hands on my shoulders and twisted me away from him, walking me out of the kitchen. "There's no way you are going to dress in nothing but my shirt and be anything but a distraction. Change and stop being so fucking sexy—for just an hour—while I make us some dinner."

I grinned at him over my shoulder and went and found some of my own clothes to put on. When I came back, he leaned across the counter and kissed me. "Still too sexy, but you'll do. Peel these." He handed me some carrots.

"So, what's going on with Jules?" he asked.

"What do you mean?" I replied, mouth half full of raw carrot.

"With Adam. Is she into him?" Most of the time Joel couldn't give a shit what was going on around him, so his question took me a little off guard.

"Why do you ask, Mr. Wentworth?" I squinted at him, exaggerating my suspicions.

"Dunno. Just wondered if they were likely to become a thing." He was concentrating hard on whatever he was doing with the chilies in front of him.

"Do you care?" I asked.

"Not really, but Adam asked me to ask you, so I'm trying to do that and be subtle at the same time."

I let out a throaty laugh. "You boys are hilarious. So how is that subtle thing working for you?"

"Not so good. I have Sherlock Holmes for a girlfriend, apparently. She doesn't let me get away with anything."

I threw a carrot at him. "Sherlock Holmes? I couldn't be one of Charlie's Angels?"

"Charlie was creepy. Why would you want to be his angel?"

"Better Cameron Diaz than some crazy man in a deer-stalker." I grinned. "So Adam really likes her, then?"

"I guess," he said, as he shrugged.

"She said she gave him the night of his life."

Joel guffawed. "There's no false modesty for Jules, is there?"

"I don't think she's fallen madly in love, if that's what Adam wants to know."

"Before I knew you, I thought you and he might have had a bit of a thing going on." He squinted at the chilies.

"Me and Adam?" I scrunched my eyebrows, still concentrating on my carrots.

He nodded. "You seemed to get on well together, and you all are such a tight group. I thought it was bound to have happened or happen at one point." He dusted off the chilies he'd chopped into the frying pan on the hob and then headed to the sink.

"Well, it hasn't. Ever. And it wouldn't have, ever."

"I know," he said simply, soaping up his hands.

"You sound very sure."

"I am."

"Because?"

"I asked him. After that first day at the library." He dried off his hands and slung the tea towel over his shoulder. I couldn't keep my eyes off him.

"You asked Adam whether or not he and I had ever been involved?"

He nodded as he began to unwrap an onion.

"After we studied together that first day at the library?"

He nodded again as if this was no big deal. Had he been interested in me all the way back then?

"Why did you ask him?"

He looked at me and raised his eyebrows. "Are you fishing for compliments, Miss Elliot?"

I tried to bite back my smile. "No. Well, kinda."

"You shouldn't need to fish. I should be giving them so often that you never have to. They're there in my head all the time."

God, I loved it when he said stuff like that to me. It made my stomach flip and my knees weak.

"I liked you," he continued. "I had for a while, but as I said, you lot are such a tight-knit group of friends, there was never a time when I saw you without the others. And then when you came and sat with me, it seemed a perfect opportunity for us to, you know, get to know each other."

Heat spread across my cheeks and down my throat. I looked down, chopping already chopped carrots.

"Are you embarrassed?" he asked.

I shrugged but I wasn't embarrassed. I was just surprised. He'd liked me before we'd become study partners and friends. I'd assumed it was time and my personality that had won him over, but apparently it was more than that. "Is it a shock to you that I like you?" He laughed. "The permanent hard-on I have doesn't give me away?"

I couldn't look at him.

"You are just too cute sometimes."

"So, you don't feel like you're part of our group?" I asked.

He pursed his lips and thought about it for a second. "More so now. But I don't know how much of that's because of you."

I'd finished the carrots, and I went to the fridge to take out some wine. This place felt more and more like my home. *Our* home. I hitched myself up onto the stool and watched Joel work, his muscles flexing in his arms. He loved to cook; the whole creative side of it really lit him up.

"And what did Adam say when you asked him?"

He shrugged. "He made some kind of Adam-type comment, but I knew he hadn't gotten in your pants."

"He said something about me dying an old maid, didn't he?" Adam always said that about girls who weren't interested in him.

"Something like that."

I let Joel's confession marinate. It had taken me by surprise he'd wanted to find out if I had been hooking up with Adam—he'd been trying to find out more about me before we really knew each other. Before studying and the library. I couldn't quite believe it; he was so cool and handsome and popular. Even now that I knew him, he was still all those things to me, and I found it so hard to think that he'd be attracted to someone like me—someone who was the opposite of him.

"Unsurprisingly, I don't think Jules is interested," I said. "I don't know how you'll break it to him."

"Hmm, it's a shame. I think he really likes her."

"He obviously wants to be dominated," I said.

Joel raised his eyebrows. "You might be on to something there. God, I could get some real mileage out of that theory." We chuckled. "I'll just tell him that you were telling about some other guy she has her sights on. And anyway, he's got exams to worry about."

"Haven't we all." I had to get a handle on my trusts module or I wouldn't graduate.

"There's only a few weeks left, and then we've got the rest of our lives to think about." He smiled but didn't push.

I didn't tell him I liked the thought of having the rest of my life with him. I just wasn't sure if it was realistic. We were so young and on such different paths. Somehow knowing he'd liked me for longer than I realized made me feel surer in his feelings for me, but I just didn't know if it would be enough.

THE RITUAL WHEN any of our circle finished their exams was that the others who had already finished would meet them outside the exam hall and then we all would spend the rest of the day drinking and celebrating. My last exam had been the day before and tomorrow was Joel's. Despite the fact Joel wasn't quite at the center of our group, everyone sat in the cafeteria over lunch, discussing the blowout for the following day after Joel's last exam.

"We could get on a plane and fly to Vegas," Adam said as if he'd just come up with the perfect plan. Everyone ignored him and continued to jabber away. "Hey! What about it guys? Vegas?"

"We're not going to Vegas, Adam," I said. For such a smart guy, some of Adam's ideas did a really good job of disguising his intelligence.

"Why do you get to decide?" Adam asked.

"Fine. You go to Vegas. Have an awesome time. No one is coming with you." My head hurt from last night's excess and my tolerance for Adam's crazy had all but disappeared.

"Joel might."

"He will not," I replied, quite certain the last thing that was going to happen tomorrow was Joel boarding a plane for Vegas with Adam.

"What won't I be doing?"

I turned as Joel arrived at our table with a tray in his hand. He looked exhausted. He set his lunch down in the spot next to me and climbed over the bench to sit down. When we were in public, I avoided sitting next to him, afraid I would give our relationship away with a look, a touch. But today I wanted him close.

"How did it go?" I asked. Joel hadn't been confident about his exam this morning, and I'd been thinking about him all day.

"Who knows? I had things to write, so that's a start."

I slid my hand across to his thigh and squeezed. He looked at me and smiled a tired but grateful smile.

"Anyway, what am I not doing?" he asked again.

"Going to Vegas tomorrow," I said.

"How awesome would that be?" Adam asked. "We should definitely do it. Even if it's just the two of us. We would have such a wild time. Just think of the booze, the women. And you need to get laid. How long's it been?"

Warmth spread across my cheeks as I concentrated on moving food around my plate.

"More recently than you might imagine," Joel replied.

"I might have known that you had some girl. But I like your style. You keep it discreet. Nice."

Christ, Adam could be a dick at times.

"Shut up, Adam," Jules cut in, listening to the conversation from the other end of the table. "And none of us are going to Vegas."

"Maybe another time," Joel said, taking the edge off Jules' put-down.

Adam looked disappointed but quickly bounced back. "So, we're all going to come down and meet you tomorrow, right?"

Joel nodded, then finished his lunch, almost inhaling his food. "Guys, I'm heading back to the library. See you later." He stood and stepped over the bench.

"Good luck," everyone chorused. "See you tomorrow."

Tomorrow would be the end of exams. The end of university. Graduation would be the only ritual left.

And then what?

I couldn't decide if I was being weak or sensible. I desperately *wanted* to go to New York with Joel but something was stopping me from saying yes. Was it wrong for my dreams to be so intermingled with Joel and his? Should I strive for more independence? My dad was right—there was a risk that twelve months would become five years. When would be a good time to start *my* career? My parents had raised so many good questions that had made me think, made me worry. And the picture of Joel and I and our future together was growing fuzzier with each passing day.

THIRTY-THREE

Past

Joel had told everyone his exam finished at five, but it actually finished thirty minutes earlier. He'd told me he wanted me to himself for the first half an hour.

I sat on the grass outside the exam hall, with the other students waiting for friends, my chin resting on my knees. I kept my eyes firmly on the door. I wanted to see him before he saw me. I wanted to see the look in his eyes when he found me—to see how much he loved me. His announcement about him going to New York had shaken my trust in him and I wanted to still my concerns.

I'd told the others I had to take a book back to the library and I would meet them in the pub. It was as if I was stealing something. Maybe I was just taking time for Joel and me.

When he appeared, my heart tripped as if I'd not seen him for weeks. This was it. We'd both finished. And it was the beginning of something. Or the end of something.

He scanned the grass, looking for me, and I uncurled my legs and stood, pausing, just for a moment. He found me quickly and grinned so wide he could make me do anything, almost.

I raced over and flung myself at him, wrapping my legs around his waist, pulling him closer. I didn't want anything between us. I didn't care if anyone saw. Not today. Not now. Just for a second all that mattered was the two of us in that moment.

Joel didn't let go. I expected him to first, but he didn't so we just stood there in our Joel and Ava bubble.

"Ava?" he asked eventually.

"Yes?" I mumbled into his neck.

"Shall we go get a drink?" He still didn't let go and neither did I.

"Okay. Do I have to let go?"

"Nope." He started walking in the direction of the pub. Giggling, I slid down his body and let go.

"So, how was it?" I asked.

"Okay. The two things I really wanted to come up did, so that was good, and that was the last exam, so who cares? I'm done."

I nodded. I'd nearly walked out of my last exam. I was so over it I hadn't cared at that point if I failed. We got our drinks and found a table big enough for all of us, then sat.

"That didn't last long," Joel said with a resigned smile when Adam's voice rang out behind us. "I just want to spend the evening with you."

"Give me your keys," I said quickly. Joel looked at me but didn't ask for clarification as he reached into his pocket and pulled out his keys.

"When I leave, give it thirty or forty minutes, then I'll see you back at yours."

His answer was a simple panty-melting grin just as Adam reached our table.

"Here he is. Geek of the week," Adam said, slapping Joel on the back. "What are you drinking?"

An hour or so later, I slipped away, avoiding any big goodbyes. Most of the group was so lost in their alcoholic haze they didn't notice. I went to Joel's via the supermarket and arrived with two bags full of food, wine, and candles. I let myself in the front door. It felt odd being here without Joel, but I was excited to have the whole evening with him, without the pressure of studying hanging over either of us. We were in a delicious limbo that would only last minutes, maybe hours, before we had to start thinking about what came next.

I unpacked the shopping and quickly put the wine in the fridge and the chicken into the oven. Joel would be here soon and something told me he wouldn't be late.

Leaving the potatoes steaming, I went into his bedroom and was immediately hit by how it smelled of him. It was like a gigantic memory enveloping me. I smiled and went to the wardrobe, pulling out his favorite shirt. I quickly changed then headed back to the kitchen to find the candles. I dotted them about and dimmed the lights.

Joel, perfect as usual, arrived just at the right moment.

"Ava," he called from the hallway.

"In here."

"I hope you're naked."

"I'm not naked. I'm cooking. I thought you'd prefer food to sex."

"You were wrong." He stood leaning against the door frame, arms folded, watching me. "You're wearing my favorite shirt," he said.

"Do you mind?" I asked, knowing his answer from the darkness in his eyes.

"I do."

Oh.

"Take it off."

Ohh.

"Joel," I said softly.

"Take it off, Ava."

I LAY in the crook of Joel's shoulder, my head and hand on his chest. We had our best talks like this. Our best silences. Our best fun. It was my favorite place in the world.

I would miss it.

So much.

As much as I told myself that I could go to New York, I knew it was impossible. For other girls it might be a dream come true. But not for me. My confidence had been shaken in Joel and me as a couple because he'd kept such a life changing opportunity from me. I'd thought we shared everything but this time, when he was expecting so much from me, he'd decided to be less than open. The shock had allowed me to see things clearly. There were other reasons I wouldn't follow him—reasons that were about me rather than us. I struggled with giving up so much with no certainty about my own future. My parents had been right. We were too young to think about marriage. And I'd worked too hard to work in a bar when I had law school and a job waiting for me. I wanted Joel but I also wanted to be a lawyer. I wanted the job that I had lined up and the life I'd been looking forward to for the last three years. Surely he'd understand, wouldn't he?

His hand stroked absentmindedly up and down my back. His chest rose as he took a deep breath.

"You're not coming," he whispered. "To New York. Are you?"

My throat tightened and blood pounded in my ears. I didn't speak, couldn't form the right shapes with my mouth.

How would I survive without him?

He pulled me closer. "It's okay if that's what you decided. I just hope it was. I hope you weren't persuaded by your parents or what anyone thought."

I willed my tears not to fall.

"I love you," I said. "For infinity."

"I know," he said. "I love you. For infinity."

"I can visit. And you'll be back too, right?" I asked. We could see each other every few months, surely.

Joel closed his eyes. "I can't do that, Ava. I can't watch what we have die in slow motion."

"Who says it has to die?" I asked, lifting my head to look at him. My heart began to thud. It could work with me in London and him in New York, especially if he was only out there a year.

"I would rather quit while we're ahead. While we still have this amazing thing."

He wanted to end things? Just like that?

"If it's so amazing, isn't it worth trying to maintain?" I asked. I hadn't expected him just to want to give up on us.

The dullness in his eyes told me I'd lost him. Worse, I'd given him up.

"Do you want to punish me? For this decision?" I asked.

He sighed. "I'm really not. I just think a clean break will allow us both to make the most of what's going on right in front of us."

"You mean other women?"

Joel frowned. "No, I mean life. You know I'm not suggesting this because I want to shag other girls."

Of course he wasn't. He could do that in England. He didn't have to fly to New York if he wanted to be with someone else.

"You could just try it. Give us three months. It might work," I said.

He smoothed his thumb across my bottom lip. "I think it's best for both of us if we start with a fresh slate. It will be like ripping the Band-Aid off. And I might move my flight up so I leave just after graduation. There's no point in . . ."

He was going to go in two weeks? Just like that, he'd disappear from my life?

"No, Joel." My voice cracked and I pressed my hands into his chest.

"I think it's best," he said simply.

It was as if he was delivering a long awaited punishment. He was angry with me, but more than that, he was disappointed in me. I could feel the resignation in his body, his eyes, his words. He'd lost the fight he didn't think he'd ever win. He'd asked me to have faith in him, in us, and I'd refused. I'd decided to let him go rather than take a risk on him. That was a betrayal for Joel. I understood that but I couldn't change my mind.

I had no right to ask anything of him anymore.

I shifted out of his embrace and headed to the bathroom. I needed to be able to breathe. The idea that he was no longer mine had stolen all the oxygen in the room and made me numb. What had I done?

I'd wrecked him.

I'd wrecked me.

I'd wrecked us.

THIRTY-FOUR

The silence between us was deafening as we sat together on the sofa. I'd just told Joel I still loved him. After eight years. And he'd not said a word, not moved a muscle. Every second that ticked by magnified the ache in my chest. What was he thinking?

Joel sat forward and put his head in his hands, then slumped back, then forward again. Had he not expected me to say what I said? Did he not realize I was still in love with him? Was he trying to find a way to tell me I was an idiot and it was all so long ago that he'd forgotten me?

Finally, he broke the silence. "I'm scared."

I wasn't sure what I'd expected him to say, but I got it. I understood fear. Loving Joel had taught me all about being scared. From the first moment he'd kissed me, I was afraid he never would again. And while we were together, I was always afraid he'd see sense and leave me. Even now, I was scared I would never see him again, that I would see him with someone else. Scared that I still loved him, that he might not still love me. Scared that he did.

"Me, too," I said. I wanted him to say more, tell me exactly what he was afraid of.

"Can I kiss you?" He spoke to the floor.

It was the last thing I thought he'd say, but the only thing that made sense.

Joel and I were the only thing that made sense.

"You've never asked before," I said.

He looked up at me, his face full of questions, thoughts, and emotions. Still as handsome as he'd been at twenty-one, but he was older now. Wiser.

His gaze dipped to my lips and then back up to my eyes. "Before, I was always sure. I never had to ask because I was always sure."

"You can always be sure. You never have to ask," I half whispered.

There was about a mile between us and then nothing. He rose, cupped my face in his hand, and I closed my eyes. *If we could just stay like this forever.*

As I opened my eyes and looked up at him, he pulled me up. I felt that familiar warmth pass from him to me. And there we were, his body an inch from mine.

He drew a breath and pushed his hands from my shoulders down my arms, reaching my fingers, linking them together.

"So," he said as we stood body to body, hand in hand.

A smile tried to escape and I bit my cheek. I didn't want to admit how it felt to be touching him again in case he changed his mind. "So," I said.

"So, I'm going to kiss you now."

I nodded. "I'm going to let you. I might even kiss you back."

"You will?" he asked, his grin coming into focus.

"I might," I teased.

"Okay."

"Okay."

He took my face in his hands and that familiar buzz covered me, running across my skin. I closed my eyes, waiting, wanting.

The slight brush of his mouth heated my skin. I bit my bottom lip to ease the burn. He kissed one corner of my lips, then the other. Then he trailed a finger across my bottom lip, releasing it from my teeth. He dipped his head and followed the path his finger just made with his tongue. It was delicious and maddening and wonderful. My mouth parted and his tongue pushed gently inside.

I couldn't just stand there being kissed anymore. I couldn't *not* touch him. I brought my hands to his waist and slid them up his back. His kiss became more insistent, pushing against mine, and he pressed his hand against my back as if he wanted to somehow get us closer when there was no space left at all.

He pulled his head back, and when I opened my eyes to see why I was being denied his mouth, I found him staring at me. Unsure, I smiled. Was he changing his mind?

"You taste the same," he said.

My stomach flipped. He sounded so . . . sexy, so like the Joel I remembered.

"You, too. You taste perfect." I pulled him back to me, less reticent than before. Memories of who we used to be flowed back into my limbs. It felt familiar and new and right.

I pulled his shirt out from the back of his trousers and slid my hands up his bare skin. His back was harder than I remembered. More muscled, wider. He shifted under me and groaned. Or was it me? I couldn't tell as our mouths molded together. It wasn't enough. I needed to feel his body.

Fumbling, I undid the first two buttons on his shirt, pausing as his mouth moved to my neck. He kissed me on my collarbone, distracting me. I brought his face to mine again, and pulled the fabric of his shirt apart and sent the remaining buttons scattering to the floor.

Joel stopped and looked at me.

"You ripped my shirt," he said.

"I did."

"It was kinda hot." He kissed me.

"I'm glad you think so. You were doing some good work there for a moment. What stopped you?"

"Well, you've got me half naked here," he said as I pushed his shirt over his shoulders.

I ran my hands over his body, tracing the contours of his skin, and placed a kiss on his beautiful chest. His head fell back. Why had he paused?

"Ava, this is fast. Are you sure?"

"I've had plenty of time to think it through, Joel. I've never been so sure about anything." Even if this was just about tonight, I'd find a way to be okay with that. I'd take every scrap of Joel I could get.

"It's just . . ."

I dropped my hands from his chest and my eyes to the floor as a chill slid down my spine. It sounded like he wasn't sure. He placed his hands on my shoulders.

"It's just . . ." he continued. "This can't . . ."

I turned away from him. I didn't want to hear his rejection. He pulled me closer, my back to his front, and wrapped his arms around my waist as I struggled against him.

"Let me finish," he said.

I relented, willing him to say something I wanted to hear.

"This can't just be about sex, Ava. If that's what this is for you, then I can't do it. This thing between us, it nearly broke me. In fact, I'm not sure I'll ever really recover. So if this is just a one-night thing for you, then we need to end this now."

I gasped. Was that what he thought? I turned to face him and reached for his face.

"Joel, I love you. I have always loved you, and I will always love you. You can have any piece of me you want. You can have me tonight or forever. I'm yours."

With his thumb, he wiped the tear that had just escaped the corner of my eye and pulled me into his chest, his hands covering my back.

After a few minutes, our breathing synchronized. He hadn't responded and I wasn't sure what was going to happen next. All that mattered was that I was in Joel's arms again and I'd told him everything.

"So, is there a bedroom?" he asked after a while.

I pulled my head from his chest and looked at him.

"Yes, there's a bedroom. Where do you think I sleep?" I said. Before I could tell him where, he'd tossed me over his shoulder in a fireman's lift and demanded directions.

He threw me on the bed and crawled over me. "We've got some catching up to do," he said as he pulled my T-shirt over my head and stared at my breasts. "We've been in love a long time, Ava. It's time we acted like it." His eyes darkened. He pinched my nipple between his thumb and his finger, pebbling it, filling me with desire. I pushed my chest toward him.

"So, for you, this is more?" I asked, barely able to form

words as his hand moved across to the other breast. He nodded before he bent his head and replaced his fingers with his mouth.

"For me, this—you—are everything." He dipped his head, kissing between my breasts, down my stomach to my underwear. His lips scorched my skin, creating a line of fire across my stomach. I pushed my hands through his hair. I'd forgotten how much I loved the feel of every part of him. Every inch that I knew so well, that I'd missed so much.

He hooked his thumbs into the sides of my underwear and pulled them down. He kneeled over me, watching me, his gaze wandering up and down and across my body.

"You are so beautiful."

Remembering what he'd said about me appearing so old, I brought my knees up to my chest.

"Don't hide from me." He pressed my knees down so my feet were flat on the bed, then pushed my knees apart and focused on what he exposed. I let him, but turned my head away so I couldn't see where he was looking. "What is it?" he asked.

"I overheard you talking to Adam—you said I'd aged." I felt silly. We'd all aged.

"Did I?" he asked, moving away to stand over me.

I nodded. "At your welcome-home dinner."

He frowned. "I only remember thinking how I didn't recognize you at first. You seemed so . . ."

"Old?"

He shook his head. "Sophisticated. Grown up. Out of my league."

I took the arm from my eyes and propped myself up on my elbows. He'd taken his trousers off and looked as close to perfect as I'd ever seen.

"No one's out of your league, Joel Wentworth."

He lay next to me on the bed and linked his fingers through mine. "I always thought you were. You were super-smart, and so funny, and you didn't seem to fall for my charms. Or what I thought at twenty years' old were charms."

"Hello? I totally fell for your charms."

"But it took more effort than I was used to. In a good way. And when I came back, you had . . . I don't know. You'd turned into this glossy, sexy, lawyer woman. I'd never known you like that. You know, as a grownup. You were never here when I came back to London."

We both lay on our backs staring at the ceiling. Our hands, hips, and legs touching. Energy buzzed and jumped between us.

He was still my Joel.

"So, because I started going to a hair salon and wearing outfits that cost more than my lunch, suddenly I'm sophis-ticated?"

"You're beautiful, but I'd forgotten just how you took my breath away. I guess that's what I was trying to tell Adam."

I sighed. "I avoided being around when you came back." I hadn't wanted to see him move on. "I couldn't bear to see you with a new life that didn't include me."

He reached over and pulled me to him. "I wanted to see you. I came back to see you."

He'd wanted to see me? I'd thought he hated me. "This time?"

"Every time. At least subconsciously. My resentment was mixed up with my love for you for a long time. But the love was always there."

Oh God. How much time had we wasted?

Before my tears spilled over, he pushed me onto my

back and climbed over me, stopping all thoughts of sadness and regret. I loved his familiar weight, and I brought my fingers up his sides, marveling at the feel of him, the size of him, the hardness of him.

"Do we need to . . .?"

He didn't have to finish his thought. I knew what he was asking. "I didn't sleep with Will, and I'm fine. Tested, on the pill. You know."

Joel closed his eyes as if in relief. "I've still never . . . only with you."

"I want you, Joel," I replied.

He pressed himself against me, hard as stone through his boxers. I pushed them off. I didn't want anything between us. We were Joel and Ava.

"I'm not going to last long, Ava."

"We've got all night."

He put his forehead to mine, reached between our bodies, and pushed slowly into me.

"Oh dear God." I lifted my hips, wanting him deeper, and it was just perfect. *He* was just perfect. He stilled, his breathing heavy, deliberate. I stroked his tense arms. His mouth found my neck, kissing and sucking. When he brought his eyes back to mine, he pulled away, then slid back in, right to the hilt, taking my breath. He began to thrust and, conscious that he was above me and inside me, my orgasm began to rumble. What started as emotion turned physical.

"Joel," I gasped as the drag of his cock pushed out every thought in my head. "Joel. I'm . . ." I bit into his shoulder as my climax shuddered through me, my entire body clenching under him. I was vaguely aware of his moan before he slumped over me. I flung my arms around his neck.

When the panting had subsided, he said, "I used to be better at this."

I giggled. "I've never come so quickly in my life. I think you did just fine."

He rolled to my side and propped his head in his hand, trailing the other one up and down my body.

"When you came back, did you think this was going to happen?" I asked.

He took a few moments to answer. "I thought you were single. Adam mentioned it a few months ago, and I guess I hoped that might leave room for something. But I didn't know if you'd moved on, or even if I'd see you."

"I thought you'd still be angry with me," I said.

"I was disappointed for a long while. But I loved you too much. I missed you too much." His fingers strayed lower. "I missed this," he whispered as he dipped between my folds, exploring my wetness. His thumb rubbed over my clit. "I was the first to make you come like this, baby."

"You're the only man that's made me come," I said honestly.

He growled in response, increasing the pressure and pressing his mouth to mine. His tongue snaked between my lips and his fingers continued their rhythm.

"You can't say things like that."

"It's the truth."

The pleasure built slower this time, starting somewhere in the tips of my fingers, just a warning at first, a hint of something. But there was no stopping it, no stopping Joel. He knew me, knew my body. He circled and rubbed and pushed with just the right pressure, just the right speed. I grabbed at his hand, as I began to lose control.

"I'm not going to stop, Ava. Let me be. Let it go."

I fell and fell and fell as his words tipped me over the

edge. His fingers kept their rhythm, pulling every last ounce of pleasure from me.

I was boneless, seeping into the mattress, when he finally pulled his hand away. I felt his lips on my forehead. "I thought I locked your face in my memory, your sounds when you came, but that was better than I remembered," he whispered against my neck. I lay unresponsive, as if he'd stolen my energy with his magic fingers.

He moved his body against mine, his lips busy against my skin.

"We are never leaving this bed," I said.

"Okay." He pushed my breasts together and took one nipple between his teeth, letting go just at the edge of painful.

"I mean, like, ever." My voice was unsteady.

"Okay." His tongue drifted down my stomach, creating a path lower.

"Okay. I'm serious. You can't go to work tomorrow."

"Okay." Words disappeared as he found my clit, circling it, tasting it, and then sucking and sucking. I pulled at the sheets as I screamed, incoherent and desperate.

His tongue pushed down and deeper and his thumb rounded my clit, rough and perfect. He sat back on his knees. I could see myself on his lips, the effect of my fingers in his hair.

He looked like he was mine, finally.

I pulled myself up and, face-to-face with him, I leaned in and licked myself off his lips.

"You like to taste yourself," he said, the words dripping from his mouth, his fingers trailing up my sides.

"I like to taste me mixed with you." I straddled his hips and rubbed myself along his shaft, him hard and pulsing beneath me. I circled my hand around him and looked up.

Slowly, he pulled his gaze from my hand to my face, then grabbed my jaw with both hands and pressed into my mouth, exploring me. I squeezed and pushed down along the length of him, then back up as he moaned into my mouth. The feel and sound of him wanting me unleashed a spasm of desire through me. I rose and positioned him at my entrance.

He pulled back, holding my gaze with his, and placed his hands on my hips. Not pushing, not rushing, but waiting, ready for me. Slowly, I slid onto him. His eyes widened a fraction, giving me slightly more of him, if that was even possible. There we were, face-to-face, our bodies connected.

"You're all I need," he whispered before he flipped me to my back and pushed back in with such blinding force I had to scramble for breath. "And I'm all you'll ever have." I gave up trying to match his rhythm and let my body be his entirely. "Do you hear me, Ava? There's no one for you but me."

I nodded.

"Say it," he said, pushing farther, deeper. A sheen of sweat coated our bodies, cocooning us against the world.

"No one but you. There never was." I wasn't sure if my words were spoken or remained in my head.

"No one knows your body like I do," he said, circling his hips and proving himself right as my back arched off the bed. "No one knows this spot." His fingertips pushed against skin just below my hipbone and a burst of pleasure released deep in my belly. I turned my head, overwhelmed at the moment we were sharing, and devastated we had wasted so my years apart.

"Tell me, Ava."

"No one but you." I cried out as he circled his thumb

around my clitoris and I clenched around him. I reached for him, desperate for something, more, and there it was.

"*Ava.*"

My name from his lips was all it took. My orgasm barreled down my spine and I heard nothing but booming in my ears, felt nothing but his fingers, his body, his tongue, wanted nothing but him. His rhythm increased and his head fell against my neck, his teeth grazed my skin and then perfect stillness.

Eventually, he moved to my side and pulled me into him, twisting his legs through mine. His warmth covered me. "I'd forgotten how it was—is—between us." I dragged my hand down his chest.

He sighed. "I knew it was good, but it feels . . ."

"I know."

Explosive and passionate and *right*. So very right.

SEVERAL HOURS LATER, Joel and I lay on our backs, our limbs tangled together, trying to summon the energy to do more than breathe.

"The stuff you were saying tonight to Harvey about thunderbolts. I mean, it's cheesy," he said.

I slapped him on his chest.

"It *is* cheesy, Ava, but it's also what it's like between us."

Words caught in my throat. He felt it too. I knew he had, but I wasn't sure if he still would—if those feelings would be quite so strong. I rolled to my side and nodded against his chest.

He wrapped his arms around me. "Are you really going to skip work tomorrow?" he asked.

"Yep. And you can't go in, either. You can't leave

my bed."

He dropped a kiss on my head. "Never?"

"Not for a while, yet." I wasn't ready to let him out of my sight.

"Do you have plans for me?"

I nodded. I did and they involved me not wearing much and getting to explore Joel's very naked body.

"Well, I have a few conditions."

"You do?" I tilted my head up to look at him. Maybe he would insist I make a huge announcement on Facebook that we were together or something.

"No clothes." His tone was serious. "If we're playing hooky tomorrow, then you're not allowed to wear a stitch of clothing. Agreed?"

"What about you?"

"Always the negotiator."

I giggled.

"If you're naked, I don't want anything coming between us," he said simply. "We'll have a naked Monday."

"I don't want anything coming between us, either." I replied. I didn't know if he had meant to say so much, but I wanted him to know how I felt.

He pulled me closer and we lay there for seconds, minutes, hours. I lost track. I must have fallen asleep at some point, because I woke up on my stomach. I grinned before I opened my eyes, remembering the delicious interruption to my sleep. Muffled voices floated in from the living room. What was going on? I sat upright, becoming aware of my body and the effects of the night before. I ached from him, for him. My stomach, between my thighs, my neck, my hips. I was covered in echoes of him.

I grabbed a T-shirt, pulled it over my head, and went to investigate. I stuck my head around the bedroom door and peeked into the living room. There was Joel, his very naked back to me, facing the sliding doors to my balcony, a mobile clamped to his ear.

My grin grew and I opened the bedroom door wider. Joel turned around, and smiled, his gaze darting down my body.

"If you look under GNO Enterprises and then this month, I'm sure it will be there," he said into the phone. He beckoned me forward. As I neared him, instead of pulling me into him for a kiss, he reached out to the hem of my T-shirt and pulled it up as far as it would go. He mouthed at me, *Arms*. I lifted them up and he stripped me bare, then looped his arm around my back and pressed me into him.

"Yes, exactly. You just need to add the logo and check the formatting, and that's it. Yes, definitely tomorrow."

He maneuvered me so I was leaning against the glass doors, his free arm beside my head.

"I'll tell you when I see you," he said to whoever he was talking to. "No, thank you, and fuck off." He hung up.

"Naked. That's what I said, Ava. We had a deal." He looked at me seriously. "Nothing between us."

I nodded.

"If I want to fuck you, I don't want to waste time having to take your clothes off."

Wetness rushed between my legs.

"Do you understand?"

I nodded, biting my lip.

"Show me you understand, Ava. I want your mouth on me."

My nipples tightened at his demand. I wanted him in my mouth, wanted to please him. I'd do anything. He placed his other hand on the glass to the other side of my head, trapping me, daring me to try to escape.

I slid to my knees and my eyes fell on his hard cock. I reached for him greedily. He pulsed in my hand and slowly, tantalizingly, I pulled my tongue from the base to the tip like I knew he liked. His stiff legs told me he was holding back when he really wanted to force himself inside me. He'd demanded this, but I was the one in control. I circled his crown with my tongue, once, twice, and then took just the head in my mouth and stilled.

"Ava, Jesus. Don't stop." He banged his fist on the glass, frustrated, impatient. I relented and slid my lips down, taking him deeper and deeper until he hit the back of my throat and he moaned. I kept him there, swallowing before pulling back, trailing my teeth against him as I knew he liked.

"Jesus. Fucking. Christ," he yelled, and pushed back into me, again and again, unable to control himself. I loved that I could do that to him. I reached between my thighs, wanting to feel my wetness, to elicit some kind of release. "What the fuck?"

He lifted me so I was facing him, my hand still between my legs. "What are you doing?" He stared at my circling fingers.

"Feeling what you do to me," I whispered. He closed his eyes and when he opened them, there was a fire there. He lifted me, pushed me against the glass, and plunged into me, ripping the air from my lungs. I grabbed at him as if I were drowning as he thrust into me with enough force to drive away the last eight long years.

No man had made me feel like Joel did. And I'd love no one but him. Eight years ago, I'd been young and foolish but I wouldn't make the same mistake twice.

I would never let him go.

I needed to understand he felt the same.

THIRTY-FIVE

Before I'd even opened my eyes, I broke out into a huge grin as I became aware of Joel's breathing. It was really true. He was here with me. I hadn't just dreamt it. I was lying on my side and I opened my eyes to find Joel on his back beside me. He turned his head.

"How long have you been awake?" I asked.

"Just a few seconds." He turned to face me and tucked my hair around my ear. "It's just past nine."

I couldn't remember which day we were on and it was only the lack of light coming through the curtains that told me it was evening.

"Your stomach was growling in your sleep. We need to get you some food."

I didn't need anything. I had everything I'd ever wanted right there. I grabbed Joel's hands as he pulled them away from my waist, not wanting him to move.

"We've not eaten all day and we've been doing some serious exercise. Let's eat."

"Urgh. Okay. We'll have to order in, though. My cupboard is bare."

Joel chuckled. It was a beautiful, familiar sound I'd missed so much. It was only the small lines around his eyes that reminded me how much time had passed.

"That wasn't a euphemism, you freak."

"You know me too well." He kissed my forehead and moved off the bed.

Joel ordered a pizza, then settled back in bed, tucking me against him, my back to his front. We fit so perfectly. Nothing had changed and everything had changed.

"Who did you tell to 'fuck off' on the phone earlier when I interrupted you? I meant to ask but we got side-tracked."

"My business partner, Ed. He was giving me shit for not going in. Told me my dick would shrivel up and fall off." In the eighteen hours since Joel had arrived, we hadn't slept much. But we had both managed to call in sick.

"Nice."

"He is, actually. You'll like him."

Thoughts of the future drifted into my head. I'd kept them out for longer than I'd expected. "So, he knows? About me?"

Joel sighed. "Yes, he knows. Is that a problem?"

"No. I . . . No." What I struggled with was me not knowing who his business partner was. He was clearly important in Joel's life and yet I didn't know anything about him.

"We need to talk about this, Ava." He didn't mean we needed to discuss Ed. He wanted to talk about my insecurities. He didn't realize I wasn't the Ava of eight years ago. He didn't know what eight years of being without him had done.

"I just want it to be okay this time. I want you and me to be okay."

My phone rang, and I shuffled to the edge of the bed to see if it had fallen off my nightstand.

"It's Jules," he said, holding it out to me. "Shall I pick up?"

I gulped in a breath. He wanted to answer my phone and announce to Jules we were together. It was a test. I wanted to know more about how Joel was thinking before I told anyone. I had to prepare.

I shrugged. He tossed the phone at me, then got up and headed to the bathroom.

"Hi, Jules, you okay?"

"Yeah, you didn't reply to my emails so I was just checking on you."

The bathroom door was open, but there were no loos flushing, no taps running. Joel wanted to hear what I had to say.

"Sorry, I wasn't at work today. I had some things to sort out."

"Like what?"

"A few important things." What I was saying was as much a message to Joel as it was to Jules. He was important, but he couldn't expect me to tell Jules I was in bed with him and had been for the last however long. Not before we'd even had a chance to discuss where things stood between us. Surely.

"What things?" Jules asked.

"I'll tell you when I see you," I replied. I shouldn't have answered the call at all, but I didn't want Joel to think I was afraid to. "I've got to go. Let's talk tomorrow."

I hung up and followed Joel into the bathroom. Sitting on the edge of the bath in his boxers, he'd broken the no-clothes rule. I moved toward him but he didn't look at me. I reached out and stroked his back. I shivered and covered my breasts with my arm, vulnerable being so naked standing in front of him.

"Let's talk. Please come back to bed," I said. The doorbell rang and without a word, Joel stood and headed out. I scrambled around, trying to find something to put on amongst the debris of sheets and pillows and bedcovers. I found his shirt, crumpled in a heap by the bed, and pulled it on. It smelled of him.

Joel was just closing the front door as I went into the living room. He still wouldn't look at me.

"Joel."

He slung the pizza box on the counter and braced himself against the surface, exhaling as if he'd just finished a run.

"Fuck," he said.

"Please talk to me." Tension gathered in the bottom of my belly. I hadn't said he couldn't answer the phone. I hadn't lied to Jules.

He straightened up and looked at me. "You have a week," he said.

"I don't understand." Was he saying we could only be together a week?

"To get your shit together and decide what you want."

Decide what I wanted? This wasn't a one-way street. "I want *you*. Joel, you know that. But we've not talked about what's beyond these few hours. Let's do that. Let's take the next steps together."

"It can't be like last time, Ava. I told you I couldn't do that again. I thought you were stronger than worrying about what everyone else thought."

"I am. But I don't know what you want from us, from me."

I moved toward him and he stepped back. My stomach churned at his distance.

"I want you to *want* to tell people! Don't you get it? I want to shout that I love you from the fucking rooftops. I couldn't give a shit what anyone else thinks. I want us to be together—forever, Ava. I want to marry you, have kids with you, grow old with you."

My heart was beating out of my chest. Finally, the words I'd been waiting to hear from him.

"I won't be your dirty little secret."

"You never were, Joel. I was different before. I didn't know how things would work out. If I could turn back the clock, I would. I want all those things, too. I promise. I love you."

"I can't risk my heart again, Ava. I need to see things are different," he said.

He turned and headed to the bedroom. I followed him, needing to close the distance between us. I felt as if I'd been stabbed in the heart as he pulled his trousers on. He was leaving?

"I need my shirt, Ava."

"Stay. Please don't be angry with me. I'll do whatever you want." My heart was beating out of my chest. I couldn't lose him again.

"I'm not angry. But I've accepted my part in our breakup and I'm here, fighting for you. I've moved back to England. I'm trying to right my wrongs. But I've got to see that you're willing to learn from your mistakes too. You told me you loved me but not enough to tell your friends or to come to New York. Not even enough to ask me to stay." He slumped back on the bed. "Words aren't enough, Ava. And

I can't wait forever. Take some space to decide in the cold light of day what you want."

"I don't need time and space! How can you know what *you* want but doubt that I know what I want?"

"Why didn't you say anything to Jules?" he said.

Christ, he wasn't giving me a chance. "We hadn't talked about what was next. And she's been trying to get into your underwear since you got here. What was I going to say? I need to see her in person."

"Jules tries to get into everyone's pants. She won't care. It's just another excuse. There's always a reason why you can't tell people I'm your guy."

"She'll care more than you think. And I'm not just using that as an excuse." I grabbed at him. "And this might have just been a one-time thing for all I knew."

"Fucking hell, Ava. I told you I couldn't make this a one-time thing."

"Well, we haven't made specific plans about what's next." It sounded stupid now that he was playing it back to me, but we *hadn't* spoken about what was next. This was all new territory and I was doing the best I could. "I didn't want Jules asking me questions I couldn't answer. Maybe that sounds weak and insecure and I get that, but that is a part of me, and if you're going to love me, you have to love *all* of me."

He stood and pulled me against his chest, then stroked my back. "I *do* love all of you. The insecure parts of you are some of my favorite parts. That's why I need to give you time and space. It's the right thing to do. Let's just take this week and see where we end up."

It was as if we were ending again, and I wasn't sure if it was new pain I felt or the memory of the old pain but either way, it flowed through me like poison. My knees buckled and my grip weakened.

I didn't want to see where we ended up. What happened if I couldn't convince him that I loved him?

"You should eat," he said, steadying me. I clung to him, hoping he'd see how much I needed him.

He peeled my arms from around him. "Come on, Ava. It's a week and you want us to be together, you just need to show me."

"I don't need a week!" I punched him in the arm and he chuckled. "What if you change your mind?" I asked.

"After eight years, what's going to happen this week that could possibly change how I feel?"

I had no answer to that. I didn't want to tell him any of the hundred things I had in my head.

"Now, let me have my shirt. As sexy as you look in it, I don't want to have to leave your flat half naked."

I swapped his shirt for the one I'd worn last night and followed him out of the bedroom. He stopped at the front door. "We'll have to live at my place. Your bed squeaks and I can order better takeaway." He grinned, and I loved him ten times more in that moment. He still had faith in me. I smiled back and he grabbed my neck and kissed the top of my head.

"I'll see you on Saturday," he said. He didn't want to see me until we had dinner at Hanna and Matt's? I'd only just got him back and he was disappearing.

"Can that be our week?" That would only be five days, but I didn't want to wait any longer.

"I need to see that you want this as much as I do, Ava."

The door shut and I stood for a moment, mentally running through what I could do in this week to show him I knew what I wanted. That I didn't care what anyone else thought. That I finally had myself together.

I raced back into the bedroom and texted Jules.

A: I need to see you. Are you free tomorrow?

I passed the phone back and forth between my hands, willing it to buzz.

It was late, but I wasn't tired, even though I probably should be. We'd not slept much and I had work tomorrow, but the adrenaline racing around my body wasn't letting up.

This time, I needed a plan.

THIRTY-SIX

I set the two glasses down on my coffee table and began to pour the wine. Jules would be here any minute, and I'd like her a glass of alcohol down before I made my confession. Joel had given me a week and speaking to Jules was the first thing I had to do. It wasn't that I was nervous about Jules telling me Joel was too good for me like I had been at university. I knew Joel and I had something special, something most people didn't have, so whether or not I was pretty, sexy, or funny enough in other people's eyes didn't matter.

I was enough for Joel.

Eight years had taught me that. He still cared about me after all this time, and I was sure that if Adam turned around and said, *What the hell are you fucking her for, you could bang a supermodel*, Joel wouldn't care.

Joel coming back to London, Joel coming back to *me*, had taught me that. It had taken eight years, and I'd learned that lesson the hard way. He thought I still had to decide but he was wrong. I just needed to show him, to convince him. Jules was the first step in my plan.

The wine sloshed over the rim of my glass as the doorbell went. I swallowed and put down my drink. This was the bit where I'd find out whether keeping the most important thing in my life a secret would ruin a friendship.

"Hey," I said, as I answered the door with a practiced grin on my face.

Jules frowned. "What are you so happy about?"

I chuckled. "Seeing you, my dear, sweet friend."

She barged past me. "I hope you've got some wine—ahhh, yes." She abandoned her stilettos mid-stride in the corridor and grabbed her glass as she flopped onto my sofa.

She wasn't in the greatest of all moods. But it was Tuesday, before wine. I suppose that had to be expected.

"That's better." She sighed. "Today has been pure hell. It's a good job I love you. I want to be at home in bed, not trying to find you a man that you don't seem to want." When I'd invited Jules over, I'd told her it was to help me pick some more online dates. It was the only way I could guarantee she'd turn up.

"I appreciate you coming over," I said, wiping the palms of my hands down my yoga pants. "But, actually, I don't need help with online dating. That's not really why I asked you here." I took a breath, trying to keep my breathing steady. Jules had reason to be really upset with me. "You're a good friend. I know we're really different, but I do love you. And Hanna."

Jules sat bolt upright. "Fuck, Ava. Are you okay? Are you sick or something? Or a lesbian? Are you in love with me?"

I couldn't help but chuckle. I shook my head. "Not you but someone. And for a long time."

"What? You're talking in riddles." Her eyes grew wider.

"I want to tell you about the man I've been in love with for the past nine years." I glanced down at my lap. "I really don't want this to ruin our friendship. I know that you've always had a bit of a thing for him."

"Who are you talking about?"

I looked up to find her staring at me.

"Joel." I winced, half expected to be hit with a shower of wine from Jules' glass.

"Wentworth?" she asked.

I tilted my head as if to say *How many other Joel's do we know?*

"Since he came back to London?" she asked. "Is that why you and Will split?"

I had to go back to the start, otherwise nothing made sense. "Since the beginning of our final year at university," I said.

"For this whole time?" There was none of the anger I'd expected. Perhaps that would come later, when she knew the extent of what I'd kept hidden away. "Does he know?"

"Let me tell you everything."

I went on to explain how we'd fallen madly in love, completely unexpectedly during that final year and how it had ripped me to pieces when he left and that we'd never seen or spoken to each other since until these past few weeks. I told her how the feelings I had for him had never gone away and he'd confessed the same but had given me an ultimatum. I kept talking and talking and Jules sat there, her wine poised at her mouth, but never taking a sip as if she were waiting for me to be finished.

"I'm sorry I kept it from you," I said finally as I sank back into the cushions.

"That's the bit I don't get," she said. She held her finger

up, gulped down some wine, and then turned back to me. "Why did you keep it a secret? At university. And how?" She lifted her palms to the air as if the heavens would respond. "No one could keep secrets from anyone."

"I think that's your answer," I said. "No one expected Joel and me to hook up, so it was easy to keep it hidden because people weren't looking for it."

Jules sucked in a breath and pushed out her lips as if she was digesting the information. "I suppose neither of you courted attention in the way that Adam or I did." She smiled. "Still do. But no one was looking for Matt and Hanna to hook up, and they did. They didn't hide it though."

"Yeah but Hanna and Matt are perfectly suited. Joel and I are . . ."

"Well according to you, soulmates."

"I know it sounds ridiculous, it's just—"

"It sounds bloody fantastic. It's what we're all looking for. I just don't get why you kept it a secret."

"I didn't want the pressure. I was scared to lose him." I shrugged. "I didn't want people to tell him he could do better and ask him what he was doing with me."

"Who the hell would say that?" Jules asked. "They'd have me to answer to."

"Come on, Jules. Even now you tell me I'm the Hermione that nobody fucks. I knew no one would understand Joel picking me."

She slumped back on the sofa. "The Hermione thing was meant to be a joke. And anyway, Emma Watson's beautiful and clever. And she kicks arse as Hermione. We all want to be Hermione, Ava. Especially if Joel Wentworth falls in love with her."

I didn't expect her to be this rational and understanding

when I told her. Her reaction was almost too nice for me to be able to bear. Why couldn't I have had this conversation nine years ago? I took a swig of my wine to stop myself from getting emotional.

"I'm sorry," I said, swallowing. "I shouldn't have kept it a secret."

She moved off the sofa to sit next to me. "No, I'm sorry. I hate to think my teasing made you think I wouldn't be supportive of you." She pulled me into a hug. "Whatever you chose or choose, I will support you. And I think you and Joel are perfect for each other. You're both overachieving, sexy, good-looking people who have kick-arse friends who just want them to be happy."

The problem hadn't really been with Jules or Adam or any of our friends. I hadn't believed in myself. I couldn't possibly see how I could be enough for Joel.

"Thank you," I said.

"And he still loves you after all this time?" she asked.

I shrugged. "But he thinks I still want to hide."

"Do you?" she asked.

I shook my head. "Not at all. He's told me that he wants to shout it from the rooftops that he loves me. I feel the same. I just need to prove it to him. I have until Saturday night to set him straight."

"Well," Jules said as she stood. "Then we better get to work."

THIRTY-SEVEN

Every single part of me shook as we got out of the taxi outside Hanna and Matt's place. I couldn't tell if it was excitement or fear. Both, maybe. This was my last chance to show Joel what had changed since he left eight years ago. I knew he wouldn't care how I looked or what I wore, but I wanted to look good. Jules and I had had our hair blow dried and our nails done. There was something about having amazing hair that was like a shot of confidence straight to your heart.

Jules promised to pick me up in a cab, despite her being closer to Matt and Hanna's than I was. It was caring and thoughtful. So often Jules hid how utterly selfless and open-hearted she could be.

Jules had been a little upset I'd not told her until now. And embarrassed that she'd so relentlessly pursued Joel in front of me. But she'd not been shocked in the way I expected her to be. She'd not told me I was going to get hurt, or that men like him didn't end up with women like me, or that I should set my sights a little lower. There wasn't even a hint of disapproval or concern. After we had shared our apologies with each other, cried a little and hugged a lot, she'd been excited for me. She was cheering for me. And I loved her for it.

I'd not told Hanna. I went back and forth on it and still didn't know if it was the right thing to tell her first or not. I didn't want to put her in a position where she was hiding things from Matt. And telling Matt would lead to telling Adam, telling Daniel, and being open. I wanted to do all that, but it seemed like they all should find out together.

I shivered in the breeze outside Hanna and Matt's place. The silk jumpsuit I'd bought especially for tonight wasn't made to be worn in the wind. It looked like a simple long-sleeved all-in-one from the front, but was completely backless. I was naked from my neck to below my waist. It suited the occasion. A little bit conservative, and a little bit shocking.

A familiar buzz slid across my skin as we went up the stairs.

"You look amazing. Go get your man." Jules pulled me into a hug just before we headed into the house.

"Wow, you two look hot. Like, man-hunting hot," Hanna said. Maybe we'd overdressed; Hanna had on jeans.

No, I was here for Joel. Nothing was too much.

I saw him from the corner of my eye, but he wasn't looking at me. If I was a betting woman, I'd say he was deliberately avoiding looking at me. Deliberately enthralled with whatever Leah and Daniel were saying. I took a deep breath and went over to the three of them.

"Hey, guys," I said breezily.

Leah and I exchanged kisses and as I leaned forward, revealing my back to Joel, I heard him take a sharp intake of breath. I swallowed a grin. Daniel pulled me into a hug, his hand on my bare back. "Wow, Ava, you look amazing," he said and Leah swatted him.

"Don't sound so shocked. Ava always looks amazing."

I smiled and turned to Joel, leaving Leah and Daniel to bicker. "You look handsome tonight." I rested my hand on his chest and tilted my head up to kiss him on the cheek. "I've missed you. I'm looking forward to having you back."

"But nothing's changed, Ava." I could tell by the dullness in his eyes he was disappointed that everyone gathered tonight didn't know about us.

"It's about to," I said. I mouthed, *I love you.* And then I turned away to help Hanna.

EVERYONE WAS SEATED and they'd clinked glasses and swapped cheers. This was it. Now was my time. I was trembling, just a little, but I'd never been so certain about anything, ever.

"So, I have something I'd like to say." I pushed my chair behind me and stood up. My mouth was dry and I took another sip of my champagne.

"How dramatic!" Hanna laughed. Holy crap. I hoped she wasn't going to be upset I'd not told her before now.

Joel looked at me as if I'd just run him over. Then he looked at Jules, who was beaming at me, and then back at me. I saw the moment he realized Jules knew. I saw it in his eyes—hope.

This was it.

"You look so serious, Ava," Daniel said, then they started chattering amongst themselves, not taking much notice of me.

"Guys, seriously, I need to say something." They settled down and all eyes were on me now. "So, as you know, I don't date."

"Yeah, because you're a lesbian. It's fine, Ava, we've known forever. This isn't news. Sit down and have another glass of wine." Adam laughed. He was never as funny as he thought he was.

"Will you shut up for once?" I was going to start throwing things in a minute. "I am not a lesbian, I am not a work-obsessed crazy person, and I'm not simply asexual or whatever you've convinced yourself, Adam. I'm just . . . I've just been in love with the same man for the last decade. And because I know I'll love him for the rest of my life, there has been no point in looking elsewhere."

I had everyone's attention now. Joel shifted in his chair.

"There will never be anyone else for me. I know that's true. He's it. The one. The love of my life. He always has been and always will be my thunderbolt." My throat tightened and tears begin to pool in my eyes. I hoped this would do it.

"I love him as much now as I did on our first date, when he cooked me chicken and refused to have sex because he wanted me to be ready. I love him as much now as I did a week ago when he walked away from me and told me to get my head together.

"What I've failed to realize, until now, is that I've always been ready for him. Nothing else matters to me. I would give up anything and everything for him. I don't need anyone else to tell me it's okay. I just need him."

Tears started to trickle down my left cheek as I thought about what I was going to say next.

"And I'm afraid I might have lost him again. I've pushed him away, trying to make everything perfect, trying to keep everyone happy, trying to keep everything in control. I've caused nothing but hurt by being so scared. I've hurt you, my closest friends, by keeping something so important to me so secret. I've hurt myself by denying myself the love of my life. And worst of all, I've hurt you, Joel." For the first time, I turned to him. "I'm so sorry."

I grabbed a napkin from the table and tried to stem the tide of mascara escaping down both cheeks. I dried my tears, took a deep breath, and looked right at Joel.

"Eight years ago, the worst thing that could ever happen to me happened—I lost you. For a long time I didn't think I'd survive. But I did. More than survived, that awful time gave me understanding and a belief in myself. I'm not the scared, insecure girl I was at university. I knew that if I ever faced losing someone so important to me again, I'd do every-thing in my power to hang on to it. Joel Wentworth, I won't let you go again. I need you. More than anything, I want you and I love you. For infinity."

As I stopped speaking, everyone turned to Joel. I followed their gazes. He shook his head. *Was I too late?* He pushed his chair out and stood, still looking at the floor. The only sound in the room was of my breath coming heavy and desperate, as if someone's hand was on my heart, squeezing. Joel stepped around the table. When he reached me, he stopped and just gazed into my eyes.

"So, you did it," he said.

My heart was thudding. "I did. I meant it, Joel. I love you."

He pulled me toward him, his arms snaking around my waist. "It only took you the best part of a decade."

I pressed my forehead to his chest.

"We've both made too many mistakes to count. But now that's over with. It's all in the past," he said. "Look at me."

I brought my gaze up to his.

"This is it. We're us now. Forever. Get it?" he asked.

I nodded.

He took my face in his hands and brought his lips to mine. My entire body relaxed.

Joel pulled back and let his hands drop to my waist. He smiled at me as murmuring erupted around the table.

"I'm really sorry if you are pissed at us, or you want to hear the whole story, but it's all going to have to wait," Joel said. "I need some time alone with the love of my life. We have some catching up to do." He took my hand and led me to the door.

"You're pussy whipped. I can't believe it," Adam said.

Joel paused and I bumped into his back. "Shut the fuck up, Adam. You think she's gorgeous," Joel responded and warmth spread through me. I tugged on his arm and he looked at me and then led me toward the door.

"Sorry about dinner, Hanna. Speak later," I called behind me. I couldn't keep my eyes off Joel. I didn't know what their faces looked like. I wasn't sure I cared. We raced out the front door and into a cab.

"Sit there." Joel pointed to the corner of the taxi. I looked at him quizzically. "Seriously. Stay over there," he said. "Don't touch me or I'll have you in this cab. Your back. What you're wearing. I mean it, stay there." He shifted in his seat, trying to rearrange his trousers. He tried to steady his breathing. Right then I understood my power over him. My ability to ruffle him. He wanted me just as much as I wanted him. I grinned.

"Don't look at me like that," he said.

"Like what?"

"You know what," he replied, his eyes dark and wide.

The tension in the car was thick, viscous. Like a spell

that would be broken if anyone moved or spoke. He stared at me as if I'd disappear if he looked away for even a second. The way he was gripping the edge of the seat gave away how he was trying to hold himself back. Stopping himself from touching me. My skin vibrated at the thought, my thighs shook. I tipped my head back and gasped.

"Fuck, Ava." He grabbed me and pulled me onto his lap. Pressed my lips to his and pushed his tongue into my mouth, desperate, hungry. His hands slid across my back, and then lower, until he could go no farther. "How do I get into this thing? Or get you out?" He slipped under the material at the side and grazed my bare breasts, then kneaded them together. "Fuck," he said again. I could feel him harden beneath me, twitching. My head was light and bright and full of him, of his hands and his tongue.

The cab came to an abrupt halt and Joel pulled away to check where we were. He scrambled about, reaching into his pockets, then flung some money at the driver and dragged me out of the car. He strode into his building, yanking me along as I clattered behind him in too-high heels.

As I stepped into the elevator, Joel pushed me against the wall, grinding himself against me, his desperate mouth against mine.

"Joel, the button. Press the button."

I needed to be in his flat. I needed him.

Without breaking our kiss, he grappled at the buttons, his tongue on my neck and his teeth grazing my jaw. When the elevator stopped, he pulled away, dug out his keys and threw the door open. Before we stepped inside, he was unbuttoning his shirt.

"Take it off, Ava. Now," he said.

I froze. I'd not seen him like this for a long time, so crazed with lust.

Stripping off his shirt, he stalked toward me, sending me backward. "Take. It. Off."

I fumbled for the zip, forcing my fingers to work, half looking behind me, trying to make sure I didn't bump into anything.

"Off," he said again, then kicked his trousers off and guided my back to the wall. I expected him to kiss me again, but he just stayed there for a second, his nose almost touching mine. Finally, he reached behind me and opened the door, walking me inside until my legs hit the edge of a bed. I shrugged my top from my arms and the whole thing fell to my feet, leaving me entirely naked.

"That's better. I can see you now." He pressed me back, and without warning or ceremony, put his hand under my bottom and pushed into me. I cried out with the shock, the ecstasy of it. I'd never felt so full of him, of love, of life.

"You are so wet, Ava."

I couldn't breathe. Couldn't speak as he moved above me, soothing me with his dirty words, made me his. There was no hiding.

"So beautiful and ready for me."

I wrapped my legs around him, urging him deeper.

"Finally, so ready for me."

I always had been. And now, I always would be.

EPILOGUE

"Stop, you're distracting me!" I said as Joel wrapped his arms around my waist and buried his face against my neck. I tried to continue chopping the onion in front of me, but all I really wanted to do was turn around and lose myself in Joel.

"You're the distracting one. I remember warning you before about cooking while wearing my shirt."

I giggled and relaxed back into him. If I was being honest, I'd worn his shirt to chop onions on purpose. I loved it when he couldn't keep his hands off me, which was most of the time. We had a lot of time to make up for.

"We only have three hours until everyone arrives," I said, trying and failing to be stern.

"So we can go out to eat, or call caterers or something. Then we can spend the next three hours in bed."

"I see you've been working on your advocacy skills, Mr. Wentworth." I dropped the knife and turned to face him, looping my arms around his neck.

"Are you nervous?" he asked.

I shook my head. "No. Not at all. Should I be?"

"No, just checking."

"Are you?" I asked.

"Of course not."

It had been a week since I'd finally found the courage to stand up and tell Joel I loved him in front of all our friends. Tonight, everyone was coming to dinner at Joel's. I'd spent the week here. After all, my bed did squeak and his place was at least nineteen times bigger than mine.

I'd spoken to Hanna to apologize for not giving her the heads-up before my confession. She'd been characteristically forgiving and understanding, and most of all, completely excited and happy for me. For us.

Joel had spoken to Adam, who intimated that he had known all along. *Whatever.*

I pulled Joel's head down to mine and pressed my lips to his.

Pulling back, I said, "I'm going to go and change, and then we're going to finish cooking and have our friends for a home-cooked meal in your flat."

"Our home," he said.

I grinned at him. Joel was my home wherever he was. "Our home."

Joel nodded. "Okay."

"Okay."

"Okay, you loser."

"SOMETHING'S BURNING," I told Joel at the exact minute the intercom sounded.

"Fuck!" Joel replied.

"You see to the door and I'll rescue the food."

Voices echoed in the corridor as I scraped off the burned skin of the roasted peppers. No real harm done.

"Hey, Ava."

I spun at Hanna's greeting, then wiped my hands on a cloth as I moved toward her.

"I'm sorry I didn't tell you," I whispered as we hugged.

"Don't be. Not on my account. I'm so happy to be here," she replied, handing me a bottle of champagne. "And it gives us all reason to celebrate."

Matt trailed in with Adam, who scanned the room, followed by Daniel and Leah.

"Where's Jules?" Adam asked as he kissed me on the cheek.

"Not sure. She's not late, though, it's only just seven. Cut her some slack," I replied. Adam nodded.

Daniel grabbed me and twirled me around as Leah beamed. "Joel's a very lucky man," he said.

"And I'm a very lucky girl."

I glanced over at Joel across the room, playing the perfect host, pouring out drinks, and hanging coats. It felt as if we were getting back to normal. A new normal.

"So what are you going to poison us with, Ava? I've never known you to so much as boil an egg," Adam asked.

"You'll find out when I serve it up."

The buzzer sounded again and Joel went to get it.

The six of us stood in the kitchen as Jules burst in, waving another bottle of champagne.

"We finally get to celebrate Ava getting some!"

Everyone laughed and I just rolled my eyes as Joel's hand discreetly found my back.

"Can I get you a drink to take the edge off?" he asked.

"There's no edge. But I'd love a drink."

"You okay?" he asked. I was pretty sure Joel was still getting used to the more confident Ava.

"I'm great. Really great." I put my arm around his waist

and pulled him toward me as he bit back a grin. I wasn't sure if it was in response to my PDA or my being more relaxed than he'd expected. Either way, I loved seeing him happy, even if he was trying to hide it.

Everyone took their seats around the table, leaving two spaces next to each other for Joel and me. Our friends' quick acceptance of us as a couple was sweet. I wanted to sit as close to Joel as possible. Not because I was nervous, but because I didn't want to be apart from him, not even for a minute.

"I'd like to make a toast to Joel and Ava, and love and friendship," Adam said, raising a glass.

I waited for the sarcastic follow-up, but it wasn't forthcoming. We all clinked glasses and began our meal. Surely Adam wasn't growing up? I looked at Jules to see if she'd noticed anything odd. She wasn't looking my way and was quieter than normal. Had they both had personality transplants?

"So, tell us the story of you guys at uni. I'm dying to hear it all. Were you secretly shagging all the time you pretended to be in the library?" Daniel asked.

"Oh. My. God." Realization hit me. Everyone turned to look at me.

"Sorry, Ava, I'm only kidding around," Daniel said.

"No, it's okay, I wasn't responding to you. I've just realized why these two are behaving themselves for once in their lives," I said, gesturing between Adam and Jules. "You two are totally doing it."

Jules blushed. "We are not."

"You're blushing. You never blush. Oh. My. God," Hanna said.

"Sherlock strikes again," Joel said, squeezing my thigh.

"I told you: I'm Cameron Diaz, not Sherlock Holmes." I rolled my eyes.

He kissed my cheek and I melted and reached across to grab his hand under the table, linking my fingers with his.

"So, are you two shagging?" Daniel asked.

"We kissed, that's all," Adam mumbled.

"And it's not going to happen again," Jules said.

"Yeah right," I said.

"Well, you can keep your nose out, Ava, since we didn't get to weigh in on your relationship with Joel," Jules snapped.

I held my hands up. "I'm very happy to keep my nose out as long as you make sure you call me first thing tomorrow to tell me everything." I grinned at her. Staying out of Jules' love life was the last thing she'd ever want from me.

"Okay," she said, a tiny smile stretching her mouth, "it's a deal." And then she remembered herself and sobered. "But there's nothing to tell. I was really drunk, and like I said, it's not going to happen again."

I looked at Adam as he concentrated on his plate, not saying a word.

I squeezed Joel's hand. *Jules and Adam.* That would make everything even more perfect, if that was even possible.

"Let's change the subject and let these guys off the hook for the evening, shall we?" Joel said.

There were murmurs around the table, and then Adam and Matt started arguing about something. In no time at all, we fell into our familiar rhythm of friendship.

"You guys look good together," Daniel said as he passed me the potatoes.

"Thanks," Joel and I answered in unison. We grinned at each other.

"I might have to vomit," Jules said with a smile.

I shrugged as I caught Leah scowling, though I knew Jules was joking.

"But it's true, you do," Jules followed up.

"Of course they do. They're perfect together," Hanna said. Matt rolled his eyes at his wife's relentless romanticism.

"So, are you guys going to do the whole white wedding thing, or what?" Adam asked.

"I don't need a ring and a white wedding to know we're going to be together forever," I replied.

Joel squeezed my hand and looked at me with a question in his eyes. "But you'd wear a ring if I bought you one?"

I shrugged. "I guess."

"You guess?"

A wedding was never part of my plans. I'd only ever wanted Joel. Being married to him didn't seem important. "I haven't thought about it, but sure."

"Your enthusiasm is overwhelming." He grinned at me. "You'll have a ring at some point. You're *so* going to marry me."

"I am?" I asked. I'd do anything he asked me, so he wasn't wrong.

"You are."

"Okay."

"Okay." It was Joel's confidence that was his most seductive trait. But he had every reason to be confident about me marrying him.

Joel

I'd been waiting for this girl who sat next to me in the car for the whole of my life. I glanced across at her as she fixed her gaze forward out of the windscreen. As if sensing my stare, she reached across and squeezed my hand. We'd always been perfectly in tune like that—almost as if we were two halves of the same person. I knew when she was close, even before I saw her—I felt her in my bones. The woman who had stood next to me yesterday as we'd exchanged our wedding vows meant more to me than she'd ever know, however hard I tried to explain to her. I'd make it my life's work to show her how much I loved her.

I'd worked hard to get over her in the eight years we'd been apart—tried to take my heart back from her grasp. Nothing had worked. I'd done everything I could think of from throwing myself into my business to dating some of the most beautiful women in the world.

But there was nothing and no one that could stop me from loving Ava Elliot.

"Oh my God, what have you done?" she asked me as we pulled up at the marina. "Tell me you didn't hire a boat?" She grinned as if she wanted to hear the exact opposite.

I chuckled. She'd have something to say when she saw what I had planned. I'd insisted on keeping it a secret as it was a wedding gift as well as a honeymoon.

Throwing myself into my job may not have cured me from needing Ava, but it had meant that my business had grown into something I could never have imagined. I had more money than we could ever need.

"Well, you used to talk about the Joel and Ava bubble." I snapped open my seatbelt and got out of the car. The heat of the Italian Riviera beat down on my back immediately. I rounded the bonnet and caught the door just as Ava opened it.

"But I'm not trying to hide us anymore. You know that, right?" she asked.

She tilted her head and I cupped her face, smoothing my thumb over those luscious lips that belonged to me now. "I think the two hundred guests at our wedding yesterday might have given me a clue."

"You think they had a good time?"

I nodded. I didn't care if they had a good time as long as Ava did. I was pretty sure my wife had overcompensated on the guest list to prove to me she was happy for the world to know about the two of us. As long as I got to marry her, I didn't mind if twenty or two hundred got to see it.

"I'm just trying to say that I liked the bubble too." As much as I loved that we didn't have to hide our feelings anymore, I missed the sense it was us against the world sometimes. "I thought this would give us a chance to escape and just be us every now and then."

She shook her head. "You're crazy."

The squawk of seagulls overhead brought me back to why we were here, by the sea. "Come on." I took her hand and led her out along the jetty.

I glanced behind as Ava scanned the boats either side of us. They got bigger, the further along we got.

As the boat I'd bought the day we got engaged came into focus, I began to smile. This was perfect.

I stopped as we got to the correct dock. "What do you think?" I asked.

"It's huge," she said. "Do we have to drive it?"

"It's a 122.4 foot yacht. We're definitely not *driving* it. In fact no one will drive it. But we do have a crew." I bent and kissed her on the head. "What we're going to do is eat, sleep, swim, and make love for two weeks on this thing."

She sighed and then glanced up at me. "Sounds like it's about to be the best two weeks of my life."

She snapped her head around. "Hey! You found one with that name?" she asked as she noticed the writing on the side of the yacht.

She frowned and I circled my arms around her waist. "Not quite. I called it *Infinity*. It's your wedding gift."

Her eyes widened. "You bought it?"

I nodded. "So we can escape to our Joel and Ava bubble whenever we want to."

She jumped into my arms and tightened her legs around my waist. "Did I tell you how much I love you?" She bent down and kissed my neck and I began to walk toward the captain waiting at the walkway.

"I'm never going to get tired of hearing it," I replied.

She slid down my body and we greeted the captain and the rest of the crew.

"The main bedroom is up here," I said as we entered into the main salon. "And there are three bedrooms downstairs."

"There are four bedrooms?" she asked, looking around. "This place is huge."

"I'm thinking ahead. When we have kids, we're going to need more room. And we can always have Hanna and Matt, Jules and Adam, and Daniel and Leah to stay in the meantime."

She beamed up at me. "Kids?" she asked.

I shrugged. We hadn't talked too much about it. But we'd both discussed in the abstract about wanting a family.

"Sounds perfect," she said.

I pulled her into the master suite. "This room is ours."

"I can't believe you bought it." She sat down on the bed, bouncing, as if to test the mattress.

"We're married. If that's true then anything can be." I sat next to her on the bed and we lay back.

She slid her fingers over my lips as I lay on my back and she leaned over me. "It's the only thing I need to be true in my life. As long as you are here by my side then nothing else matters."

"I'm here for infinity, Ava. We're together forever. There will be nothing that separates us now."

She nodded. "I know." She exhaled as if the thought relaxed her. "We're for infinity. We always were."

PLAYLIST

Up All Night
Kip Moore

Last Time
Taylor Swift ft. Gary Lightbody

Say Something
A Great Big World and Christina Aguilera

Limbo No More
Alanis Morrisette

Some Other Time
Jill Scott

I Miss You
Kacey Musgroves

Who Knew
Pink

Love Me Still
Chaka Khan

What About Now
Daughtry

Brave
Sara Bareilles

Living Inside My Heart
Bob Seger

Added to the revised version, 2017
When We Were Young
Adele

ACKNOWLEDGMENTS

To my readers - nothing is more thrilling than hearing how someone loved the book that you wrote - that they brought the characters, which you simply scribbled onto a page, into life through their imaginations. Thank you for reading. Thank you for reviewing. Thank you for supporting and encouraging me. Every review, message, like, share, retweet lifts me up and I'm on top of the world.

Thank you to the wonderful community of bloggers and reviewers who want nothing more than for indie authors to thrive and flourish. You are amazing and generous and kind and wonderful and none of us could do it without you. If you're reading this and wondering if I mean you – I do. Thank you.

I am so lucky to have hoodwinked a fantastic group of beta readers to give me their thoughtful, careful and creative thoughts on this book. They were very kind and I am very grateful. Karen, Slick, Darby and Renee – thank you.

Slick, your generosity knows no bounds.

To Lisa Walker, Megan Fields, Lucy May, Jacquie Jaxs,

Barbara Campbell, Tina Haynes-Marshall, Helen Waller, Susan Ann Whitaker and Ashton Williams Shone - you Babes are wonderful. Thank you for making time in your day for me.

Thank you Karen Booth. There's no salt in that pedestal. I can't wait for London Calling.

Thank you to Heather Way. You have such a good heart.

Thank you to Twirly. Are you actually still alive?

Added to the revised version, 2017

This revision has been a complete labor of love for me. As many of my readers know, this is one of my favourite books I've written. I wrote it too early, when I knew nothing about anything to do with writing. I wanted to try and improve it—to do Joel and Ava's story justice. I have so much affection for them just as I do for Frederick and Anne. I still don't think it's everything I wanted it to be but it is somewhat reflective of where I am now with my writing. It's been wonderful going back into their world. I hope I haven't ruined it for anyone.

Elizabeth, the reason I'm able to make these revisions is because I have learned so much since I wrote this book. That's all down to you. We've come such a long way! Thank you for all that you do and everything you put up with from me.

To everyone one of my supporters that I've gathered since the last time I added words in this section—thank you, thank you, thank you!

OTHER BOOKS BY LOUISE BAY

Sign up to the Louise Bay mailing list to see more on all my books. www.louisebay.com/newsletter

Hollywood Scandal

HE'S A HOLLYWOOD SUPERSTAR. SHE'S LITER-ALLY THE GIRL NEXT DOOR.

One of Hollywood's A-listers, I have the movie industry in the palm of my hand. But if I'm going to stay at the top, my playboy image needs an overhaul. No more tabloid headlines. No more parties. And absolutely no more one night stands.

Filming for my latest blockbuster takes place on the coast of Maine and I'm determined to stay out of trouble. But trouble finds me when I run into Lana Kelly.

She doesn't recognize me, she's never heard of Matt Easton and my million dollar smile doesn't work on her.

Ego shredded, I know I should keep my distance, but when I realize she's my neighbor I know I'm toast. There's no way I can resist temptation when it's ten yards away.

332 OTHER BOOKS BY LOUISE BAY

She has a mouth designed for pleasure and legs that will wrap perfectly around my waist.

She's movie star beautiful and her body is made to be mine.

Getting Lana Kelly into my bed is harder than I'm used to. She's not interested in the glitz and glamour of Hollywood, but I'm determined to convince her the best place in the world is on the red carpet, holding my hand.

I could have any woman in the world, but all I want is the girl next door.

A standalone romance.

Duke of Manhattan

I was born into British aristocracy, but I've made my fortune in Manhattan. New York is now my kingdom.

Back in Britain my family are fighting over who's the next Duke of Fairfax. The rules say it's me--if I'm married. It's not a trade-off worth making. I could never limit myself to just one woman.

Or so I thought until my world is turned upside down. Now, the only way I can save the empire I built is to inherit the title I've never wanted-- so I need a wife.

To take my mind off business I need a night that's all pleasure. I need to bury myself in a stranger.

The skim of Scarlett King's hair over my body as she bends over . . .

The scrape of her nails across my chest as she screams my name . . .

The bite of her teeth on my shoulder just as we both reach the edge . . .

It all helps me forget.

I just didn't bargain on finding my one night stand across the boardroom table the next day.

She might be my latest conquest but I have a feeling Scarlett King might just conquer me.

A stand-alone novel.

Park Avenue Prince

THE PRINCE OF PARK AVENUE FINALLY MEETS HIS MATCH IN A FEISTY MANHATTAN PRINCESS.

I've made every one of my billions of dollars myself—I'm calculating, astute and the best at what I do. It takes drive and dedication to build what I have. And it leaves no time for love or girlfriends or relationships.

But don't get me wrong, I'm not a monk.

I understand the attention and focus it takes to seduce a beautiful woman. They're the same skills I use to close business deals. But one night is where it begins and ends. I'm not the guy who sends flowers. I'm not the guy who calls the next day.

Or so I thought before an impatient, smart-talking, beyond beautiful heiress bursts into my world.

When Grace Astor rolls her eyes at me—I want to hold her against me and show her what she's been missing.

When she makes a joke at my expense—I want to silence her sassy mouth with my tongue.

And when she leaves straight after we f*ck with barely a goodbye—it makes me want to pin her down and remind her of the three orgasms she just had.

She might be a princess but I'm going to show her who rules in this Park Avenue bedroom.

A stand-alone novel.

King of Wall Street

THE KING OF WALL STREET IS BROUGHT TO HIS KNEES BY AN AMBITIOUS BOMBSHELL.

I keep my two worlds separate.

At work, I'm King of Wall Street. The heaviest hitters in Manhattan come to me to make money. They do whatever I say because I'm always right. I'm shrewd. Exacting. Some say ruthless.

At home, I'm a single dad trying to keep his fourteen year old daughter a kid for as long as possible. If my daughter does what I say, somewhere there's a snowball surviving in hell. And nothing I say is ever right.

When Harper Jayne starts as a junior researcher at my firm, the barriers between my worlds begin to dissolve. She's the most infuriating woman I've ever worked with.

I don't like the way she bends over the photocopier—it makes my mouth water.

I hate the way she's so eager to do a good job—it makes my dick twitch.

And I can't stand the way she wears her hair up exposing her long neck. It makes me want to strip her naked, bend her over my desk and trail my tongue all over her body.

If my two worlds are going to collide, Harper Jayne will have to learn that I don't just rule the boardroom. I'm in charge of the bedroom, too.

A stand-alone novel.

Parisian Nights

The moment I laid eyes on the new photographer at work, I had his number. Cocky, arrogant and super wealthy—

women were eating out of his hand as soon as his tight ass crossed the threshold of our office.

When we were forced to go to Paris together for an assignment, I wasn't interested in his seductive smile, his sexy accent or his dirty laugh. I wasn't falling for his charms.

Until I did.

Until Paris.

Until he was kissing me and I was wondering how it happened. Until he was dragging his lips across my skin and I was hoping for more. Paris does funny things to a girl and he might have gotten me naked.

But Paris couldn't last forever.

Previously called What the Lightning Sees

A stand-alone novel.

Promised Nights

I've been in love with Luke Daniels since, well, forever. As his sister's best friend, I've spent over a decade living in the friend zone, watching from the sidelines hoping he would notice me, pick me, love me.

I want the fairy tale and Luke is my Prince Charming. He's tall, with shoulders so broad he blocks out the sun. He's kind with a smile so dazzling he makes me forget everything that's wrong in the world. And he's the only man that can make me laugh until my cheeks hurt and my stomach cramps.

But he'll never be mine.

So I've decided to get on with my life and find the next best thing.

Until a Wonder Woman costume, a bottle of tequila and a game of truth or dare happened.

Then Luke's licking salt from my wrist and telling me I'm beautiful.

Then he's peeling off my clothes and pressing his lips against mine.

Then what? Is this the start of my happily ever after or the beginning of a tragedy?

Previously called Calling Me

A stand-alone novel.

Indigo Nights

I don't do romance. I don't do love. I certainly don't do relationships. Women are attracted to my power and money and I like a nice ass and a pretty smile. It's a fair exchange—a business deal for pleasure.

Meeting Beth Harrison in the first class cabin of my flight from Chicago to London throws me for a loop and everything I know about myself and women goes out the window.

I'm usually good at reading people, situations, the markets. I know instantly if I can trust someone or if they're lying. But Beth is so contradictory and confounding I don't know which way is up.

She's sweet but so sexy she makes my knees weak and mouth dry.

She's confident but so vulnerable I want to wrap her up and protect her from the world.

And then she fucks me like a train and just disappears, leaving me with my pants around my ankles, wondering which day of the week it is.

If I ever see her again I don't know if I'll scream at her, strip her naked or fall in love. Thank goodness I live in

Chicago and she lives in London and we'll never see each other again, right?

A stand-alone novel.

Anna Kirby is sick of dating. She's tired of heartbreak. Despite being smart, sexy, and funny, she's a magnet for men who don't deserve her.

A week's vacation in New York is the ultimate distraction from her most recent break-up, as well as a great place to meet a stranger and have some summer fun. But to protect her still-bruised heart, fun comes with rules. There will be no sharing stories, no swapping numbers, and no real names. Just one night of uncomplicated fun.

Super-successful serial seducer Ethan Scott has some rules of his own. He doesn't date, he doesn't stay the night, and he doesn't make any promises.

It should be a match made in heaven. But rules are made to be broken.

The Empire State Series is a series of three novellas.

When the fierce redhead with the beautiful ass walks into the local bar, I can tell she's passing through. And I'm looking for distraction while I'm in town—a hot hook-up and nothing more before I head back to the city.

If she has secrets, I don't want to know them.

If she feels good underneath me, I don't want to think about it too hard.

If she's my future, I don't want to see it.

I'm Blake McKenna and I'm about to teach this Boston socialite how to forget every man who came before me.

When the future I had always imagined crumbles before my very eyes. I grab my two best friends and take a much needed vacation to the country.

My plan of swearing off men gets railroaded when on my first night of my vacation, I meet the hottest guy on the planet.

I'm not going to consider that he could be a gorgeous distraction.

I'm certainly not going to reveal my deepest secrets to him as we steal away each night hoping no one will notice.

And the last thing I'm going to do is fall in love for the first time in my life.

My name is Mackenzie Locke and I haven't got a handle on men. Not even a little bit.

Not until Blake.

A stand-alone novel.

Faithful

Leah Thompson's life in London is everything she's supposed to want: a successful career, the best girlfriends a bottle of sauvignon blanc can buy, and a wealthy boyfriend who has just proposed. But something doesn't feel right. Is it simply a case of 'be careful what you wish for'?

Uncertain about her future, Leah looks to her past, where she finds her high school crush, Daniel Armitage, online. Daniel is one of London's most eligible bachelors. He knows what and who he wants, and he wants Leah. Leah resists Daniel's advances as she concentrates on being the perfect fiancé.

She soon finds that she should have trusted her instincts

when she realises she's been betrayed by the men and women in her life.

Leah's heart has been crushed. Will ever be able to trust again? And will Daniel be there when she is?

A stand-alone novel.

KEEP IN TOUCH!

Sign up for my mailing list to get the latest news and gossip
www.louisebay.com/newsletter

I'm on social media

Twitter
Facebook
Instagram
Pinterest
Goodreads
Google +

www.louisebay.com

24247137R00207

Printed in Poland
by Amazon Fulfillment
Poland Sp. z o.o., Wrocław